MIDNIGHT AT THE EIFFEL

Rebecca Randolph Buckley

First Printing – June 2007
ISBN-13 978-0-9791701-0-2

R.J. Buckley Publishing
Queen Creek AZ

www.rjbuckleypublishing.com

Works by Rebecca Randolph Buckley

NOVELS - Rachel O'Neill Series

Midnight at Trafalgar
Midnight at the Eiffel
Midnight in Brussels
Midnight in Moscow
Midnight in Malibu

COLLECTIONS – Short Stories and Plays

Love Has a Price Tag
Bits & Pieces of Me
My Dramedy
Shoe's on the Other Foot

Acknowledgements

First of all and once again, I thank Jim Buckley for his generous support and for making it easier for me to do the geographical research for this book.

Bob Abrams, my expat friend in Paris who is the photographer of the cover photos, is next on my list of thanks for offering his knowledge of Paris and for allowing me to stay on his exotic Bateau Simpatico. Thank you, Bob. See you soon.

www.quai48parisvacation.com

AND . . . very special thanks go to Viv Goff, Jim Buckley and Mary Matejcek for their valuable input and edits.

Dedications

I dedicate this book to my precious sons and daughter and to their
loving spouses – Barry and Kellie, Micheal and Elaine, Tami and
David. As the song says, "You Are Always on My Mind . . . "

AND so is your little brother, Mark Ray, who flew away with the
angels before he knew his mother had become an author.

A Few Favorite Quotes

"Writing is the only profession where no one considers you ridiculous if you earn no money."

Jules Renard

"There are three rules for writing a novel. Unfortunately, no one knows what they are."

W. Somerset Maugham

"One ought to know a lot about reality before one writes realistic novels."

John Barth

"A sequel is an admission that you've been reduced to imitating yourself."

Don Marquis

"Literature is an occupation in which you have to keep proving your talent to people who have none."

Jules Renard

"I often quote myself. It adds spice to my conversation."
George Bernard Shaw

"For me, to write is to live."

Rebecca Randolph Buckley

MIDNIGHT AT THE EIFFEL

PART ONE
"By Myself"

PART TWO
"I Love Paris"

PART THREE
"Will You Still Love Me Tomorrow"

PART ONE

"By Myself"

"I'll go my way by myself; this is the end of romance . . ."

(Song by A. Schwartz and H. Dietz)

Rebecca Randolph Buckley

CHAPTER 1

Swiftly Shellie used her arms to shield her face from the impending blow and figured as long as she could live through this one last onslaught of punches and could prevent cuts and bruises to her face, she would gladly take it. But this would be the end of it, there would be no more.

Jerold swung in a drunken rage at the side of her head and Shellie could swear he had broken her wrist as his iron fist smashed into it. She had become adept at dodging and averting most of his maiming violence, but on occasions like this, when he was wild and furious that she had not been home offering up his dinner the moment he had walked in the door, his level of abuse could escalate to a point of unpredictability. Sometimes he would only shove and slap her around, sometimes he would only verbally abuse her, and other times he would land into her as if she were a punching bag in a gymnasium. She never knew which way it would go whenever he was sloshed and angry, for his wrath could surface for the minutest reason or for no reason at all. She had learned long before tonight that there didn't have to be a reason for him to lash out at her. She also knew it was all about him, not her.

So she had expected it tonight because on top of the usual afternoon after-work beers, this was the boys'-night-out in the

3

marina. Today, like every day, Jerold and his buddy construction workers would spend a couple of hours of heavy drinking before going home to their wives and girlfriends. It was their excuse for rewarding themselves for working so hard for their "little ladies." A macho thing to do. But Jerold didn't treat Shellie like a lady. He treated her the only way he knew how, learned it from his father who beat the crap out of him and his brother as well as their mother. As much as Jerold hated his father for what he had done to them, he had followed suit and carried on with the violent tradition that had been handed down from father to son for four generations.

So, she knew he would be raging the minute she walked through the door. One thing for certain, though, she would not be there going through another brutal attack if she had not forgotten the damn envelope. She would have been long gone by now.

Abuse wasn't new to Shellie Singer. Before marrying Jerold, she had been physically abused by her own mother who had been a tyrannical single mother raising an only child. Her mother had been an alcoholic with boyfriends too many to count, so it was inevitable that Shellie would land in a dysfunctional relationship after she fled her mother's ever-changing nest, for she believed that was the way people lived and she didn't expect any better.

That is until earlier in the week when she took a sick day from work and happened to watch the Oprah television talk show. Rachel O'Neill, a guest on the show, had explained why women stay with abusers year after year. She had said that it wasn't love that kept them there. Her very words were "No one loves being beaten and you don't beat a person if you love them."

The show had caught Shellie's attention because Rachel O'Neill had been the key witness in a high profile case in California two years before. It was in all the media for weeks when a California politician was convicted of murder, attempted murder, and multiple rapes. Rachel O'Neill's testimony helped put him behind bars; she had been one of his victims.

Shellie remembered Rachel saying, "If a man can verbally abuse a woman, he can just as easily hit her, and if he can hit her, he can just as easily kill her. All it takes is one angry punch connecting with one vulnerable spot and abusers don't quit at one punch."

Another guest who had made an impression on Shellie that day was one who had been beaten to the point of plastic surgery and had been literally stolen from her home by two of her closest friends to tear her away from her tormentor. Oprah's words echoed in Shellie's mind for hours after the show on that Tuesday morning, "If you're watching this show and this is happening to you, get out and get help before it is too late!"

Shellie made up her mind that day that she would leave Jerold on Friday, which was pay day, which was today.

Jerold grabbed Shellie's elbows as she held her arms close and tight covering her face and head. He lifted all of her 110 pounds and tossed her through the air towards the dining table.

Her back struck the hard wooden edge of the table, right across the middle rib cage, the impact scooted the table a few inches. She crumpled to the floor into a fetal position. Pain shot in every direction - up out in and down - the kind of pain that comes from broken ribs. She had felt that pain before, oh yes; she knew what that pain was.

As she burrowed her face into her knees, with her arms still protecting her head, she began whimpering like a wounded puppy. The sounds were barely audible for she knew if she made too much noise or cried out or screamed it would make him worse. Thank God they had never had children. She had lived in fear that he would find out she was on the pill and had kept her pills in her desk drawer at work so he wouldn't know, for he had wanted a son.

But now all she had to do was get through this one night, just one more time. *Please, God. Help me.*

Jerold kicked her in the back, and then stomped on her side. An involuntary muffled scream burst through her clinched teeth.

He stepped over her feet in his steel-toed boots and headed for the door, glancing back as he growled, "I'm going

5

across the street to the fucking deli to get some take-out since you didn't have the decency to fix my goddamned dinner. So I suggest you get your fucking self up and we'll finish this when I get back." With that, he walked out and slammed the door.

Shellie knew she didn't have much time to get out of there, and she was ready. She had given notice at her job on Wednesday, two days ago. There was a part-time girl who'd wanted to work full-time and knew the job, so Shellie hadn't left her employer in a bind. All he had to do was hire a temp until he found another part-timer. The false reason she gave for quitting was that she had been hired to tour as a singer with a band and they were leaving on Friday afternoon. Her boss knew how much she had wanted to become a professional singer, so he believed her and gave her an unexpected bonus of $500 in addition to the final paycheck earlier that afternoon.

She had hurried home and packed her belongings, taking nothing that would give a clue to Jerold that she had left. Then she spaced the remaining clothing in the closet so he wouldn't notice anything was missing, and had done the same in the chest of drawers. She took only things she felt she really needed and packed them in borrowed suitcases and left the apartment for the last time. At least that had been the plan.

Shellie had been confiding with Janet Corrigan, one of the regular patients at work, who had already guessed Shellie's situation. Janet had empathized with the bruises, swollen lips, and black eyes over the past year. She had been a victim herself at one time and had recognized all the telltale signs in Shellie's behavior and demeanor even before she saw the bruises. She had told Shellie that her own injuries by an abusive husband were what led her to the chiropractic clinic and to support groups and finally to freedom.

Janet had pleaded with Shellie to get away from Jerold and had even offered her a place to stay. She lived in Glendale which was far enough away from Marina del Rey, so when Shellie made her decision, she took Janet up on the offer. He certainly wouldn't be looking for her in Glendale, it was on the northeast side of L.A. and he knew nothing of Janet, had never even heard her name.

Earlier that day, after Shellie collected her final checks and bid farewell to her boss, she went to the bank and drew out her savings on the way home. She was on an adrenalin high as she cashed her checks and purchased travelers checks and then hurried to the apartment to pack her things in the suitcases Janet had brought to her that morning at work. It took her no more than thirty minutes to get everything she needed before she began the escape to Janet in Glendale.

At last she could breathe freedom air. As she drove the 45 minutes across town, it had felt as if a terrific weight had been lifted off her tiny being. She had felt giddy and happy. She sang. She wasn't sure what was going to happen or how she would manage and she didn't really care because at that very moment she felt better than she had in years.

Janet Corrigan was in her late 50s, a divorcee, had worked for Coldwell Banker Real Estate in Los Angeles for years and had made some hefty real estate investments that enabled her to live very comfortably. She was an attractive, sexy woman, blond, went to the gym every day, to the chiropractor, masseuse, and to a hair and nail salon once a week – a very self-pampered woman and a very caring one. She had welcomed Shellie with open arms that afternoon on her doorstep and had taken her inside and tried to make her feel at ease.

"Honey, you're free now, you can stop your shaking," Janet said as she hugged her after they had put Shellie's things in a guest room. She took her into the kitchen and poured her a cup of coffee. "You never have to see the bastard again. You're free."

"I know," Shellie said as she took the cup of coffee, spilling some in the saucer as she sipped. "I don't know why I'm shaking. It's just so sudden, I guess. I don't feel like I'm totally free yet. Thank you for this coffee. I needed it." She continued to sip while she ran the day's events in her mind, going over a mental checklist. Suddenly she stiffened. "The envelope! I left the envelope, Janet!"

"What envelope, hon?"

"My ticket, my money . . . I left it at the apartment on the desk! What am I going to do? I have to go back and get it!"

She stood up and began pacing frantically on the pristine kitchen floor in Janet's upscale home on the golf course, almost crying.

"Now, honey. Let's take a deep breath and figure this out. Okay? Just calm down. Let's talk about this."

"But it's all I have in the world. I just have a small amount of cash on me; I converted all my savings and put what was in my checking account into traveler's checks. I have to go back and get the envelope and that's going to put me there after Jerold gets home. I have no other choice."

"Yes, you do. I can loan you the same amount of money you have in that envelope. And you can leave me your key and I'll go get it when he's at work. He'll never know the difference. I think we need something a bit stiffer than coffee to drink." She pulled a bottle of champagne from the refrigerator.

"No, I can't do that. I can't take money from you. He'll go through my things if I don't show up tonight. He'll find it. He'll see the plane ticket – when and where I'm going. I have to go back and slip out while he's sleeping."

"I can't let you do that, honey. Please! If you aren't there before he is tonight, you know what will happen, and it's too late now anyway. You can't afford to go through another beating, Shellie. Sweetheart, you never know when that fatal blow will come. Listen to me. Cancel that flight, take another. Don't go. Please don't go back there."

"I have to," she said as she grabbed her purse.

"Oh, honey. I wish you'd think some more about this."

"I have to go, Janet."

"Okay, wait here for a sec. Don't leave yet." Janet went to her office and came back with her purse. She pulled out a gun she had been carrying since she had had to protect herself from her ex-husband. At the time, he had threatened to kill her if she left him. "Here, take this with you. I'll show you how to work it."

"Oh no. I'm afraid of guns. I'm sorry. I can't take that."

"Honey, that man is dangerous. He might kill you. This

8

might be the night."

But Shellie didn't heed the warning; she drove right back to Marina del Rey and right back to another beating.

Her thoughts became a painful blur as she tried to get up from the floor. She knew she had only a few minutes to get out of the apartment before Jerold returned. The horrible throbbing pain encircling her body's ribcage was almost unbearable now, but she had to move, regardless of the pain. Blood had surfaced just under the skin on her hand and wrist where he had slammed his big fist into it. It was numb, probably broken. Still bent over and struggling against the rib pain while cradling her injured wrist against her body, she reached for her keys and purse and grabbed the envelope from the desk. She carefully peered into the corridor on the Thirteenth Floor of the apartment building. Around the bend at each end of the long corridor there was an elevator that lowered to the parking garage fourteen floors below. The one to the left – the east elevator – was the one they always used when coming to and fro. They usually parked their cars near it on that side of the garage. But she had been wise and this time parked on the street at the west end behind the complex, out of sight, just in case she needed the leverage.

After glancing to the left, making sure he wasn't coming back down the hall, she rushed to the west elevator, the one they never used, the one at the opposite end of the hallway. She decided the stairs would be too difficult for her to manage in her condition, and would take much too long. She couldn't envision herself going down the stairs with the worsening pain she was experiencing. At the elevator she leaned against the wall for support and winced as she pushed the down button. She closed her eyes, feeling as if she was about to pass out as the inflamed throbbing spread throughout her body. It was a total effort to move, and it seemed as if the elevator had taken the night off. *Come on! Come on!*

Now she was getting nauseous. She thought she might have to telephone Janet to come get her if she ever got out of the building. She could be bleeding internally and was afraid she

9

would pass out while driving to Glendale clear across town. Maybe she should just drive to some safe spot and wait there for Janet. She could call her on her cell. But first she had to get away. She heard the elevator at the other end of the corridor slide open and sheer panic consumed her. She could hear children's voices, laughing, yelling. She relaxed. They were the grandkids of one of their neighbors who had come to spend the weekend.

What is taking so long?

The elevator door opened.

CHAPTER 2

Adrian von Allman picked up the empty pails on the stone stoop of his grandmother's back door. He could hear her stirring in the kitchen, could smell the coffee brewing as he tapped on the window and gave his usual morning grin and salute to her on his way to the barn.

It hadn't been easy for his mother and grandmother after his father died, and it certainly hadn't been easy for Adrian. He was the only one left to help with the chores, the dairy cows, and the family's meager farmland. It certainly hadn't been his desire to stay in Gimmelwald where he was born and raised, where his father and grandfather had been born before him. The van Allman's had lived in the Swiss Bernese Oberland for two centuries and maybe more.

Gimmelwald was a sleepy, traffic-free, remote village high in the Swiss Alps on a steep grassy slope - accessible only by the Shilthorn cableway or by foot. It was a favorite off-the-beaten-track destination for skiers in the winter and hikers in the summer - the locals rented out rooms in their homes to the travelers, some rented out hay lofts in their barns. The tastiest Swiss cheeses originated in Gimmelwald. Some were made by the van Allman family, who was one of the three core families making up the 300 plus inhabitants of the mountainside hamlet.

The families sold their cheeses and products in the local farmers' shop.

But now Anna van Allman's Gimmelwald descendents consisted only of her grandson Adrian. Adrian's two older sisters had already flown the Gimmelwald coop. They'd gone off to school and married and made their homes in England and Italy. There were van Allman cousins, aunts and uncles - near and far removed - in Gimmelwald, but Anna's family had dwindled, having had only one son – Henri, who was Adrian's father.

When Adrian was in his early twenties, he had dreamed of leaving Gimmelwald to become a world-renown artist. His dreams were to live in Paris to be near the masters at the Musee du Louvre, to study with the most acclaimed artists in Europe, and to one day see his own paintings hanging in impressive galleries all over the world.

But there seemed to be too many obstacles and reasons why he couldn't go. First it was to stay and help his father after his older sisters vacated, while at the same time it was always in the back of his mind to break away as soon as he could. His father had built him an artist's studio separate from the house. Adrian slept there and painted in every spare moment he could steal away from his chores during the hours from four in the morning to four in the evening. His drawings and paintings were all over the village, in homes, in the restaurant, in the farmers shop. But he couldn't make a complete break from his family to pursue a career in art, they still needed him too much.

Of course he felt compelled to stay more than ever when Henri van Allman became ill. During the six years his father languished with a fatal disease, Adrian lost all hope of ever achieving a serious career in art. Now he was in his thirties and he felt it was much too late to chase childhood dreams.

He opened the barn door and set the pails near the first milking machine. Then he grabbed a rope and walked out of the far end of the barn to fetch his grandmother's milk cow that was separate from the rest of the small herd that belonged to the family.

"Tessa, c'mon girl. That's a good Tessa." He rubbed the

smooth black and white fur of the giant Holstein as he looped the rope over her head and tugged gently to secure the slip knot. "That's a girl. Let's go give Mama Anna some milk, shall we?" He posed a tall, handsome figure beside Tessa - his hair was as black as her spots and he was head and shoulders above her.

Adrian resembled his Italian mother, although his immense size was that of his Swiss father. His mother had met his father on a ski trip when she was 19 and it had been love at first sight. They both spoke German and English, so a language barrier was non-existent from the first. They fell madly in love with each other and it lasted till the day Henri died - never had there been a more loving match.

While Adrian was in the barn milking Tessa, Gina bounced down the stairs of the expansive three-story centuries-old Swiss cabin into the kitchen, smiling and wide awake, ready to face another glorious day. There was no way of knowing she hadn't slept all night, for she looked fresh and brilliantly alive. This was the day she was going to tell Mama Anna about her plans. It had to be today. She couldn't put it off any longer.

"Good Morning, Mama Anna. Lovely day, isn't it?"

"Ah, it is, child. It is. And how did you sleep? I thought I heard you up and about a few times during the night."

Gina reached for the cup of coffee Anna had poured for her. "Oh, it was nothing. Just woke up a few times thinking of things."

"Thinking of things?"

"Uh, yes, thinking of things." She had to tell her now. She must. "Anna–"

"Anna, is it now? Not Mama Anna?" Anna sat at the table with Gina and sipped her coffee.

"I'm sorry, Mama Anna. Uh, well–"

"What is it, child?"

"I . . . uh . . . well, I don't know how to say this. Just give me a moment, please, to gather my thoughts." She gulped the coffee, burning her tongue. "Mama Mia, that's hot!"

"Here, I'll get you some water."

"No, no. Please, sit down. Please. I must talk to you."

13

Anna sat back down even more curious at what was going on with her daughter-in-law. She had noticed a change in her the past few weeks; she had seemed happier and brighter, full of energy, laughing more, actually cheerful - a complete turn about in the four years since Henri's death. She was glad to see that Gina was finally recovering from the deep sadness they'd all experienced. It had worried Anna that Gina might not ever get over Henri's demise, but in the past few weeks a definite change had been taking place. She wondered if what Anna had wanted to tell her had anything to do with her new behavior. Now she was worried. She frowned.

"Mama Anna, I don't know if you've noticed, but something happened to me three months ago that has changed my life."

"You have gotten spiritual?"

"No, I haven't gotten spiritual," she replied as she smiled and reached across the table to touch Anna's arm. "I am in love."

The silence was beyond silence. If ever there was anything quieter than quiet, and stiller than still, this was it. The two of them searched each other's eyes for what seemed like minutes, but was only seconds.

"I met him in Interlaken, Mama Anna. When I went down for supplies. And we've been seeing each other every week since we met three months ago. He's a newcomer, a widower, lost his wife two years ago. His children are grown and he opened a business in Interlaken. A gift shop with art and antiques. Collectibles. We plan to be married. Right away."

Anna hadn't taken her eyes from Gina's. She hadn't moved, hadn't breathed, and hadn't blinked.

"Please say something. Please be happy with me."

Anna sighed heavily and looked away. All of a sudden she felt more than her 87 years of age.

"Mama Anna?"

"I– I– what do I say? I don't know what to say. This is so sudden. I didn't know– why didn't I know? What about Adrian?"

"Adrian is a grown man, Mama Anna. I can't put my life on hold because of Adrian."

"But he has put his life on hold because of you, my child. And not only for you, for me. For Henri. Adrian stopped living his life because we all needed him here with us. Oh, I understand you must go on with yours. I do, yes, I do. And I am happy you have found someone. Now I worry about Adrian. Have you spoken to him?"

"I intend to tell him today."

CHAPTER 3

Shellie held her breath as she stepped back and the elevator doors opened slowly.

Hank Schwartz's eyes brightened when he saw her waiting to board. "Hi, Shellie," he cheerfully greeted and moved out of the elevator while holding the doors open for her. "You going down?"

"Uh, yes. Yes, I am. Thanks, Hank." She forced herself to straighten up and walk onto the elevator as normal as she could, while at the same time hiding her injured wrist behind her.

"Good seeing you, Shellie. Tell Jerold I said hello." He rounded the corner and headed down the corridor towards his own apartment next door to the Singers.

Just before the elevator doors had completely closed, Shellie couldn't believe what she heard.

"Oh! Hi, Jerold. I just told Shellie to tell you hello."

Jerold was standing with his hand still on the door knob after having opened his door. "You just spoke to Shellie?"

"Yes, she got on the elevator just as I came out." Hank motioned towards the west elevator.

Jerold threw the bag of food into the apartment, pulled the door shut and rushed back to the east elevator he had just exited. He figured he would get down to the garage just after she would and he would find out what the fucking hell she was up to. He thought it was strange that she would take the west elevator.

"Damn it," he said as he watched all the floor numbers light up above the elevator doors. He grumbled as he impatiently waited for the elevator to return to the fourteenth floor. "If one of you brats is pushing all the God damn buttons again, I'll kill you." He stood for a few more seconds, and then thought about taking the stairs. It was a fleeting thought. Running down fourteen flights didn't really appeal to him. "Hell, who gives a shit!" He sighed and walked back to the apartment muttering that when Shellie returned she'd have a lot of explaining to do this time. He was eager to eat his pastrami sandwich and go join the boys at Casa Escobar. Friday nights were hot in the Marina, especially at the Casa. They had a live band and Latin dancing till 1:00 a.m., and he and the guys got off on watching all the women shake their stuff. They even got out on the dance floor and joined them on occasion.

Shellie was running through the garage for all she was worth. She hurriedly took the steps leading to the street on the west side of the complex, and then rushed to her car that was parked a block away near an alley. She could hardly breathe. Her chest was hurting so bad it felt like she was having a heart attack. She was convinced her ribs were broken and feared that one might puncture a lung or some other vital organ with all the violent movement, but she felt she had no other alternative. She had to get out of there as fast as she could. If she died trying, it was better than not. At least she had made a decision to leave that animal. And strangely enough no one was in the garage or on the sidewalk to witness her painful lopsided manner of running.

She glanced back at the garage through the rear view mirror as she put the key in the ignition and started up the car. No sight of him. *I'm almost free, I'm almost free!*

All of a sudden the adrenalin drained a bit and the torturous, stabbing pain made her dizzy. She pulled away from the curb, and headed down an alley towards the beach. Then she drove down Pacific Street crossing Washington Boulevard going towards Santa Monica.

17

She fumbled the cell phone from her purse, blinked back the tears that had begun to cloud her vision, and pushed a number. She waited and spoke as the first sob surfaced.

"Janet, I'm– I'm driving in the car . . . he beat me up pretty bad and I don't think I can . . . make it . . . to Glendale. Where? Yes, I do . . . I know where that is. Okay . . . bye."

The floodgates opened. She cried all the way to Santa Monica.

CHAPTER 4

Gina van Allman rinsed her cup in one of the refitted double sinks in the kitchen as she gazed across the sloping pasture to the snowcapped peaks of the Jungfrau.

After her husband had died, they had used some of the insurance money to finish the kitchen remodel he had begun - had put in a large window, installed the new appliances. It was a tribute to him more than anything else to finish the job. He'd wanted the women he loved to live in modern comfort, in spite of the house being over 100 years old. The exterior was in keeping with its history and environment, but the interior had all the modern conveniences of today's world.

"Good morning, Mother, Mama Anna." Adrian greeted them both in the same breath as he entered the kitchen carrying the two pails of milk. He set the pails on a table at the end of the countertop, where he put them every morning for his grandmother. "And how are my two favorite sweethearts in the entire world this happy sunshiny day?"

Mama Anna continued sipping her coffee, staring straight ahead, not looking at Adrian and not saying a word.

Gina stammered in reply, "Uh . . . well . . . we were just having our morning coffee, Adrian. Would you like coffee or milk with your muffin?" She reached towards the stack of plates

19

near the pan of muffins cooling on the table, and then she sat and placed one on a plate for Adrian. It was Mama Anna's morning ritual, making fresh muffins for Adrian.

"Coffee, thank you. Are you alright, Mama Anna?" Adrian scrubbed his hands and wondered why she was so quiet. She usually chattered away about something or another without any prompting.

Mama Anna stood and joined him at the sink. "I'm quite alright, Adrian. How was my Tessa this morning? Any problems?" she asked as she rinsed her cup.

"None at all. It's just like I said. Yesterday was just a bad day for her, must have been a hormonal thing. She's back to normal today." He dried his hands and hugged his grandmother. "You needn't worry about her."

"I worry about all my loved ones, Adrian." She leaned back against the counter watching him sit at the table. Then she glanced towards Gina and gave her a nod.

Gina sighed and wished she hadn't said anything to her mother-in-law just yet, because she wasn't ready to tell her son. She reached for another muffin and began eating it like an apple. Adrian had already eaten half of his, and was washing it down with the coffee.

"Your mother wants to tell you something, Adrian. Don't you, Gina, dear?"

Gina's heart sank and the blood rushed to her head so fast she was feeling dizzy. *Why did she do that?* She couldn't believe Mama Anna took it upon herself to start the dreaded conversation. Sure she'd planned to tell Adrian, but she wanted to do it privately, just between the two of them. She didn't want to hurt Mama Anna with what she might want to say about her feelings for George.

George Schmidt was his name and he wasn't at all like her Henri. George was soft-spoken and gentle. Henri had been strong and aggressive, although very loving in spite of his gruff manliness. George loved art and antiques. Henri was a farmer and a carpenter, although a good provider and of course an excellent father to their three children. But now the girls were

20

married and had children of their own and Adrian was 32 years old. Now it was time for Gina to begin a new life of her own. Not that she'd disliked the life she'd had, it was just that she'd raised her children and had lived in her husband's village with his Swiss family since the day they were married.

"What is it, Mother?" Adrian asked curiously as he took another bite and made eye contact with his mother.

She reached across the table for one of his hands. He grasped hers and they both sat there looking at each other, wondering.

"Yes?"

"What do you want out of life, Adrian? If you had your choice what would you do?"

He looked over at his grandmother who was still leaning against the sink, now drinking a glass of water.

"I don't know, Mother. Why are you asking?" He reached for another muffin and began munching.

"Would you choose to be somewhere else, away from here? She tilted her head genuinely interested in what his answer might be.

"Well, I–I did at one time. I had dreams - dreams of youth - like everyone does. You know. But, now it's different. I'm older. I guess you might say I'm settled."

"Are you truly happy here in Gimmelwald?"

"Yes, of course, I'm happy. Yes. Although the prospect of ever finding a wife here isn't the best." With a broad smile he continued, "I may have to do what father did, go to another country to find the perfect wife. Is that what you're getting at, Mother?"

"No, no. Not at all."

"Then why are you asking these questions? What's wrong?" He released her hand and questioned his grandmother. "What's going on, Mama Anna?"

Anna moved to the table and sat near Adrian, patting his arm. "Just be patient, Adrian. Go on, Gina, my dear."

Gina smiled at Anna's endearment, silently forgiving her for initiating the subject at hand. "Thank you, Mama Anna." She

21

took a deep breath and folded her hands in her lap. "I met someone, Adrian. I've met a man and we've fallen in love."

Adrian's jaw dropped, his eyes widened. He could say nothing. The world stopped. No sounds were heard. No sounds at all. No outdoor noises. No indoor noises. It was as if he were deaf. He continued to stare at his mother. He saw that her lips were moving, but he couldn't hear what she was saying.

"He's a lovely man, Adrian. He owns an art gallery and antique shop in Interlaken. We see each other every week when I go for supplies. His name is George Schmidt. He's from Germany. A widower. We understand each other."

The color drained from Adrian's face and his eyes glazed over.

"He's having a spell, Gina." Anna placed her hands on his shoulders.

Gina moved quickly to the sink and dampened a cloth.

"Adrian, can you hear me?" his grandmother gently asked as she stroked his hair.

"Here, Mama Anna, let me apply the cloth."

He'd had one of these spells the day his grandfather died and one when his father was diagnosed with Cancer, and then another when his father died. He had one when his childhood sweetheart Andrea had told him on graduation day that she was leaving Gimmelwald, and that she couldn't marry him as they'd planned. He had yet another when he got the news that she'd married one of her professors at the Sorbonne in Paris.

The local doctor had run tests on him when the spells first began and told the family that Adrian had a form of Epilepsy - complex partial seizures which occurred through the larger part of the brain and would cause him to lose consciousness, although his eyes would remain open and he wouldn't experience bodily jerkiness as with full seizures. In Adrian it manifested itself as a stoic demeanor and would usually occur when he was overly tired or stressed. He was prescribed *Trileptal*, but sometimes the low dosage wasn't sufficient.

"Adrian, darling, can you hear me?"

Mama Anna joined Gina's pleadings and stood on the

opposite side of Adrian as she rubbed his neck. "Adrian. Adrian. Look at me, baby. It's Mama Anna." She continued to massage the base of his neck as she looked at Gina and shook her head.

Finally, Adrian blinked and turned his face towards Mama Anna in confusion.

Mama Anna clasped his hand, "You left us for a few moments, my dear. Are you all right?"

"Just a bit groggy. What were you saying, Mother?"

"We don't need to talk about this now, darling."

"Did you say that . . . you've fallen in love?"

"Yes, my darling, and please don't be sad. You and I will still be together. I'm not going far. George and I are going to be married in three weeks, and we'd both like you to give me away at the ceremony. Will you do that for me, darling?"

Adrian quickly looked at his grandmother. Her eyes were steadfast upon him.

"B–but, how did this happen? Who is this man? Did you know about this, Mama Anna?"

"No, child, I didn't. Your mother just told me this morning, right before you came in."

He looked back at his mother with a heartbreaking frown, "You will be leaving Gimmelwald?"

"My dearest, this is why I am asking you what you want to do. Yes, I will live with George in Interlaken. I'm asking if you want to stay here. Are you happy here? "

"Of course, of course. I have my own house that papa built for me. What else would I do? Where would I go? Who would take care of Mama Anna?" He put his strong arm that was so much like his father's around his grandmother.

Mama Anna was worried about her grandson. He had been his grandfather's pride and joy, a jewel in his father's eyes and was her favorite grandchild. She loved her granddaughters, yes, but Adrian was a very special boy. She'd do anything in the world for him, and it saddened her that he always felt he had to take care of everyone else, never himself.

"But that's just it, Adrian," Gina replied. "George and I would take care of Mama Anna. There's a lovely cottage behind

23

his house and shop. It belonged to the mother-in-law of the family who lived there before. Mama Anna, this place is much too much for you to manage. It's so big. And you live in only three of its rooms. Why not rent out the rest of it and come live with us in Interlaken? You could spend part of the summers here; visit with your friends if you want. I can still help you with the rental and we can hire a cleaning woman."

Mama Anna and Adrian stared at Gina, as if she were a stranger. Here she'd been living day in and day out as she always had, never giving a clue as to what was really going on in her mind. Sure she was a very attractive woman of sixty, very handsome as a matter of fact - tall and slim with a touch of gray in her thick coal-black hair. Her dark eyes were as mesmerizing as her broad white smile against her olive skin. They both could see how she would turn a man's head. But how could it have happened without them knowing it? Both of them fooled. She went to Interlaken once a week, on Saturday, and spent the entire day. Usually went early, right after her morning coffee, and returned most times after dinner. They knew she sometimes went to a movie or to hear a favorite local musician in one of the restaurants. It was her day away from Gimmelwald to do just as she wished, and she'd been doing it for a couple of years now, but little did they know or suspect she'd been there with a man.

Gina stood up and went for another cup of coffee. "Think about it, Mama Anna. You'd be near the grocer, the shops, the cafes; it'd be perfect for you. Think of the possibilities. And I'd be right there if you needed me." She turned and put her hand on her mother-in-law's shoulder. "Please give this some serious thought, Mama Anna. Please."

Adrian was dazed. "So you've made up your mind, you are actually leaving?"

"Yes, my son. Three weeks from Sunday. Actually I'll move my things down the day before, with your help, I would hope. Please be happy for me, Adrian. I need you to be with me on this. And you too, Mama Anna. I love and need you both." Gina reached up and with the back of her hand; she wiped away a tear that was trailing down her cheek.

Mama Anna reached up and took Gina's hand in hers and rested her cheek on it. "I want you to be happy, Gina. You have been such a devoted daughter to me, and of course I want what's best for you. I'll think about your offer."

"Adrian, what about you?" Gina ruffled his hair as she bent and gazed directly into his eyes. "What's it to be? Will you give me away?"

Adrian reluctantly smiled, then hugged his mother. His watery eyes gave away his true feelings. But in spite of the reservations he had about his mother remarrying, he would do nothing to hamper her happiness. Of course he would give her away. But he didn't like that phrase at all, because it simply didn't apply - he wouldn't give her away; he would lend her to George *what's-his-name* for as long as she wanted. And he would always love his mother, more than any other man ever could.

CHAPTER 5

It was cold for a midsummer's night, unusually cold as she waited in the car. Shellie was wearing a pair of jeans with only a tee shirt and sandals. Normally that would have been enough for the warm weather in Southern California, but she was having chills and it seemed to be getting worse.

She looked at her watch, half past seven. Janet should be there any minute. Friday night traffic on the freeways was normally heavy, and Janet would be driving from Glendale to Santa Monica on I-10, the busiest cross-town freeway in Los Angeles.

Shellie reached up to adjust the rear view mirror so she could lean back on the headrest and still see who was coming into the parking lot of the beach park. Her wrist was hurting so much she couldn't move it, and it had swollen considerably since she got away. The pain around her middle seemed to have subsided somewhat. Now it was more of a strong dull ache rather than sharp, throbbing pains. She had been sitting in her car for forty-five minutes, watching the people come and go, some walking in the moonlight on the beach, some throwing Frisbees in the sand and on the lawn, some playing with their dogs.

It amazed her how an entire world of people could walk by unaware of what was happening in the lives of thousands of unhappy couples, unaware of the cruelty and madness that inhabited those houses. No family unit was safe from pain. She learned that from her mother, and even more-so from her husband - the only two people she'd ever loved. So the trick was not to love.

Oh, thank God, there she is!

Janet pulled up next to Shellie and jumped out of her car with the speed and determination of an Olympic champion and reached for Shellie as she opened her door.

"Oh, Baby! What has that bastard done to you?"

"I'm alive at least, but I think my wrist is broken. It feels like it is anyway. And something's going on inside me, may be the ribs. I don't know."

"C'mon. We'll leave your car here and pick it up later." She carefully supported Shellie as they slowly made their way to Janet's navy-blue Lincoln SUV. A blanket was draped over the passenger seat and Janet tucked it around Shellie. She was worried after recognizing the tell-tale signs of shock, the involuntary shaking and paleness. "I've called one of my doctors here in Santa Monica and he's waiting for us. You're going to be fine, honey. He'll fix you right up. Do you want a pillow? I brought one for you."

Shellie's teeth chattered as she replied, "No, this is okay. I'm just cold. Thank you for the blanket, I can't stop shivering."

Janet locked and closed the door and hurried to the driver's side. She hopped into the vehicle and lost no time speeding away to the small 24-hour women's clinic on Santa Monica Boulevard that she had frequented quite often once upon a time.

CHAPTER 6

Where is she? Still in his jeans and polo shirt, Jerold sat on the bed for a few minutes, and then he jumped up and paced some more, wracking his brain. Was she all right? Had he injured her? He didn't think it would've been bad enough for her to go to a doctor, but if she did go to a doctor, who would it be? Maybe she called her boss. But if she hadn't, he certainly didn't want to call him at this time of night. His mind was wound up as tight as his body. He was shaking and sweating. This had never happened before. She'd never left like this.

He reached for his jacket and grabbed his keys. Outside the door he stood for a moment, thinking, then walked to his neighbor's door and rang the bell. He knew it was three in the morning and didn't care.

Hank opened the door slowly, wearing a robe and slippers. "What is it, Jerold?"

"I'm sorry to bother you, Hank. But I just need to know if Shellie said anything about where she was going when you saw her in the elevator earlier."

"Say anything? Well, no. I don't think she did."

"I just thought you might know where she is. She hasn't come home. I'm worried about her."

"Oh dear, I don't recall her saying much at all. She

28

seemed a bit different though. Quiet. A little pale. Has she been sick?"

"No. Well, I just wondered. Thanks. Sorry for bothering you. Sorry."

Hank watched as Jerold walked towards the elevator. He wondered if she'd finally left the prick. The walls were paper thin between the two apartments and he'd heard the yelling and screaming many times over the years. He had even considered reporting them to security, but had decided to keep his nose out of it. He figured if she got tired of it, she'd leave. He hoped to God she had, poor girl.

Jerold decided to take a ride along the beach. Sometimes she would go there; it seemed to be her favorite place to brood after they'd have a row. Maybe she had fallen asleep in her car at the beach, since he couldn't find it in the parking garage.

He drove out on the Marina del Rey peninsula first, checking out the parking spaces along the entrance to the harbor. No sight of her. Then he decided to drive towards Santa Monica. He knew of a beach park there she liked. Normally no one was allowed in the parking lot past 10 p.m., but he'd look anyway.

As he drove along glancing down side streets in the diverse Venice Beach neighborhood, questions flooded his mind. What if he couldn't find her? What if she was gone for good this time? Why had he hit and kicked her? He didn't know why he did that. Something would just come over him and he had no control over it. He had hated his father for beating his mother, and here he had been doing the same thing to Shellie. She was so tiny, so harmless and helpless.

"God!" He hit the steering wheel with the heels of his hands as he cried out, "Why! Why! Why!" He rested his head against the steering wheel at a stop sign and prayed aloud, "God, bring her back to me, please bring her back. I know I've been wrong. I'll get help. I want to make it up to her. Please help me find her."

He could see the street that lead to the beach park up ahead. By the time he turned, he was choking back the tears. As he pulled to the entrance that was closed, he could see her car parked on the front row near the sand.

"Thank you, God!" He jumped out of his car and ran towards hers, calling out her name, "Shellie? Shellie, I'm so sorry."

The car was empty. He used the spare key on his key ring to open the door and then he searched for some clue or indication of where she might be. He found nothing. The beach was deserted and void of noise except for the calm rolling waves slipping up the slope and then back down again. The thought entered his mind that Shellie may have committed suicide, may have walked into the Pacific and slipped away. But he rejected the thought almost as quickly as it came to him. Not his Shellie, she wouldn't do that. He decided to wait in her car for her. She'd be back. She'd at least come back for her car. She needed it for work. And when she did he was going to beg her for forgiveness. And he would promise to see a therapist and would never hit her again as long as he lived. He loved her and he wanted to prove it.

On Monday morning after a highly emotional weekend, Jerold drove to Shellie's workplace. Over the past two days and as he had sat and waited all night in Shellie's car, his feelings had run the gamut.

He hadn't noticed the Lincoln SUV that had passed by early Saturday morning at the beach as he had waited in Shellie's car. So he hadn't seen the blond woman driving it and his own Shellie half sitting half lying in the back seat. It had slowed down for only a moment and then sped off in the opposite direction. He'd spent the rest of Saturday and all day Sunday berating himself for all he'd done to Shellie. He had gone through four twelve-packs of Budweiser in two days.

Now his head was throbbing and his eyes were swollen and bloodshot as he opened the door that led into the reception area of the chiropractic clinic where Shellie had worked. He was surprised to see Julie sitting at the reception desk where his sweet Shellie usually sat. He'd run into Julie quite a few times on his Friday night outings at Casa Escobar and they had struck up a friendship.

"So where's Shellie, Julie?"

Julie looked over at the new temp who was sitting at the computer next to her, and then back again to Jerold.

"Uh, well, she doesn't work here anymore, Jerold."

"What do you mean she doesn't work here anymore? Where's the doc? Get him out here!"

"He's with a patient. Can I help?"

"I said get him out here!" He slammed his fist onto the desk. "Right now!"

She stood up and backed away towards the adjoining office door as she tried to reason with him. "Please, calm down. Okay? I'll get him."

Jerold took a deep breath and turned towards one of the chairs in the waiting area, but decided not to sit down. He stood instead, shifting from one foot to the other, glancing at the new temp and at the door Julie had just gone through. He looked at his watch. It was 9:15 a.m. The office had opened at nine.

"Hello, Mr. Singer," Doc Roos said as he entered the reception area from his office. "What can I do for you?"

"I want to know where Shellie is. Why isn't she working here?"

"She gave her notice last week, said she was going on tour with a band that was leaving on Friday."

"What band?"

"She didn't say." He saw the wild and frustrated look in Jerold's eyes, and the nervousness and edgy mannerisms that Shellie must have so often feared. Many times Doc Roos had wanted to report the bruises and obvious beatings to the police, but Shellie had begged him not to, said she didn't want to press charges and swore she wouldn't.

"Did she have any friends who visited her here?"

"No, can't say that she did, but then I wasn't watching."

Jerold squinted as he stared into Doc Roos disapproving eyes. He could detect the attitude he knew so well - the looking down of one's nose, the obvious disdain.

"So may I gather she left without telling you?

"You may gather anything you want. If she calls or turns

31

up here again, I'd appreciate it if you'd give her a message."

"If she calls, I will."

"Tell her I need to talk to her. Tell her it's very important and something she'd want to hear."

Doc saw tears gather in Jerold's sad eyes and for a moment he felt sorry for him. He felt that the poor fool probably did love Shellie, even if he didn't deserve her. "If she calls, I'll give her your message."

"Thanks," he said as he headed for the door, suddenly lifeless and limp with exhaustion. "I'm sorry I barged in on your morning."

His hang-dog look got to all three of them.

"Poor guy," Doc Roos sighed after Jerold shut the door behind him. "Get me Janet Corrigan," he said as he headed back to his office.

CHAPTER 7

The wedding day had arrived in Interlaken. It was Sunday. The festivities had begun at the five-star old-world Grand Hotel, which was the most exquisite hotel in Interlaken and according to George Schmidt, the best in the region. Adrian had to agree with George on that score. The Grand Hotel was absolutely elegant. The moment one entered the huge wood and glass doors that were flanked by doormen, it was evident one had stepped into a world of grandeur. Tall columns, spaciousness, marble everywhere, live trees and shrubs, magnificent floral arrangements, chandeliers, molded wooden wall and partition panels, antiques, etched glass, fabulous artwork – it was all there.

Adrian knew his mother was thrilled and proud to be able to have a luxurious wedding celebration and to introduce her groom to all her family and friends in the banquet hall of the hotel on this very special day.

Between the two of them–George and Gina–they successfully kept the guest list under 300. George invited friends and family from Germany and Gina invited her friends and family from Italy and Gimmelwald, and of course there were all the newfound friends they'd both acquired in Interlaken during the past three months.

Adrian smiled and nodded at familiar faces as he glanced

33

around the enormous window-lined dining hall. His mother's favorite color dominated the décor. On every table was an arrangement of purple fresh flowers including cuttings of lavender Wisteria that grew in abundance and climbed the stone walls throughout the hotel grounds.

The pale lilac five-tiered wedding cake was perched on a table in front of a massive fireplace, waiting for the bride and groom to cut the first slice.

After the private ceremony in the chapel, Adrian had joined the dinner guests while Gina and George had gone up to their suite, where they had planned to spend the night before leaving on their honeymoon the following day. During those few private moments, they had sipped their first glasses of champagne as husband and wife and had reaffirmed their expression of love and commitment to each other then sealed the commitment with a symbolic kiss and a very tender embrace. Now they were ready to face their family and friends downstairs at the reception.

"They're coming!" one of the children screamed. "They're coming!"

Excitement spread throughout the room and everyone stood facing the doorway eagerly anticipating the newlyweds' entry. The women were curious to see what Gina had chosen to wear. Would she wear white, or off white which was the custom, or would she be bold and do a color? Most of Gina's family and friends were curious about George, who was this man who'd captured their Gina's heart? And George's side was just as curious about Gina. How could she measure up to George's Hilda, who'd been his bride for 45 years before she died tragically of Leukemia? George's son and daughter weren't asking that question, though, because they were elated he had found someone, and both supported him implicitly.

Here they were, the daughters and sons of the newlyweds, all seated together at one large table - Adrian, his sister Maggie and her husband and two children from the UK, his sister Tara from Italy, who came alone, George's daughter Ingrid and his son Victor from Germany - a table of very handsome offspring indeed.

Most everyone in the room had reached for the small baskets of rose petals that had been placed on every dinner plate. They were poised to shower the bride and groom with the soft multi-colored rose petal confetti as they walked by. The energy level was high amongst the crowd who was feeling the mood of the day whether or not they approved of the marriage, because they were ready to celebrate and enjoy themselves on this splendid summer day regardless.

The bride and groom entered the great banquet hall to the sounds of applause and cheers and Mendelssohn's *Wedding March* played by a stringed quartet.

The new Mrs. George Schmidt wore a deep purple satin brocade suit, tailored to fit her lithe, perfect figure and a simple low neck lavender silk camisole underneath. A hat in violet hues swashed with lilac voile bunched in the back–held by a giant purple satin rosebud with green leaves–adorned her black hair that was gracefully pulled up in a loose style, with occasional wisps feathering her neck and face. She was wearing a pair of lavender pearl drop earrings given to her by Mama Anna, which had belonged to her mother. Pinned just below her shoulder above her heart was a large broach shaped like a heart made of semi-precious multi-colored stones in shades of purple and green. George had surprised her with the bauble the evening before. She had admired it in the jewelry store next door to his shop, and he couldn't resist buying it for her as his wedding gift.

George Schmidt stood a good six inches taller than Gina and was wearing a gorgeous light brown silk blazer dotted with tiny dark brown nubs, a cream colored shirt and a tie in bold colors–purples, greens, and bronze–and chocolate colored silk trousers. His sandy hair had blond highlights mingled with gray; he was tanned and a very attractive man.

Together they were spectacular, both sparkled as if they'd been sprinkled with fairy dust and appeared to have stepped from the pages of current issues of Vogue and GQ.

Adrian's glance went to their shoes that were of the finest Italian leathers, his mother's were amethyst and the groom's were coffee. Adrian loved shoes. He had always been drawn to shoe stores and one of the first things he noticed on a person was the shoes. He occasionally boasted that he could easily tell if a person was "well-heeled" or not by the kind of shoes he wore– the condition of them and the savoir faire in which he wore them. "Shoes tell the story," he had said many times. And if that were true, his mother had certainly made a proper financial choice in George Schmidt. At least she would not be destitute. He was happy in that for her.

He glanced at George's daughter Ingrid, across from him, who was giggling and tossing rose petals at the happy couple. She seemed to be the same age as Adrian. He hadn't said much to the Schmidt offspring. No particular reason, he just hadn't. He realized it wasn't their fault their father was taking his mother away from him.

Ingrid turned and caught Adrian's stare. "Adrian, you're not throwing petals. Why not?"

"Oh, I think they're getting enough as it is, don't you?"

She lifted her glass of champagne. "You're so right. It's time to drink." She gulped the remainder of the champagne in her glass and then asked her brother Victor to pour another for her, since the bottle was on the table near him.

Victor turned and obliged her. Then he clanked a water glass with his table knife and stood to address the entire room of people. "Let's drink a toast to the magnificent couple standing before us – your friends, your family, our parents," he nodded to those standing at the sibling table with him. "Shall we?"

Adrian's sisters and the Schmidt clan quickly poured more champagne, as did the other 250 people in the room, and lifted their glasses, holding them in mid air.

"Adrian?" Maggie questioned quietly when she saw her brother hadn't lifted his glass.

He sighed and acquiesced, but lowered his eyes in contemplation without smiling.

"To our newly combined family - the Van Allmans and the Schmidts. May we too be as happy as our father and your mother. Prosit!"

36

"*Prosit!*"

All but Adrian joined in verbalizing the toast. He sipped his champagne slowly while watching his mother kiss George before they cut the cake.

Mama Anna had seen Adrian's reluctance, his sadness. She had also witnessed his happiness earlier in the chapel as he stood up with his mother. He seemed to be confused about his feelings, switching back and forth from sad to happy to sad again. But Mama Anna understood Adrian. She knew how he must be questioning himself now. Questioning why he stayed in Gimmelwald all these years. Asking himself why he hadn't left to make a life for himself, same as his sisters.

Adrian felt Mama Anna's penetrating gaze and was drawn to her empathetic eyes. *Why didn't I leave when I had the chance, Mama Anna?*

CHAPTER 8

After the festivities, on the ride up the mountain from Interlaken, Adrian and his sisters cavorted and teased each other like old times. Maggie was the eldest, Tara was two years younger, and then came Adrian two years later. When they were growing up together they were a close-knit family. The two girls had hovered over their brother and protected him when he was a child till he shot past them in growth and took on the role of protector.

He had been heartbroken when they both left Gimmelwald, almost as much as when his childhood sweetheart left him never to return.

But today they were all together once again and as they rode the train, he was in high spirits. He joked with his niece and nephew, dished out as many riddles as they did to him. He was good with children, and had at one time wanted to start his own family. But now he felt that possibility was next to nil.

"Adrian, why don't you come back with us and stay in London for awhile? We can ask Cousin Harold to care for the farm and animals. And Cousin Mary could stay with Mama Anna. Mary says she's lonely living by herself, anyway. What do you think, Mama Anna?"

Mama Anna was grinning from ear to ear; she had been

the instigator of this abrupt invitation. She and the girls had discussed it during the reception, had all agreed it was a fabulous idea. And they'd already talked it over with Harold and Mary, who'd said they'd be happy to help.

"I think it's a grand idea, Maggie. Adrian needs a holiday. He hasn't been away from the farm since Henri took all three of you to Greece before he . . . " She stopped herself, didn't want to lower the present high everyone was maintaining by mentioning their father's death. " . . . before you girls left for school."

"Adrian?" Maggie questioned.

"I don't care to go to London. I don't even like London." Adrian retorted.

"Well, then go to Paris. You can use our apartment in Montmartre. You've always wanted to go to Paris. I remember how you used to dream of being a Parisian painter. Yes, that's it! Go to Montmartre and paint portraits!"

Tara immediately jumped into the excitement, "Yes, that's right! That's what you've always wanted to do. Oh, Adrian, you've got to do it!"

"The apartment's been cleaned; we just spent a couple weeks there. So that's no problem. You can stay as long as you wish, actually."

"And Mary and Harold can help me move my things to Interlaken after Gina and George return from Germany. You needn't be concerned about me or the farm or the animals. It's all been arranged. "

Adrian stared at his family, befuddled and confused about how they'd just come from joking and playing while riding the cog train up the mountain after his mother's wedding to suddenly planning his sojourn from Gimmelwald to Paris. Obviously this was not something that had just come out of the blue. "This is your idea, isn't it, Mama Anna?" he frowned as his eyes began to water. "You're behind this, aren't you?"

Mama Anna moved next to him by the window. She took his hands in hers, stroked them, and looked him straight in the eyes. "It's time for you to go, Adrian. I will not allow you to stay behind and be my nursemaid. Please, go. You must find your own way."

The rest of the family immediately responded with sincere encouragement in their words and actions. They all adored Adrian. He had been such a thoughtful and devoted son, grandson, brother, and cousin. Adrian was always the first one to lend a helping hand to anyone who needed it. Yes, it was his turn to follow his heart.

Adrian gently hugged his grandmother. "All right. For you I'll go. For you, Mama Anna."

They all cheered, some jumping for joy. Others in the car joined them in the merriment when they learned what was happening. Now they had more to celebrate, not just Gina's wedding, but Adrian's holiday.

"So which is to be, Adrian? London or Paris?" his sister Tara called out over the cheerful clamor.

"Paris, of course!" he gleefully shouted. He stood and stretched, took a deep breath and looked towards the forward car. "I smell smoke," he said.

The Van Allman family was on the second of two cars connected to each other on the railway that led from Interlaken up the mountain to Gimmelwald.

Maggie's husband Derek stood up to see if he could see anything ahead. They were coming to a tunnel, one of many tunnels through which the cog trains wound up and down the steep mountains. A cog train has the ability to climb a 48 percent grade and is widely used in the Swiss Alps where a two-rail wheeled train can not go. It has an additional rack or cog in between the two outer tracks to carry it forward, making it easier to make the vertical ascensions.

"There's smoke in the front car, Adrian." Derek whispered.

Adrian saw a glimmer of a flame in the middle of the smoke as they entered the dark tunnel. Almost immediately smoke began billowing towards the second car. Then the train suddenly stopped as it was programmed to do when there was a fire. It stopped just inside the tunnel with half of the second car extending outside the tunnel.

"Derek, grab the children!" Adrian tried the doors, but they wouldn't budge.

The smoke was getting blacker and heavier and beginning to seep into their breathing space. Adrian and Derek were both choking and coughing, working at the windows, trying to pry them open. Finally Derek opened one, and several other people had also.

Adrian yelled as he motioned to Maggie and Tara, "Climb out of the windows, both of you. Go! We'll hand the kids to you." He managed to get another window open, and encouraged others to jump out.

Derek quickly lifted children through the windows that had cleared the tunnel. The people that were inside the tunnel were at a much greater risk from smoke and fire. Adrian could hear the echoing screams from those who were struggling to reach safety or were trapped. He tried to block out the cries as he reached for Mama Anna and saw that she was having difficulty breathing. She was gasping, eyes clinched shut. The smoke was so thick; it was becoming a chore for Adrian to hold his eyes open. People all around were panicking and screaming now and clamoring out the windows any way they could, not fearing how their bodies impacted the ground. The flames had reached the second car.

With squinting eyes and gasping for smokeless air, Adrian lifted his grandmother and threw her over his shoulder. Derek was standing below the window at the rear of the car crying for Adrian to jump out. Adrian followed Derek's voice until he opened his eyes briefly and saw him standing below the open window. Without a moment's hesitation he pushed Mama Anna through the window into Derek's arms, and immediately dove out and landed smack on top of them.

They tumbled down the embankment where his sisters and other family members had been huddled in terror and shock waiting for their beloved Adrian and Mama Anna. The family frantically pulled the three of them farther away from the tracks and the train, which was now totally engulfed in flames.

41

* * * * *

The cause of the fire was under investigation. It was suspected there'd been a leak of some sort of flammable material on the tracks, although the cog trains were supposedly fireproof. How it could happen was truly a mystery. Fourteen people had died in the fire. Some had survived with massive to less serious burns; some suffered broken bones and sprains from falling and jumping through the windows, almost all experienced a degree of smoke inhalation.

Mama Anna died one day after the accident - the day Gina and George were to leave on their honeymoon. The day Adrian was to leave for Paris. The van Allman family and friends were devastated.

Mama Anna lasted twelve hours after a heart attack immediately after the train disaster, and then had silently, peacefully faded away as a result of congestive heart failure.

Adrian and Gina were at her bedside that morning when the final puff of breath escaped her lips.

Adrian shivered as he stood looking at Mama Anna, he felt a coolness overtake him, "She's still here, Mother. I feel her!"

"Darling, she'll always be by your side. She loved you more than life itself, and she wanted you to be happy." Gina put her arms around him while at the same time trying to squelch her own sobs, to console Adrian when she needing consoling.

"I tried to save her, Mother. I tried—" His quiet weeping grew into uncontrollable gut-wrenching moans. His mother tried to calm him, but he broke loose and fell across Mama Anna's body. "I love you, Mama Anna. I'm so sorry."

Gina couldn't bear it. She lost control as she watched her heartbroken Adrian mourn his grandmother. George and Derek rushed into the hospital room; Maggie and Tara were right behind them.

George instantaneously grabbed Gina and held her tightly in his arms, stroking her hair as she wept. Derek gently pulled Adrian off Mama Anna and Maggie and Tara held their little big brother tightly between them.

Six days had passed since his grandmother's death and Adrian's train was about to leave for Zurich where he would catch a plane to Paris. A large group of family members and friends from Gimmelwald came to see him off. His mother held his hand as the others greeted him and wished him the best in life.

He had decided to move away from Gimmelwald, not just go for a holiday as was originally planned. It would be too difficult to live in Gimmelwald now that his father, mother and grandmother weren't there anymore. He couldn't stay in the house with all the memories. It was too much for him, at least for now.

He missed the smell of Mama Anna's morning coffee and muffins; and he knew he would worry about Tessa the cow, but being around all the mementos and memorabilia in Gimmelwald was overwhelming. So he had been staying in George's guest house in Interlaken because he couldn't bear being reminded of his grandmother's tragic death. He felt if he had handled her more gently, she would have lived. He felt he was such a lummox and blamed himself for her death.

"Darling, it's time for you to board the train," Gina said as she gently squeezed his hand.

"I love you, Mother," he said as he hugged her. "George is not a bad guy, you know. I think I like him." He smiled mischievously at his mother.

"He likes you too, darling. Now you must get on the train. Go."

Adrian waved at all the bitter-sweet expressions on the faces turned towards him as he sat near a window and the train pulled out of the station. He was overwhelmed by the abundant expression of love and felt so lucky to be a Van Allman from Gimmelwald. He wanted to make his family and friends proud of him, to make the Van Allman name famous. He didn't know how he was going to do it, but in his heart he knew he would find a way.

CHAPTER 9

A month had passed since Shellie had given herself over to the loving care of Janet Corrigan and since Jerold had burst in on Doc Roos. The doc had returned Janet's earlier call that same morning telling her Jerold had appeared at his office as they had figured he would.

It was unfortunate Jerold had found Shellie's car because she had planned to sell it to help finance the start of her new life. And then her plans had been altered even more at the insistence of Janet and the physician at the Santa Monica clinic. As it turned out, her wrist wasn't broken; it was badly bruised and now was beginning to look and feel normal. Although she had a couple of cracked ribs, using a binding support and moving around as little as possible had aided in the successful healing of the painful damage.

Shellie threw the covers back and stretched, testing her mending injuries as she did every morning. She stood in the sunlight that was streaming through the French doors. She had been very comfortable in Janet's lavishly decorated guest room. She could become accustomed to living the good life - lounging around the expansive country club mansion, lying in the sun, floating in the swimming pool, or watching television and reading, eating only the healthiest foods prepared by Janet who

44

was a health nut. But in spite of it all, Shellie was eager to get on with her own life.

When Doc Roos had told her how distraught Jerold had been, Shellie became upset once again and was terribly unsure that she was doing the right thing. At first she felt she should at least telephone him. But then Janet had reminded her of all the days, weeks, months, and years he had been abusing her, and how he had always apologized the next day and told her how much he loved her and wouldn't hurt her ever again. He said it every time, so no, she wasn't going to call him, and no, she wasn't going back. Remembering made it easier for her to put him out of her mind as she recuperated and became stronger.

Today was the day she would be putting Los Angeles and a lifetime of horrible memories behind her forever. She knew she should never say *forever*, but that's exactly how she was feeling at the moment. She couldn't care less if she ever California again.

Of course the recovery days she had spent with Janet had been wonderful, and she would always be grateful to her. Janet was a fun person to be around, and had made Shellie feel like a necessary human being. It was going to be difficult to say goodbye to her. She had no clue how she would ever repay her for her kindness.

Shellie touched the outfit she had laid out the night before next to her packed suitcases. This was it. The time had come.

Paris! I can't believe it! She had dreamed of going to Paris her whole life. She had studied and read about all the musicians who'd started out in Paris, and she longed to experience the Jazz scene in the City of Lights. Five years ago she had almost left Jerold and had applied for a passport without him knowing. Now she was thanking her lucky stars for having the foresight.

Janet had rescheduled Shellie's flight and had paid the penalty for changing dates. She had even slipped a sealed envelope containing a *good luck* note and 5000 Euros into Shellie's suitcase after it was packed. Shellie had refused the extra money when she had offered it to her, but Janet knew she would need it. She had traveled to Europe several times and knew it wasn't going to be easy for Shellie to find a job, especially since she didn't speak French. So in the note she offered assistance anytime she needed it, told Shellie she was sponsoring her, and pleaded with her to contact her immediately if she was in a bind of any kind. Janet was sure they had formed a lasting bond and felt they would be friends for life. It was like having the daughter she had always wanted. And why not, she was lonely living by herself in such a big house, which was one of the reasons she felt the urge to take Shellie under her wings. Actually, she was hoping Shellie would stay with her.

After college, Janet had married her fiancé of two years who was gorgeous and a gentle man, an up-and-coming young corporate attorney. At the same time she had entered the corporate world of real estate finance and investment. She and Dave had a successful relationship the first seven years of their marriage, at least that's what Janet thought, until one day Dave came home and asked for a divorce. Unbeknownst to Janet, he had been having an affair with another attorney - a male attorney. She was devastated and became confused about her own femininity. She wondered what within her had driven her husband to a man. After several sessions with a therapist, she forced herself to *let it go* and ten years later she married a rugged, macho man who turned out to be the "King of Abusers". Thank goodness during the ten years prior she had built herself quite an investment portfolio and when the time came for her to divorce her second husband she was already set financially. She didn't need him or his money.

Since then her life had become easy and comfortable, and she felt it was time to share that comfort with someone else. She felt that that someone could be Shellie. She wanted to give her a chance to experience the good life too. And although she was hoping Shellie would stay with her in California, she admired her for setting out to follow her own dream.

CHAPTER 10

Jerold had been at the bar since noon. He was restless and had agreed to meet some of his cronies to watch a football game on the wide-screen television at El Toritos - a popular watering hole in the marina for sports enthusiasts as well as Mexican food lovers. It sat on the edge of the main Marina del Rey channel and people loved to congregate there and watch the pleasure boats maneuver along the waterway. He felt it might help take his mind off Shellie. He hadn't given up the hope of her returning to him because he just couldn't believe she would walk out without ever contacting him again. He felt she at least owed him an explanation.

"Hey, Julie!" he called out as Julie entered the bar looking around for a place to sit. The restaurant and bar were already full as usual on a Sunday.

Julie waved and headed towards Jerold. He hadn't seen her since he had gone to the clinic the Monday after Shellie disappeared.

"Hi, Jerold," she called out over the noise and continued to walk towards him.

Jerold motioned for her to join him and pulled a chair from another table for her. He'd been sitting alone at a small table along the wall, waiting for his friends to arrive.

"So, how's it going?" she asked as she sat.

"Oh, I can't complain. What good would it do? Haven't seen you around lately."

"I've been pretty busy, my folks have been here from Chicago. They come out for a month every year to drive me crazy." She laughed. "So have you heard from Shellie?"

He lowered his eyes and became silent.

"Oh, I'm sorry. I didn't mean—"

"Nah, that's okay."

"Did she call you that day you came into the office? I know the doc called the lady she's staying with."

"Lady?"

"Janet Corrigan. One of our patients. Evidently Janet had called the doc earlier that morning before we opened to let him know that Shellie was with her. That she hadn't left on a tour like she had told him. So after you came in, he called her back to give her your message. I just figured—" She saw the confused and surprised look on Jerold's face. "Oh dear."

"No, no. That's alright. I mean– well, uh– she called, yes. She called and left a message, but we've been playing phone tag ever since. Uh– what was her name again? Your patient?"

"Janet Corrigan. They were friends. She brought suitcases to Shellie at work that Friday."

Jerold rubbed his hands through his hair; he quickly stood, almost knocking the chair over. "Excuse me, Julie; I have to make a call. I just remembered something I was supposed to do."

"Sure. I'll just order a drink. You want another?"

He didn't answer as he rushed from the bar.

CHAPTER 11

Janet handed Shellie a hi-tech cell phone as they were preparing to leave.

"Here, honey. I want you to have this. You can use it anywhere in the world. It takes pictures and does email. I imagine it'll do almost anything. I haven't looked at the instructions. You can upload and download data too. I put the manual in your carryon bag, so you can read it on the plane. It's my gift to you. I'm paying for it."

"Oh, Janet, I can't, let me—"

"No, I'll pay for the calls. The bill will be coming to me anyway. You just get settled and when we see what happens, then we'll talk about who pays for what. Okay? Let me help you, honey. I've got no one to splurge on. Let me splurge on you."

"But you've already done so much. You gave me a place to stay, bought me clothes, shoes, suitcases. Found me a place to stay in Paris. I just don't know how I can ever repay you, Janet."

They both hugged each other for the umpteenth time.

"Oh, wait. I need to write the number down. Here, let me see what it is." Janet took the phone from Shellie and went through the French doors to the covered area by the pool where her notes along with her appointment and address books were scattered. She did most of her work there in the summer, preferred to be outdoors rather than in her home office. She picked up a pen and wrote. "Shellie: 213-699-8209. There. Okay. Now I can call you. Here you go," she smiled as she handed it back to Shellie. "You'll call me as soon as you land, right?"

"Of course I will. I've already written your numbers in my address book."

"Okay then, let's be on our way, hon. I'm going to miss you so much. But I know you have to do this, and I'm very proud of you. I really am."

"I wish you were going too."

"Well, be careful with what you wish," she said as she ushered Shellie back into the family room.

"I mean it. I'm excited but at the same time I'm scared. I've never been anywhere by myself."

"Hon, you'll do fine. Just get a taxi at the airport, don't mess with the Metro till you have time to figure it all out. It's pretty simple, though. You'll see, once you get used to it. Take a cab right to the houseboat. You have the address. Come on, now. We don't want to miss your plane."

Janet locked the door leading into the garage as they left. She had already loaded the luggage earlier and then they were on their way. She drove to the I-5 from Glendale and then cut over to the 110 to the I-10 heading for the 405. Traffic was light and they made good time.

Jerold opened his cell phone as soon as he left El Toritos. He called information for Janet Corrigan and not only got her number, they gave him her address in Glendale. He couldn't believe a woman would have her address listed in this day and age. But who was he to figure out how a woman thinks. He certainly miscalculated Shellie.

He dialed the number as he pulled out of the parking lot heading for Glendale. The message machine came on.

Hello, I'm away from the phone at the moment, but please leave your name and phone number. Your call is important to me. I'll get right back to you.

He didn't leave a message.

As he drove a bit faster than usual, he thought again of how much he loved Shellie. He knew he had been a bastard. He knew he needed to control his anger. Maybe he could go to an anger management group. Yes, he would do that. He had seen the movie that took a rather comical view of anger. Yes, maybe he should seek counseling, although he felt that Shellie should share some of the responsibility. She should always be home when he got there. It was her duty as a wife to be there for him. Yes, she would have to do her part, too.

He took the I-10 from 405 going east. Figured that was the best way to get to Glendale quickly.

A few miles further on I-10, going in the opposite direction at the exact same time, Shellie and Janet were heading for the airport to catch a plane to Paris, France.

"Who did you say is going to be there to let me into the houseboat? Does he know when I'll get there?"

Janet reached across to the passenger seat and patted Shellie's arm. "Hon, don't you start worrying now. My friend Bobby will be there to let you in. He knows when you'll be arriving, and he'll explain how everything works. In fact, we were a thing at one time. But living half way around the world sort of cooled it off. He owns the houseboat where you're staying, honey. Okay? So don't worry. Relax."

"I'm so excited, Janet. I can't believe I'm on my way to Paris. I just can't believe it! Too bad this isn't April."

They both burst out in song, "*April in Paris*" at the very same moment which pitched them into laughter.

Jerold turned onto the street he had located in the Thomas Guide. How could anyone do without a Thomas Guide - the surefire way to find addresses in Southern California.

There it is. He was lucky; he entered the gated community right behind someone else who triggered the electronic gate, perfect timing. He drove up the winding driveway to Janet Corrigan's house. Again he couldn't believe she was listed in the phone book. There were too many crazies loose in the L.A. area; Jerold didn't even list his own address. *Now that is one fuckin' big house!* He gaped at the pillared entrance and sat for a moment staring at the impressive front doors.

It didn't look like anyone was around. At least no cars were parked in the driveway. *She probably keeps it in the garage, wherever that is. Must be off the alleyway.* He got out of his car and walked up the marble steps to the entry and rang the doorbell. He waited. No answer. He rang it again, still no answer.

He decided to walk around the house and peered through windows until he reached a brick wall. He found a gate, unlatched it and entered a garden area with a swimming pool beyond near the back of the house. Maybe they were at the pool and hadn't heard the phone or the doorbell.

Jerold felt a bit uneasy, not knowing what to expect, but then Shellie was his wife; he had a right to be there. When she married him it was for keeps, till death do they part. That's how he felt about it. He would never let her go. Never.

Not a soul in sight. He noticed one set of French doors was wide open. He called out, "Shellie?" He listened. "Come out here, Shellie!"

No answer. He walked noisily to the doors, clearing his throat, whistled, and then leaned through the open doorway, but decided against going inside. He felt like he had taken enough liberties as it was, being in the back yard, uninvited. Then he glanced over to the covered area of the patio and the table strewn with papers and notebooks. There was a phone there, too. He went to it, picked up a few sheets of paper; saw that Janet was an agent with Coldwell Banker. He wondered if maybe Shellie had gone to work at Coldwell Banker. He would call them Monday morning.

An address book was lying open on the table and he saw Shellie's name next to a telephone number he didn't recognize. It was a local number. He quickly wrote the number down and hurried back to his car to use his cell to dial it.

"Okay, hon. This is as far as I can go. So you have

everything? Do you need anything else? Got enough cash?"

"Now you quit worrying, Janet," Shellie said as she hugged her one more time. "I'm fine. More than fine, thanks to you."

"Okay then. But I'll trust you to let me know if you need anything. And I mean anything. You understand?"

"Yes, I understand. I'll call you as soon as I get there."

"Phone's in your purse?"

"Yep, it's in my purse. And I'll call you as soon as I board the plane like you said. Okay? I'm anxious to use my new phone. I have an hour and a half to kill, so I'll just roam through those shops you told me about; maybe grab a sandwich and a book before I get on."

"All right, hon. You get going. I love you, Shellie. And I'll miss you." She wiped her eyes quickly, trying not to appear to be a blubbering idiot.

"Me too. Bye." Shellie turned to hide her own emotions and hurried through the first checkpoint. She looked back and waved to Janet who was wiping away the tears that had finally spilled down her face.

Be happy, my sweet, Janet silently wished as she blew Shellie a kiss.

Shellie passed through the next two security checks without a hitch and then made her way to a coffee shop where she ordered a cup of green tea and an egg salad sandwich. She was starving. All the excitement up to that point had taken her appetite away. She hadn't been able to eat breakfast, just had a quick slice of toast, so the tea and sandwich tasted yummy.

Her cell phone rang. She answered.

"Hi, Janet. That was fast," she laughed. "Janet?"

There was a dead silence on the other end. Then came a jolt that almost caused Shellie to regurgitate the last bite of her sandwich.

"Where are you, Shellie?" Jerold asked.

Shellie couldn't believe it! Her eyes darted, scanning the terminal, expecting Jerold to jump out at her from one of the shops or leap from around a corner with his fist doubled and his cell phone to his ear.

"God damn it! Answer me, I know you're there!"

"How did you get this number?" she whispered. Her voice faltered. She put her hand over the transmitter to block out the airport noises.

"It doesn't make a goddamn bit of difference how I got this fuckin' number, Shellie. Tell me where the hell you are!"

Her breath came in short spurts, and she had difficulty swallowing. She began coughing.

"God damn it, Shellie, you're making me mad! Why are you doing this to me?"

She pushed the button to cut the communication, and sat staring at the cell phone. It rang again. She let it ring. Four rings. When it stopped she quickly reached into her carryon bag for the address book where she had entered Janet's number. She was shaking and having trouble finding the cell number. She accidentally brushed against the cup of tea and knocked it askew on the saucer, almost spilling its contents.

There it is. She dialed the number. As she waited for Janet to answer, she lifted the cup and gulped the dregs.

"Jerold just called me, Janet! What am I going to do? He's going to find me. I can't get on the plane yet. How did he get my cell number? Maybe he's already here."

"Shellie, calm down. He doesn't know where you are. Take it easy, honey. I don't know how he got your number, but he couldn't know where you are. You're all right. It's almost time for your flight. He can't get to you even if he is in the airport, but I know he can't be there. You're safe, honey. Don't answer the phone anymore. In fact, turn it off. I won't be calling you till you're in Paris, anyway. I can leave a message and you can call me back, okay? So leave it off and just check for messages. I'll have the number changed or send you a new phone. Sweetie, there's nothing he can do to you now. You hear me, Shellie? You're safe! He'll never hurt you again."

Shellie glanced at the people who were sitting around her, who had most likely overheard her distraught conversation. She was embarrassed and leaned her forehead against her hand while bowing her head, trying to shield the rest of her conversation from the onlookers.

"I know you're right. I'll turn off the phone. I'm okay now."

"All right, hon. Go to the restroom and freshen up, throw some cool water on your face, do some deep breathing and visualize yourself in Paris. You're on your way to Paris. Paris, France! You hear me? That's exciting, isn't it?"

"I think so. I think it is. Yes. It is. Do you mind if I still call you when I'm on the plane right before take off?"

"Of course, baby. Call me when you're buckled up and ready to take flight."

As Shellie buckled up and sat in her seat on the plane, waiting for departure, she began humming. She noticed the plane was half empty and there weren't any passengers within her view. She was happy again and her humming became singing, though very softly, *"Come fly with me, let's float down to Peru."*

A couple of passengers startled her by moving to the seats in front of her.

No more singing. She looked out of the window and her thoughts automatically switched to Jerold, for no matter how much he had hurt her, she still felt guilty for running out on him.

Here she was abandoning her handsome 6'4" high school sweetheart, the boy she had adored all through her teens, who had looked into her brilliant green eyes with his azure blues when they were seniors in high school and had asked her to marry him. Yes, she believed he had loved her then, and he had shown no signs of violence. He had even encouraged her to pursue a singing career which was what she had wanted more than anything. She loved the jazz and blues clubs in Kansas City and most of them were also restaurants so from the time she was a teen, she had gone to them. Kansas was their home state. Shellie enrolled in junior college right out of high school and studied the classics and Jazz and music composition. During the first two years of marriage, Jerold was one of her biggest fans when she would sit in and sing at the local jazz clubs. Then they moved to

Los Angeles, where she got a job as a part-time receptionist while continuing college and singing in clubs on the weekend. But then one night the inevitable happened.

It had been at a club in Redondo Beach. She had been invited by a saxophone player, who she had sung with before, to sit in with his band at the Redondo Pier Club. Jerold was to meet her there later in the evening after he finished drinking with his buddies. So when he arrived she was already on stage standing near the sax player with one of her hands on his shoulder, singing into the microphone that was held by her other hand. She was in a black cashmere off-the-shoulders sweater and tight black satin capris and heels. A massive bundle of curly auburn hair topped the tiny curvaceous chanteuse and sparkled under the stage lights framing her dazzling face; a face that many had said resembled the film star Ava Gardner. Her voice was as sultry and jazzy as she appeared.

After she sang and during the applause of a full house, Shellie and the sax player embraced – a bit too long in Jerold's opinion. He stood at the back of the house and watched her romance another song that ended with another embrace, and that's when he spun on his heels and left the club.

When Shellie got home later that night Jerold slung her across the room as she came in the door, screaming that she couldn't fool him, he knew she was having an affair with the sax guy and that her singing career was over. Kaput! Over! And then he slugged her.

Yes, she still remembered that first slug, and how the slaps and hits and shoves and pushes and kicks and the fists to the face and other parts of her body continued after that night. She thought about how Jerold was so quick at finding a multitude of reasons to beat her over the next seventeen years. Sometimes he would just come home and hit her. *Hello.* Bam!

And her social circle had certainly dwindled, a circle of one, just as the victims on the television show had said. She had no family and no friends other than the few patients she would see at the office. She quit school and began working full time as a receptionist in the chiropractic clinic. Out of her dedication and loyalty through the years, her boss had awarded her a beautiful gold wrist watch. She kept it in her desk drawer at work, as she did with all the other trinkets, terrified that Jerold would think the gifts meant something other than what was intended.

Very seldom was she late getting home from work in fear of the consequences. Not only did she make it a point to get there before Jerold, she squandered that private time alone to rehearse – to sing and play her electronic keyboard – before he fell through the door for the night and made her walk on eggs.

Over the years she continued to study and listen to Jazz greats at home, whenever she was alone. But there were times they would go out to a club when Jerold felt like it, and there were times he would want to show off her singing, so of course she would oblige. She eagerly sang in public every chance she could, but it was always at Jerold's discretion. And no matter how he felt and what he did to her, Shellie Singer had been a promising songbird cooped up in a cage, who one day would take flight.

She noticed the time and quickly took the cell from her bag and punched in the code for Janet. She had learned how to program the phone while she had waited in the terminal. She listened as the phone rang.

Janet answered.

"Oh, I'm glad you're there. I'm on the plane."

"Honey, that is fantastic! See, I told you you'd be safe. Now just sit back and enjoy the beginning of your new life. You go, girl! Take Paris by storm! And remember, I'm right here if you need me, just a keypad away. I mean it."

"I–I hope you don't think I'm silly, Janet, but I–I love you. I mean, not like a man woman—"

"I know what you mean, Shellie. Like a daughter mother kind of thing. Right?"

"I don't know what that's like; I think you're much more to me than that. You're a very special friend, my best friend, my only friend as a matter of fact. You saved my life, Janet, and I'll miss you."

"Hon, I'll see you in Paris before you know it. You just

keep your head up and your eyes wide open and gazin' forward and don't let anyone tell you *no* or get in your way. That's my motto. It's worked for me and it'll work for you. You hear me?"

"Yes, I hear you."

"Okay then, so turn this off when we hang up and I'll be talking at you in Paris. Up, up, and away!"

They both laughed and said goodbye.

As Shellie waited for the Boeing 767 to take off, she couldn't understand the mixed feelings she was experiencing–sadness, happiness, fear, excitement, dread–all at once.

Sadness because no matter how Jerold had treated her, she remembered the Jerold she first loved. The Jerold who made her feel safe and secure and loved in high school and through the first two years of their marriage. When he wasn't drinking he was kind and loveable. That is, if nothing was bothering him. If his day went well. If she did what he wanted her to do. If the weather was good. If she cooked the right food. If she catered to him. Yes, he could be loveable, but the key word here was *if*.

She looked out of the window and watched as the baggage was still being loaded onto the plane. She wondered why they were still loading while all the passengers were in place and the plane was supposed to be taking off.

The captain's voice boomed over the PA system. "There'll be a slight delay in departure, looks like 15 minutes, and then we'll be off to Paris. So, please be patient. It shouldn't effect our arrival time.

Shellie pulled her cell phone from her purse and punched the code for Janet's home number. No answer. *That's strange; she said she'd be home all day*. The answer machine beeped for a message.

"Hi, Janet. It's Shellie. There's been a delay in take off. 15 minutes they say. I hope that's all it is. Maybe you should contact the guy on the houseboat in Paris and let him know I'm running late. I'd hate to keep him waiting. He might need to go somewhere. I'm a little scared, Janet, but so excited. I can't believe I'll be living under the Eiffel Tower. Well, not exactly under it, on the river." She laughed. "Anyway, I'll call you as soon as I get there. Thank you so much, Janet. I really mean it. I just don't—" The words stuck in her throat. Her emotions took over. "I love you . . . will call you . . . bye."

She turned off the phone and held it in her lap for a few moments while she tried to pull herself together which was becoming a repeat effort lately. She considered calling Janet again, but instead, she stuffed the phone into the side pocket of her carryon.

The seats next to her were vacant, which pleased her to no end, for she could imagine how cramped it would be with everybody sitting so close to each other trying to share arm rests. She lifted the arm rest between her and the empty seat and made herself comfy. It was going to be a long flight, a direct flight. She had never flown before, so the excitement of flying and looking out the window at the cities and countryside below had heightened her anticipation. She hadn't realized that when the plane reached its targeted height in the sky, all she would be seeing would be a floor of thick, billowing clouds.

She smiled as she thought of Janet and wondered what she would have done if Janet hadn't been there for her. She couldn't have pulled it off by herself, she knew that now. Janet was the strongest, sweetest, nicest person she had ever known. Why hadn't her mother been like Janet? She wondered what her mother was like at the beginning, before the booze had taken control. She couldn't remember her ever being sober. Surely she must have been when Shellie was first born. Shellie wondered if her mother had loved her father. *I wonder where she is. I wonder who my father is.*

The flight attendant appeared out of nowhere and asked Shellie if she could do something for her. "Do you need another pillow, a blanket?"

"I'm fine, thank you. I have plenty." She pointed at the two of each on the seat beside her. "Will we be leaving soon?"

"Yes, in about five minutes."

"I wondered why the baggage was still being loaded into the plane after we'd been seated, shouldn't it have already been loaded?"

"That's the problem. We've a shortage of baggage security and handlers today, and it's taking longer than usual. But we're almost ready for take off. Would you like some magazines? We've quite a selection on board?"

"No, no. I brought some things to read. Thank you."

"And of course you have several movies of your choice to watch, if you wish. If you need any help with the controls after we've taken off, just buzz me."

"Thank you, I will."

Shellie looked at the remote control embedded in the arm of her seat. *This is great! I have my own movie screen.* Suddenly she felt comfortable and safe.

But she dreaded having to look for work in Paris. *Will anyone hire me without a green card? Do they have green cards in Europe?* She recalled one of her favorite movies with Andie MacDowell and Gerard Depardieu and smiled.

She didn't know anyone in Paris. Janet had said her friend Bob would help. Not to worry. But still she was afraid she wouldn't find work and would have to come back to the States. That frightened her more than anything. She didn't want to be on the same continent as Jerold. He would find her and would make her come back to him. Before she would let that happen, she would kill herself first. Never would she be with Jerold again, no matter what.

She remembered what Rachel O'Neill had said on the Oprah TV show. She had emphasized the fact that abusers do not quit. They get worse, if they don't get professional help; once an abuser, always an abuser. Of course, Shellie knew Jerold would never go for therapy. And he had gotten worse as each year passed, just as Rachel had said. Now she could look back and see the escalation. It was as if it really didn't involve her. She just happened to be there. She knew now that anyone would be the object of his abuse. *I can't help him, but I certainly can help myself.*

CHAPTER 12

Jerold pulled over to the curb, engine still running. He dropped his head to the steering wheel; and gripped the wheel till his knuckles looked like they were about to pop through his rough, tanned skin.

He had been driving ever since Shellie hung up on him, trying to figure out where she could be. He knew she had been staying with this Janet Corrigan woman, but what had confused him were the airport sounds he had heard in the background when Shellie had answered the call. He could have sworn he had heard gate and flight announcements. But he couldn't make out the exact words. Maybe Janet was flying somewhere. Well, he knew where Shellie was staying and knew the phone numbers.

I'll find her and I'll make damn sure she won't be running off again. He lifted his head and took a deep breath while wiping the tears from his eyes with the heels of his hands. He knew just what he had to do.

As he drove back across town towards Glendale to Janet's home, thoughts of his mother flooded his mind.

It had been years since he had thought of her lying in the hospital bed, gasping her last breaths. He had tried to remove those memories from his brain and thought he had been successful. But even now he could see the mixed looks of fear and hate she had directed towards his father as they had walked through the door that day, not knowing it was the last time they'd see her. She died that night. She died as Jerold held her hand and she told him she loved him. From that moment on Jerold called his father Warren, not dad.

At home the violent beatings continued. Warren seemed to be possessed by a rage stronger than before. Jerold felt that he and his younger brother, Erin, were taking up the slack of Warren not having their mother around to pound to a pulp. It was as if they were absorbing not only their share but her share of his hostility. Jerold became angry at his mother for leaving them.

When Jerold met Shellie in a school to which they'd both been transferred, he latched onto her, first by simple observance, then with conversation, then with dating. He was obsessed with her. He needed her. The longing for his mother transferred to his desire for Shellie. It was a mixture of love for his mother and love for Shellie. He wanted her so much that at the time he had felt like kidnapping her and taking her far away so no one could ever hurt either one of them again.

The last time Jerold's father attempted to hit him, he was seventeen years old and was already consumed with Shellie. Jerold had come home late one night, after a hot and heavy date with Shellie, and Warren was waiting for him. He swung at Jerold as he let some the most vile, obscene words fly, but Jerold intercepted, twisted Warren's arm and unintentionally broke it. Jerold's size and strength had surpassed his father's. He could hear Erin whimpering in his bedroom, obviously the victim of an earlier barrage of degrading wrath by their disturbed dad. Jerold picked up Warren as easy as a sack of potatoes and shoved him up against a wall. With one of his huge hands tightening around his neck, he punched him in the face with the other one.

"You god-dammed piece of shit, if you even so much as touch Erin or me again, I'll kill you." He punched him again, this time breaking his nose. "Do you understand me, you fuckin' loser?"

Warren choked on his own blood as Jerold slammed him hard against the wall again, jarring his broken arm. He screamed.

"Say something, you shit-faced prick! Do you fuckin' understand me?" He drew his fist back poised to smash Warren's face.

"I, I— please, yes—", he spit the words out with the blood just before Jerold bashed him in the face again.

"I mean it, you bastard! I'll kill you!"

The bastard knew he meant it.

Jerold shook his head violently in an effort to slough the memory from his brain. All he wanted to think of now was how to get Shellie back. He would take her to Canada. He would buy the cabin above Vancouver that one of his buddies was selling. The guys had been up there hunting and fishing several times, and it'd be perfect to live in, away from civilization. Shellie wouldn't have to work. He would get a job as a logger, or maybe a wilderness guide. They could have a good life in Canada. There would be no interference, and he would have Shellie all to himself. Yes, that's what he would do. They couldn't survive in a city. There were too many distractions.

He parked across the street from the entrance to Janet's gated community and waited for someone to open the gate.

Janet used the remote to open the gate. She didn't notice the vehicle parked across the street. She didn't notice that the car had been driven through the gate after her. Her mind was on Shellie.

As she drove she momentarily switched from thinking of Shellie to making a mental note to have a cocktail party and invite all her neighbors, whose mansions lined the curvy road leading up to hers. She socialized with the Aspen Glen community regularly, not only at the Aspen Tennis & Golf Club, but in her own home. She frequently threw parties, in an effort to keep her name and face in the mix, just in case someone was contemplating selling their property and needed a real estate broker. The method had brought quite a few sellers her way.

At first she had been looked upon as an outsider in the community. Her southern, down to earth, crass speech and mannerisms were foreign to yuppies of Glendale and Pasadena.

Most of them were the offspring of the native California "old money" parents who traveled back and forth between their lavish mansions of Pasadena to their palatial desert retreats in Palm Springs.

When she had first moved into her home, she had met an architect of a very wealthy Italian family that had settled in Pasadena in the 1920s. She thought she was in love with him and had said yes to everything he asked. But he was only toying with her, she realized, because it appeared he only felt she was different and amusing and he enjoyed showing off her difference to his pals and acquaintances.

She finally accepted the truth the last time they were together. He had taken her to the Jonathon Club at the Beach, which she called the *Junior Jonathon* because it catered more to the younger members while the downtown L.A. Jonathon catered to the older. It was a charity event, an outdoor lobster feast. One thing she had always avoided was to be in a situation where she would have to remove the shell of a lobster herself. When she was out and ordered lobster, she always ordered it shelled. But here she was with a huge, spidery-looking lobster sitting on a platter in front of her with supposedly the proper utensils to get to the meat of the moment. She watched Paolo expertly dig into his lobster as she lifted her glass of champagne.

"Aren't you eating?" he asked as he wiped his hands with the linen napkin.

She leaned forward and whispered to him across the long picnic table - one of 100 that had been set up. "I don't shell lobster. I always have someone do it for me. I don't know how."

"You don't know how to shell lobster?" He laughed loudly, almost as loud as he had spoken and garnered the attention of all those around them. "She doesn't know how to shell a lobster. That's amazing. Refreshing, actually. I don't know anyone who doesn't know how to shell a lobster. Oh! I take that back, I do now."

Janet was embarrassed and wanted to slide under the table. Instead, she excused herself, took her purse, saying she was going to the ladies room inside the clubhouse. But she didn't go

64

to the ladies room. She went to the front desk and called a cab which arrived within five minutes. During those five minutes she wrote a note to be delivered to Paolo, thanking him for introducing her to things she had never tried, and for introducing her to interesting people. She had had fun, but now it was time for her to move on. She was sorry she had embarrassed him with her inexperience; she knew she had a lot of catching up to do. She told him not to call her again. She said she was going in a different direction which required her full attention. She signed it . . . *from a friend always, but nothing more, Janet . . . P.S. Who's laughing now?*

After that she had delved into International real estate and met Bob Benton, an expatriate living in Paris. He owned several houseboats on the Seine River. One of which would house Shellie until she found her niche. He lived on one of his boats near the Eiffel Tower. But most times during the wettest and coldest Parisian weather he traveled to warm weather climates. One of his favorites was Vietnam.

Janet thought of Bob on his houseboat as she pulled into her driveway and used the remote to open her three-car garage. She owned a red Chevrolet F150 super cab pick up truck and a Jaguar sedan in addition to her Lincoln SUV. She figured she had all the bases covered - a vehicle for every occasion, every terrain.

She thought again of Bob, or Bobby, as she called him. They had met on the phone. He called her one day out of the blue, said someone had referred a dynamite International real estate broker and had given him her number. He said he was interested in property in the U.S. and wondered if she would represent him. Then he asked if she would be willing to come to Paris to meet with him and discuss his requirements. He said it was a bad time for him to get away, and he didn't particularly care to travel to L.A. anyway. Janet was in Paris two weeks later.

She thought of their first meeting as she carried the bags of groceries through the door leading from the garage into her house. When she first saw Bob she was stunned at how handsome he was. And when he spoke she was stunned even more. He not only looked like a younger Clint Eastwood, he sounded like him - the same sexy, raspy voice. It hadn't been easy to hide the instant attraction.

Janet set the groceries on the kitchen counter and immediately noticed she had left the doors to the patio wide open.

"Damn! I did it again!"

After checking the contents of the main rooms to see if anything had been stolen, or anyone had come in, she returned to the car to get the rest of the packages. She had stopped off at a department store to buy some clothes for herself and for Shellie. Which reminded her, she should check her messages in case Shellie had called.

Jerold crept quietly along the back of the house towards the open patio doors. Janet walked through the doors to the covered section of the patio which was in the opposite direction from where Jerold stood. He ducked down behind the shrubbery. It was too late to retreat now.

She pressed the message button on her answer machine. There were two calls from clients then Shellie's voice came on loud and clear.

Jerold had difficulty restraining himself as he crouched in the ferns listening to Shellie's voice. He couldn't believe she was on her way to Paris, France. How could she do this to him? He looked at his watch and shook his head, knowing it was too late to pull her off the plane. It would be gone by now. *This is Janet's idea. Shellie couldn't plan something like this.*

His father's words echoed in his mind - *Ruthless, conniving, deceiving cunt!*

He stood up and started for Janet with hatred in his eyes.

CHAPTER 13

Shellie looked at her watch and saw that the delay had been much longer than they'd said. Now it was 45 minutes past takeoff time. She nervously looked out the window. The baggage carriers had disappeared. So that must mean they were going to take off any minute. *Thank God!* Every moment of delay created more tension and anxiety in Shellie's mind. She knew Jerold didn't know where she was, but she had a horrific nagging fear that he would show up on the plane before it took off. *That's impossible. How could he do that? I wonder if Janet's home yet.*

She reached in the bag and pulled out the cell phone to call Janet.

An announcement came over the sound system, "This is Armand, your pilot. We're now ready for take off. So, please return to your seats and buckle up. Turn off your cell phones and any other electronic devices you might have, and lean back and think only of the City of Lights where the weather is warm and clear this week. Perfect for whatever you have in mind. Have a pleasant flight and now if the stewards and stewardesses will please take over, I'll bid you adieu for the moment."

Oh, this is so exciting! Shellie smiled as she put her phone away and tightened her seatbelt. She smoothed her clothing while the engines revved and the plane vibrated. She was wearing a gray tailored pant suit that Janet had given her and red lizard shoes to match the red silk blouse underneath the short fitted jacket. She had never owned an outfit like this and certainly had never worn red shoes. Janet told her the red was just enough added spice and was fashionable, said it made her seem more Parisian. Shellie had giggled with pleasure at the time when she had seen her reflection in the mirror with Janet beside her, pampering her, and had realized at that very moment just how fond she had become of Janet. She already missed her. The saving grace was that Janet had said she would come to Paris as soon as she could get away. Shellie was already looking forward to that.

"Excuse me," she said to the passing stewardess. "Could you please tell me where the restrooms are?"

"They're at both ends of the section, but you'll have to wait now till we're in the air and the seatbelt light indicates it's safe to unbuckle. Will you be all right?"

"Oh yes, I was just wondering. Thank you."

The stewardess could tell she was a bit nervous. "Would you like a glass of water?"

"No, no. I'm fine. Thank you." *I'll call Janet as soon as I land in Paris.*

CHAPTER 14

Janet gasped and backed up against the table when she saw the man coming at her from across the patio. "What do you want?" She reacted in fear at the cruel look on his face. She reached back for her bag with one hand and the phone receiver with the other.

"Don't try it, lady. Don't try it," Jerold ordered as he gestured in warning. "Don't touch the fuckin' phone!"

She stood still in front of the table hiding the fact that she was slipping her hand into her purse behind her.

"You want money? I don't have any here, but you can take whatever you want in the house. Go ahead." Her hand found its mark. She slipped the safety on the gun and grasped the handle, waiting to see if she would have to use it. It was always loaded - an old habit of hers to check it every morning before she left the house.

"I want to know where Shellie is staying in Paris. You're going to write down the address right now." He took another step towards her, still holding out his hand, gesturing. "Take it easy, Bitch. Just write it down."

Janet's hackles rose instantly for more than one reason. "Okay, okay. *You* take it easy." No one called her bitch anymore. Her first thought was to kill the bastard, get rid of him once and

69

for all for Shellie. Then she thought, no. She would write down a bogus address. The good-for-nothing jerk wouldn't know the difference. But something warned her that he wouldn't be grateful at all. No, this man had blood in his eyes. She had seen that same hate-filled look many times before. "Here, I'll write down the address for you. It's in my purse." In one quick motion she lifted the gun from her purse and stepped back poised to shoot.

"You fuckin' cunt!" Jerold growled as he rushed Janet, but not fast enough to prevent her from shooting off three rounds. At first he was surprised and felt nothing. But then he looked down at his stomach and saw where the bullets had entered and the blood that had begun to spread around the wounds. He looked at her, took a shaky step towards her and dropped on the tiled floor just inches from her. He raised his head and gave her his most evil, threatening look. "I'll get you . . . both . . . for this . . . you . . . fuckin' whore . . ." His voice trailed as his eyes closed slowly and his threat was nullified.

After the ambulance and police left Janet's home, she sat alone in her living room, wrapped in a fur throw. She told the police she didn't need anyone to stay with her, even at their insistence that she call somebody. Who would she call? She led a solitary life, in spite of all the social and business events she attended and staged. She had been as close to Shellie as she had been with anyone since her relationship with Bob in Paris the previous year.

As she leaned her head on the high-back over-stuffed floral sofa, she gazed up through the skylight into the starry skyscape, wondering how and when she was going to tell Shellie what had happened.

The paramedics said they didn't think Jerold would make it. He had lost a lot of blood and had gone into shock and was unconscious before they had arrived. Janet hadn't telephoned them right away, and didn't feel any remorse for shooting him, because she knew he was aiming to hurt her. She had to shoot him to stop him. That was the only way she could protect herself.

She truly believed that. It had conjured up all the years of pain and injuries she had succumbed to when she had been married to the tyrant from hell. The police didn't seem to disbelieve what she told them; although they said the detectives would be coming around in a day or two to ask more questions. They told her not to leave the city until the investigation was complete.

She ran the day's events through her mind once again. She couldn't imagine tiny, delicate Shellie being manhandled by the likes of Jerold. *The poor child. Forgive me God, but I hope he dies!*

She shook herself from her paralyzing reverie and she tossed the fur aside. *I need a hot bath, damn it!*

Rachel O'Neill

CHAPTER 15

The phone rang.

"Rachel O'Neill speaking."

"Hello."

"Well! For heaven's sake! What a surprise! How are you, Ethan?"

"I'm doing well, and you?"

"I'm fantastic!"

"I always knew that," Ethan chuckled. "So, how is your writing coming along?"

"Finished one novel began another," Rachel said as she hurried to the kitchen to fetch another cup of coffee. "What's happening in your life?"

Ethan walked to the kitchen in his country manor house outside of Stamford in Cambridgeshire, "I'm about to take a holiday down your way, thought maybe we could have dinner while I'm there." He plugged in the electric tea kettle. "I'm at home right now, just finished unpacking my bags from a trip to Ireland. I just negotiated a contract there. Now I have some inquiries from Cornwall near the Eden Project as well as the

Eden Project. That isn't far from you. You know the Eden Project?"

"Oh yes, I do," Rachel rolled her eyes as she thought of the handsome Pete Bell and how he had become such a devotee to the Eden Project and how his trips back to her in Newlyn had dwindled nearly to nothing in the past few months. But she was okay with it. They'd had a meaningful, sensual relationship as long as it had lasted, and they were still very good friends. She knew that neither had expected more than what was given and felt that they both knew the other would be there if the need arose to lend a helping hand or a shoulder to cry on. But their relationship wouldn't be going any further than it had.

"I'll be there next Friday, am spending two days in London." He lifted the kettle and poured steaming water into a cup holding a silver tea strainer filled with tea leaves. "So are you still involved with the women's group? W-T-A . . . what do you call it?

"W-U-T-A-V. Women United Together Against Violence. Yes, I'm still involved, but not as much as I was. Belinda and I are both pulling back from it, now. We got in over our heads, actually. But we've replaced ourselves with two very capable women and a staff to support them. They're trained in that sort of work. We weren't." She stood in front of the bay window of her cottage on the cliff and looked out at the south-western view through her garden overlooking the Atlantic. "But we started a good thing, and now it's off and running. I'm proud of that."

"Yes, you always were good at organizing," he smiled as he remembered how she had helped his struggling company when she first came to England. He wouldn't have covered as much ground as quickly as he did without her. The bio-degradable field was an innovative, tough business these days. He had been maneuvering for twelve long years to make his mark taking green waste from farmers and food factories to convert it to viable products for resale. And now, finally, he was beginning to reap the rewards of his bio-process, reaching potential customers throughout Britain and on the continent.

"Well, I needed to get back to my writing. The foundation was taking all my time. You can't imagine how much time it took. Belinda felt the same way. She needed to spend more time with Baby Jake and Paul, and her sculptures. We created a monster, you know, with that company." She laughed and took a sip of the hot coffee.

"Yes, I've noticed how well known it's become. And I've seen Belinda's sculptures in London, by the way. The ones with the Ammolite? They're the rage now, you know. I'd like to buy one. Maybe while I'm there, I can select one to bring back with me."

"Oh, that would be great, Ethan. Yes! We'll go to the studio in Mousehole. She and Paul both have a studio there, now. And they have a baby. Oh, I already said that. You did know they have a baby?"

"No, I didn't. They weren't married when I met them. And as I recall, she had just moved to Cornwall, he still lived in London."

"Right. Well, they were married last year. They bought a fabulous house on the hill between here and Penzance, and had little Jake who they named after Paul's twin brother that died at birth, and Paul quit his job with the ad agency in London and they both work in their studios in Mousehole together. She's downstairs, he's upstairs. Paul's a painter. Wait till you see his work. I know you'll want one of his paintings, too. They're incredible." She couldn't believe she was talking to Ethan after all this time. It felt right. "So how's your family, Ethan? How's Adele? Is she better?"

Ethan sighed and sat down on a dining chair. He reached for a chocolate covered biscuit to dunk in his tea and began munching. "She's doing all right. At first it was difficult. But she's mending, now. Lives in Oundle. Works for a solicitor."

"That's fantastic, Ethan. She must be okay to be able to do that. I'm glad to hear it. You know, when you have a chemical imbalance like she has, it's a must to be on medication if there's no other way to correct it."

"Yes, yes. She knows that now. She stopped drinking,

which is good. Alcohol and medicine don't mix. She's bi-polar, you know."

"Yes, I know. So how is your other daughter? You're a grandfather now, aren't you?"

Ethan laughed, "Yes, yes. I finally have another male in the family to chum with."

"Well, I'm glad you're coming to visit, Ethan. The timing is perfect. I'll be looking forward to seeing you. Friday, you say?"

"Yes, Friday, late afternoon. Is that all right?"

"Of course it is."

"Then I'll call you from Eden when I leave to come to Newlyn. Shall I call your mobile or your home phone?"

"Mobile. I promise I'll answer."

They both laughed on that note. He remembered how she disliked answering phones and usually never turned on her cell phone unless she wanted to use it in an emergency and never checked it for incoming calls until then.

"I'll call you around three o'clock on Friday."

"Okay. I'll be waiting."

"Okay. Bye." He hung up as abruptly as he had always done.

Rachel held the phone to her ear, smiling, listening to a dial tone.

CHAPTER 16

A few days later Ethan packed a large suitcase, although he thought he might buy some new clothing in London before he drove to Cornwall. A recent weight gain had caused most of his garments to fit tightly. It seemed he was constantly struggling to keep the pounds off. He loved food, there was no getting around it. And since Rachel had left him, he hadn't cared how he looked anyway. Now he wished he had been more careful.

He wasn't sure how long he would be on the road this trip, so he packed extra pullovers and jeans regardless of what he might purchase in London.

Verde Victory, his ecological company, was more successful than ever and was taking him all over Britain for sales meetings with prospective clients. He had positioned himself as the sales director even though he was the CEO and creator of the company. Since the beginning everyone had been telling him that he was best at selling the idea of the company's processing facilities, and that sales should be his primary function until the company got a strong foothold on the sustainable waste problem throughout Britain. Landfill containing green waste had become a huge concern to countries around the world because of the chemicals emitting into the atmosphere as a result of the live waste being buried in mounds of refuse. The *Environmental*

Protection Act 1990 and the *Environment Act 1995* had both made his business offerings very lucrative and desired. Many such environment companies had surfaced over the past 10 years, but Verde Victory was a leader in the innovative manner in which it not only processed green waste, bypassing landfill, it turned it into salable products – fertilizer and animal feed. So Ethan had sales at both ends. He generated a monthly fee for regularly hauling waste from food processing plants, markets, and farmers to regional Verde Victory plants or he sold portable onsite processing plants to the respective companies to process their own waste and Verde Victory would then take that end product to convert to animal feed or fertilizer - a very profitable business, indeed, and a very time-consuming, intricate effort to implement.

As he closed the suitcase he thought of Rachel, wondering about her seemingly friendly and positive reaction to his wanting to take her to dinner while he was in Cornwall. He thought about Pete Bell. Rachel and Pete had been living together when he last spoke to her on the previous New Year's Eve. Ethan's mind quickly reverted to the New Year's Eve he and Rachel had spent together the year before that – the millennium. The one and only time they had made love. He remembered it like it was yesterday. How he had longed to have her in his life once again. But he knew it wasn't meant to be, at least not for the present, and had moved on, had even begun a new relationship with a woman who had been sent to him as a sex-a-gram for his birthday in March.

Visions of Roxanne immediately replaced his thoughts of Rachel. Roxanne was a tall, slim, good-looking woman, considerably younger than Ethan, but more mature than her years. She had just received a doctorate degree in the environmental field, and had paid for her education working for an "escort" service up until her final assignment which happened to have been on Ethan's birthday. She had been paid to arrive at his house on his birthday with a "gift" he would never forget.

As opportunity would have it, the liaison was not only sensual and sexual, it was enlightening - a truly beneficial time for both of them. Ethan had been depressed and lonely without Rachel, and Roxanne had been in the throes of making a decision of where she wanted to reside to pursue her new career. After that first meeting, she and Ethan spent several intimate evenings together. They hit it off quite well, as it turned out. She decided to relocate to Cambridge which was near Ethan. It had been uncanny how it turned out that they were in the same line of work. And now their relationship had evolved to one of conversational intimacy as well.

Ethan hadn't thought much about Rachel over the past three months because of Roxanne, until he began planning his trip to Cornwall to meet with prospective clients and visit the Eden Project. Then the old yearning surfaced once again.

Ethan sighed. *Rachel's just a friend - mustn't expect otherwise.* He lifted his suitcase and carried it down the stairs to the kitchen.

He was hungry and poured himself a bowl of cereal and made some toast. While the toast was browning, he downed a glass of orange juice and looked out the window at the variety of trees and flowering shrubbery in his garden. *I wonder how her garden has grown on her cliff overlooking the sea and the docks. She says it's perfect and she loves it.*

They'd been exchanging emails since he had telephoned her, getting caught up on what had been happening in each other's lives. So today he would be driving to London, then on to Cornwall. In three days he and Rachel would be having dinner together. Just two friends having dinner, that's all.

CHAPTER 17

The sign read 'Newland Gallery Near Newlyn,' and as Rachel entered she was struck by the beauty of the sunlight streaming through the window onto Belinda's delicate face and pale, short platinum blond hair as she worked pieces of Ammolite into her latest metal sculpture. Rainbow rocks, Belinda called them, although Ammolite is fossilized shells, not stones. When cut, they are like flat, brilliantly colored opals, or bright colored pieces of abalone shells - reds, blues, greens, yellows and all the hues in-between.

"Good morning, you incredible artist, you."

"Oh, good, you're here," Belinda looked up from her work. "We're having a reception on Friday at seven to show Paul's latest. Just decided this morning. And we'd love to have you come. Will you?"

Rachel headed straight for the coffee pot which was always running for customers and friends alike, "Of course. I'd love to. I wouldn't miss it for the world," she gleefully replied as she poured a cup. "In fact, guess who's coming to dinner . . . on Friday?" They both laughed at the familiar pun.

"Who, dare I ask? The Lord of Charlestown, again? Our own Pete Bell of Eden? Don't tell me he's coming for a visit, is he?" Belinda mischievously grinned, eagerly waiting for an answer.

The name-dropping caught the attention of the young married couple who was browsing in the gallery, as well as the mutual admiration displayed between the two women.

"Ha. No, I'm afraid not Pete. He's too-too busy for me, you know that. And I'll be going to Charlestown next week to see our fine distinguished Lord. He has something to show me, he says."

"I bet he does," Belinda mischievously giggled.

"Belinda!" Rachel gave a quick glance at the shop patrons. "I can't believe you said that."

Laughing, Belinda said, "Well, it isn't a secret to anyone what's on his mind. How he looks at you. You should really think about that. You'd have a title, you know. Lady Rachel, living in a grand manor house in Charlestown where your ancestors lived. I mean, where you lived in a past life. You'd be returning home in either case."

"You're not serious, of course," Rachel replied as she ran her fingers along the lines of a new sculpture of a family of deer.

Belinda's works of art were large metal sculptures depicting families of nature's creatures. She used several types of metals in her pieces and gave her subjects eyes of rainbow rocks. She had become quite well-known in the short time since she began showing her work, and sales were abundant.

"Ethan is coming to dinner and I'm bringing him here to buy one of your pieces. So he can come to the reception with me."

"Blimey. I've invited Pete and Lord Evans, too. Is that all right?" She frowned at the thought of all three of Rachel's admirers appearing at once.

"I don't see a problem with it. Ethan and I are just friends. And if Pete comes, well, I don't think we'll be spending the night together. We haven't done that in weeks. Although I wouldn't be opposed, I must say. I miss him."

"Yes, I know you do. Even when you say you don't. But remember you are the one who contends the relationship isn't going anywhere. You should find someone who wants you,

Rachel, just you. Like Paul does me."

"Any woman in her right mind would want a man like Paul." She laughed.

"Yes, I know. I'm so lucky. I still have to pinch myself that he chose me." She lowered her voice as she turned back to her art piece and murmured, "We're going to have another baby."

"What? How? I mean, when did you find out? Are you sure? What did the doctor say?"

"Yesterday, and the doctor said I should be all right. I'll have to be off my feet the last three months. I'm three months now, so I've got another three to work like the devil before becoming horizontal and useless."

"I thought you'd been taking precautions. What happened?" Rachel was frowning.

The young couple was at the door, ready to exit.

Belinda lifted her head, suddenly remembering they were in the store. "Oh, I'm so sorry I've ignored you."

The man said, "That's quite all right, we're just browsing today. We'll leave you to tell your friend your good news. Congratulations."

His wife added, "We just found out we're pregnant, too. I hope you're as happy as we are. Bye-bye." They exited.

Rachel poured more coffee and stood quietly watching Belinda secure an Ammolite eye to a grizzly bear cub.

"Is Baby Jake upstairs with Paul?"

"No, Paul had some things he needed to do, some calls to make, so he thought it would be easier on me if he took Baby Jake home to nap while he works. You know. Business. He's created a tremendous marketing strategy for selling his paintings and my sculptures. His time spent as an ad exec is paying off," she murmured without looking up from the sculpture.

"Honey, look at me," Rachel said as she cocked her head and squinted her eyes at Belinda.

"What?" Belinda turned and her tear-filled eyes met Rachel's facial inquisition.

"Oh, Belinda." She quickly moved and held Belinda in her arms.

"It'll be all right, Rachel. It will. I'm just a bit frightened. But, I'm going to do what the doctors tell me. This will be our very own baby. Paul's child. His only child."

"But he feels that Baby Jake is his child. You know that."

"Yes, he does. But there's a difference when a child is your very own. I can see it in his eyes, Rachel. He's thrilled about having the new baby. And he's frightened, too. For me. But it's going to be all right, I know it." She drew back and reached for a tissue to wipe her nose and eyes. "Be happy for us."

"Of course, I'm happy for you. That goes without saying. I'm just worried. I'll always be here to support you and Paul. What's a good friend and godmother for?" She laughed as she wiped her own eyes and nose. "Or maybe you have someone else lined up to be the godmother this time?"

"We want you and Dudley. Again."

"Where is Dudley, by the way? I saw the sign on his window saying he's closed. "

"Oh, he took an extra day off, said he had some business in St. Ives."

"Did you invite Margaret and Philippe to the reception?"

"Oh yes. Wouldn't be the same without them, would it? You know they just spent a month in Spain visiting Philippe's family. First time since they've been married. Evidently it was quite a feat to go back and face his family after he had gone against their wishes when he moved to England and married a commoner. They came in yesterday afternoon and told me all about it."

"Well, Margaret is blueblood, too. She's a St. Albyn. Let's face it, Mount St. Micheal's was the St. Albyn's home and they still have quarters there even though it's a castle for tourists now. For god's sake, when are these royal families ever going to learn? It's all about love, not lineage. Those days are over.

"Right." Belinda looked up at Rachel with wide eyes and a wide grin, "And when you marry Lord Evans, they'll just have to accept you."

Rachel burst out laughing.

"I mean it. Why not? He adores you. Pete's gone on his

way, soon to be forgotten. Right?"

"I don't know." Rachel seemed to drift for a moment, and then blurted out, "What do think about Ethan?"

"I thought you said he's just a friend."

"Well, he is. I mean, of course he is. But isn't that what makes good relationships, being friends first? Look at you and Paul."

"I was madly in love with Paul long before we were friends. We didn't get along at all. He wouldn't give me the time of day till his heart attack."

"Well, you know what I mean."

"So, you're saying you might be interested in Ethan after all? I don't believe it."

"Well, it felt good hearing from him again. Something stirred in me when we were talking over the phone."

"Maybe it was gas."

"Belinda! He's really a nice person. I just wasn't ready for marriage. His proposal was too soon and too scary for me. I needed to do more healing."

"And so now you're ready? Or are you just lonely?"

"Oh, I don't know. I told you that I believe we've connected before in a past life. Same with Pete. Paul, too, as a matter of fact. You know how I feel about those things. And all along I've been wondering if it's Pete or Ethan who will surface as the flaming soulmate, the victor."

Belinda laughed out loud. "The victor? Like they're doing battle for you?"

Rachel was as amused at her own reference. "Well, something like that. But then again, maybe not. I certainly don't see anyone fighting for me. So guess not." She began laughing and couldn't stop.

"Maybe . . . we should buy them . . . rubber swords to joust with," Belinda managed to spurt between guffaws while she held her sides.

Rachel fell into the same mode, "Visions of Pete and Ethan sword fighting . . . is too much . . . rubber swords . . . can you just imagine?"

Their hysterics produced more belly holding and tears streaming. Rachel flopped onto a loveseat next to Belinda's chair, took a few deep breaths and attempted to gain her composure as new customers entered the gallery.

"Oh boy. I needed that laugh. Felt good," she said as she stretched and grasped Belinda's arm and gave it a squeeze. "I can't remember when I've laughed so hard."

"Me, either." Belinda wiped her eyes with a tissue and stood to greet her new patrons. "Hello. If you have any questions, please feel free to ask." The customers thanked her and continued to browse.

Rachel lowered her voice to almost a whisper, "I don't know why I'm even thinking of marriage. I'm not in love like you and Paul or Margaret and Philippe. I don't think I ever have been. Although I felt close to it with Pete at first. Maybe it's just not in the cards for me. Maybe I'll never fall in love."

"But you were feeling that way with Pete."

"Oh, it was probably just a physical attraction. We had a good friendship. We enjoyed each other's company. He's sexy. Kind."

"Well, my god, what's left?"

"But he isn't able to commit, Belinda. He warned me about that upfront. Said he wasn't marriage material. He told me that first day we had a date, when we went to Eden for the first time. He said he had too much to see and do in the world. And I didn't want to pressure him, to scare him away. Besides, now he's totally involved with the Eden Project. That's where his heart is. He hardly comes around anymore."

"So how do you feel about that? Are you sad, do you wish it could be different?"

"That's the strangest part. I'm not sad. I don't know how I feel. So, I guess I'm not in love with him. But I do think of Ethan. More than I think of Pete these days."

"What about Lord Evans?"

"Belinda! He's just a good friend and we have a history in common. Besides, he's in his 90s. I'm half his age."

Belinda giggled. "He looks pretty virile to me."

"That is one thing I will never find out, thank you very much. No way, Jose. Not on your life."

A man opened the gallery door and stuck his head in, "Belinda, when you have time, come by the house. I have something to show you."

"Tom, come in, I want you to meet Rachel."

He stepped inside the shop. "So this is Rachel the writer I've heard so much about," he said as he looked her over from head to toe. He reached to shake her hand. "From the U.S., I understand. What have you written? Would I know it?"

Rachel obliged with a hand shake. "Not yet, but you will. If not the first novel, maybe the second or third. Fourth, fifth, sixth. One of them is bound to catch your attention. So, you live here in Mousehole?"

"Yes. My partner and I remodeled the stone house up the lane. We're at 12 Brook Lane, on the other side of Dudley," he said as he poured himself a cup of coffee.

Belinda stood and stretched. "Did you solve the fish pond problem, Tom?"

"I could if Peter would let me."

Rachel questioned Belinda with raised eyebrows.

"Another Peter, not yours," Belinda said

"Oh, you have a Peter, too? Well, he has to be the boss, you know. Thinks he has to tell me how to do everything. I thought it looked rather shallow and put more water in it and he had a monstrous fit. I don't know what I ever did without him before we met. I must have been utterly useless, it's a wonder I reached this grand golden age all by myself."

Belinda and Rachel both laughed, thoroughly enjoying Tom's humor.

"I'm surprised I haven't met you before. I'm in here almost every day," Rachel said to Tom.

"I've only begun staying in Mousehole during the week. We usually come down for the weekend. Don't you just love Cornwall? Especially this dramatic, craggy nook by the sea. I'm so glad to be able to come here every other week, now. Peter still comes down from London on the weekends."

85

Belinda touched Rachel's arm and said, "Peter is an artist, too. He and Paul are planning to do some shows together. You'll love his work, Rachel. Brilliantly colorful! But then you know how I love bright colors."

"So, bring Rachel over with you when you come, Belinda. I want to show you the progress I've made in the garden. You'll adore your sculpture on its most unusual pedestal. That's what I really want you to see. We'll have a glass or two as you are astonished and mesmerized by it." He gulped the rest of his coffee and headed out the door.

"You're coming to the reception, aren't you?" Belinda called out after him.

"With bells on my toes, and Peter in my hair." He disappeared around the corner.

"Isn't he fabulous?" Belinda sat back down on the stool, laughing.

"What a character! Is Peter as much fun?"

"Oh yes. The two of them together are very entertaining. Peter is always correcting Tom and telling him what to do. And when you see them, it's like the odd couple. Peter's the yuppie, younger of the two. They're incredible. Nice guys. And Tom's artistic, too. He's a designer in London. Commercial and residential. Wait'll you see their house. It's amazing what they've done."

"I'm so happy you're meeting people, Belinda. And you know what? You are the amazing one. Going through what you've gone through and coming out of it the way you have. I've never seen anything like it."

"Well, I know it appears I've managed to shed those horrible images and memories, but I still have some dark moments. Especially at night when I'm alone, when Paul's away, delivering his paintings and my sculptures. Sometimes it's dreadful, Rachel." A troubled frown wrinkled Belinda's forehead. "I thought I'd worked through it, but it seems to come back at the most inopportune moments. I wake up from nightmares seeing their masked faces over me while they're tugging at me, hurting me. The one with the orange hair is the worst."

Rachel reached for her and hugged her. "Oh, Belinda. Call me when that happens when Paul is away. I'll come right over and stay with you. We'll sit up and talk all night. I mean it. If I'm at home, I'll come right away. Will you promise me you'll do that?"

Belinda leaned back and smiled sadly at Rachel. "I will, I promise. If only they'd find the bloody blokes and hang them, I'd feel better."

CHAPTER 18

Ethan Philips shook hands with the director of operations and with Pete Bell, the newly appointed assistant director.

"Congratulations on your appointment, I had no idea you were part of the Eden Project. As I recall you were running the Swordfish Pub in Newlyn last time I saw you," Ethan commented, remembering that he had actually last seen Pete at Trafalgar Square on New Year's Eve. Ethan had been watching from a hotel window, knowing Rachel would be there. He remembered how his heart withered as he watched the two of them kissing in the square at the final moment of counting down to midnight.

"Yes, you are quite right. I've come a long way in such a short period of time. But I've studied and felt the pull of the project for several years. I feel as if I've been involved more than just the past year.'

"I'm on my way to Penzance when I leave here. Am meeting a prospective client there, and then plan to have dinner with Rachel, if you don't mind. But then I suppose she's told you of our plans."

"Oh, I don't mind. I'm sure Rachel will be happy to see you. Give her my love, will you?"

"Thank you, I will. Will you not be going to Newlyn?"

"If I can get away I'll be going to an art reception tonight in Mousehole, but I have a place here now, in St. Austell. And I usually do research on the weekends. There's so much still to learn about the earth's environment and the vegetation in all the various climate zones on earth. It's fascinating and a challenge to re-create the earth's climate zones and install all the plants indigenous to those regions. I'm going to be taking a trip to South America soon to arrange for shipment of more exotic plants."

"Well, it's been a pleasure to speak to your group, and I hope you'll consider my solution to your green waste dilemma."

"I believe we'll be able to come to some sort of agreement right away. We have to do something about it to be in accordance with the Law. It's been good seeing you again, Ethan."

Ethan left the boardroom, running over in his mind what Pete had just said. *He lives here, near the project. He isn't living with Rachel. He lives here. Not with Rachel.* His heart began pumping faster.

CHAPTER 19

Rachel looked through her closet trying to decide what she would wear to the reception at the gallery and to dinner with Ethan. He called her from the Eden Project and they had decided to meet at the Newlands' reception, since he would be arriving nearer that time after he had met with his client in Penzance. Ethan was very familiar with Mousehole, so she knew he wouldn't have any trouble finding the gallery. Mousehole was so small he would be able to find it regardless of knowing his way around.

In fact, the first time Rachel saw Mousehole, Newlyn, and the Penzance area was with Ethan over seven years ago. She had come to the UK on a visit and they had spent the Christmas holidays in Cornwall. He had introduced her to the Cornish celebration in Mousehole of the eve before Christmas Eve and to Cornish pasties. Cornish pasties were a traditional meat pie and favorite of the droves of locals who came out for the pre-Christmas merriment and festivities. That night she had listened to the stories of the violent sea storms and the ships that didn't make it back to port and the ones who did. That week she had fallen in love with this unique section of England and felt a fiery desire to someday return to it. In fact she had chatted with a clerk in a tourist shop near the Mousehole seawall that week, an

American woman who had pulled up stakes in California and had moved to Mousehole on a whim. She had lived in Mousehole for six years and loved it.

Ever since that trip, the draw to Cornwall became stronger, and when she returned, she discovered that she may have had a history in Cornwall. Indications were that she had lived there and in Charlestown, in a past life, in Lord Evans' mansion. She wasn't sure what to believe just yet, and was still researching the possibilities. But there was a portrait painting hanging in Lord Evans house that was the spitting image of Rachel in 19th Century attire, clothing that she had seen on herself in one of her haunting dreams, long before she saw the painting.

She lifted a hanger from the closet on which hung a two piece, black, beaded sweater set. She smiled as she remembered how Ethan would tell her she should wear bright colors, not so much black. He had said that she always dressed as if she were going to a funeral.

If was a relief that they were meeting at the gallery tonight, rather than at her cottage. She felt the need to be around other people when they met again. It'd been quite some time since she had seen him, and she was nervous. She didn't know why she should be so nervous. They'd known each other for years and had been through a lot together. From when they first met in the States over a decade ago, through all the visits she had made to England, to when she lived in his country house in Cambridgeshire and worked for his company up to when they'd planned to marry and then called it off. So why was she having such anxiety about this meeting for dinner?

She selected black, satin jeans to wear with the sweater set, and laid them on the bed next to the sweaters. Then she lifted a dressy pair of black Italian boots from the shoe shelf and placed them next to the chair.

In the recesses of her mind and heart, Rachel felt she and Ethan were destined to be together some day. She didn't know when nor could she explain why she had the feeling. So it was something she never openly discussed with anyone. Not even with Belinda or with Margaret – her two best British friends.

The phone rang.

"Hello?"

"May I speak to Rachel O'Neill, please?"

"Yes, that's me," she answered as she reached for the glass of wine she had almost finished while taking her bath.

"I've been asked to call you to let you know that Ethan Philips has been in an auto accident near Truro."

Rachel's breath stopped. "Is he all right?" she nearly dropped the glass as she tried to set it on a camelback trunk that was near the foot of the bed.

"I don't know the extent of his injuries, mum, although he is conscious and asked me to call you. He said he was to meet you tonight and wanted to let you know what has happened."

"Should I come?" Her innermost gut feeling was panic. She could feel the dread increasing by the second. "What shall I do? Shall I come pick him up?"

"That I cannot tell you."

"Where is he? What hospital?"

"He's at the Royal Cornwall Hospital. Near Galweth on the A390, about five kilometers northwest of Truro."

"Hold on a minute, let me write that down." She literally ran to her study and grabbed a pen and notepad. "Okay, now give me that again."

She was almost there. After telephoning Belinda and hysterically divulging what had happened, the two of them decided it would be best if she went to the hospital. Belinda told her to take the A39 from Penzance to Truro, that it was approximately 30 miles and shouldn't take long during this part of day.

Rachel hadn't been able to find out anything about Ethan's condition when she called the hospital before she left Newlyn and when she telephoned while driving.

She turned on the A390 as she approached Truro and drove towards Galweth as the man told her. A tightening feeling in her stomach had spread to her chest and had begun to take her breath away. She inhaled deeply and exhaled with vigor, but it wouldn't subside. It felt like a huge rock in her chest. She pounded on her chest to loosen the tightening. But to no avail, fear had gripped her mind and body. She began to get dizzy as she saw the hospital sign and drove to its car park.

"Oh please, please, please, dear God. Let him be all right. This can't be happening. Not now."

Through the doors she ran, shoulder bag flailing and flopping to her side and behind her. She asked for directions to Ethan Philips, told the receptionist she was a very close friend of his, handed her a business card that she had put in her pocket earlier, told her that Ethan was probably in emergency, that he had been in an auto accident – blurted it all out in one frantic breath.

The receptionist looked through records and then picked up the telephone and pushed a button. As she waited on the line, she looked up at Rachel and saw how frightened she was. She was beginning to shake.

"Doctor Jenkins, Rachel O'Neill is here. Yes. I'll tell her," she replaced the receiver. "The doctor will be right with you. If you'll please go to the private reception area over there, the first door on the right, he'll talk to you there."

Although Rachel felt this was all wrong, that she should be going back to where Ethan was, she did as she was told. She wasn't feeling well at all now. Waves of nausea were overwhelming her and she was having cold sweats and the smell of the hospital was getting to her, as it always did.

Ten minutes passed as she sat restlessly alone in the cold air-conditioned, sterile room. There was one framed picture on the wall, a cheap print of Van Gogh's "Sunflowers." *Why do reception rooms have that atrocious print on the wall? I'm sick of it.* The door opened and a doctor entered.

"Miss O'Neill?" he said as he looked down at her business card and extended his hand to her.

She shook his hand. "Yes, I am."

"I'm Doctor Jenkins. I attended Mr. Philips."

"Will he be okay? Shall I take him home with me?"

"I'm afraid not. He—he didn't make it."

"Excuse me, what did you say?"

"We did all we could for him once we found the source of the hemorrhage, but it was too late. An aneurysm. I'm sorry." He quickly reached for Rachel and rang the buzzer near the door alerting staff when he saw her eyes begin to roll back in her head.

Ethan, Ethan . . . her own voice echoed in her brain . . . *Ethan*. She was floating underwater, then she was drowning . . . drowning . . . drowning . . .

CHAPTER 20

"Rachel, doll, can you hear me?"

She could hear a familiar voice, but it seemed so far away. Was she dreaming?

Pete Bell tenderly stroked the side of her face with the back of his fingers. "Sweet, sweet, Rachel."

Now she knew who it was. *What is he doing in Newlyn?* She opened her eyes to find Pete Bell leaning over her, just a few inches from her face. "Why are you here, Pete?"

"Belinda told me what happened when I arrived at the reception. So I rushed here and found that you'd been admitted."

"Admitted? Wha—" She quickly sat up in bed and looked around. "Why am I in this bed?"

"You've been out for a couple of hours, luv. They gave you a sedative. We've just been waiting for you to wake up to take you home. Margaret and Philippe are here, too. They're in the cafeteria having a cup of tea. Belinda had to stay at the reception, you know. But she wanted to come; she wanted me to tell you that."

"Oh my. I hope I haven't spoiled it for them. Let's get out of here." She threw back the covers and tried to stand, losing her balance. Pete caught her, and held her close. She clung to him

95

suddenly remembering why she was there. With her face nestled between Pete's shoulder and neck, she whispered hoarsely, "Ethan is dead, Pete. He's dead." She wept softly.

Pete continued to soothe her while breathing in the aroma of her hair, kissing her forehead, "That's a luv. It's alright now. There's nothing we can do. I'll stay with you tonight."

Rachel's weeping became uncontrollable. Pete nestled his chin in her hair. He hoped her pain would transfer from her body to his. He would gladly take it from her, gladly.

His thoughts raced back to earlier that day when he had been talking to Ethan about the project and about when they'd first met in the Swordfish Pub nearly two years ago. He knew even then that Ethan was in love with Rachel, and he knew Rachel had feelings for Ethan. She wouldn't admit it, but at times Pete could feel her drifting and then she would mention Ethan and how she wondered how he was doing. It was as if she was with Pete one minute and Ethan the next. He finally came to the conclusion that she couldn't love him if her thoughts were on Ethan. Pete thought of no one else other than Rachel. He loved her with all his heart. But he had sensed her confusion and recognized the fact that she was a fragile spirit, unsure of what she wanted, but wanting to make her own decisions and choose her own direction. Pete certainly didn't want to tell her how he felt, that he wanted to marry her. He was afraid if he mentioned it, she would pull away and never come back. She told him what she thought of marriage when they first met. Said it wasn't for her. So he decided to put some space between them and concentrate on the Eden Project. And if they were meant to be, it would happen. He could feel her sobs subsiding as she relaxed against him.

How he wished that she loved him. Surely they could agree on an amicable living plan involving her writing and his environmental projects. Although he had made that mistake with his first wife and swore he would never do it again, she couldn't handle him being away for weeks at a time. So after a few months of living with Rachel and beginning to feel indifference from her, he had decided to move to St. Austell and concentrate on his new career at the Eden Project. Rachel hadn't seemed very disturbed about his decision, which only reinforced the feeling in his mind that she didn't love him. Yes, he knew he spent most of his time involved with the Eden Project, but he hadn't been away any more than she had. She traveled to do research for her writing and to speaking engagements for Women United Together Against Violence. Although she was withdrawing from WUTAV, she still participated on television shows and seminars about women and abuse, and he was proud of her for doing that. So, he had his environmental causes and she had her causes, but he missed her and wanted to be with her just the same.

CHAPTER 21

Rachel turned toward the sunlight streaming in through the French doors of her bedroom. From where she was lying she could see the white wrought-iron table and chairs with hearts worked into the pattern. The set was under the huge Magnolia tree near the edge of her garden. She remembered when she first saw it. It was a gift from Pete and it was waiting for her when she had first walked through the gate of her newly purchased cottage on the bluff above the sea. It was when she had returned to Cornwall from the U.S. after her mother had passed away. Pete had met her in Newquay at the airport. That was the first day she had actually seen the cottage she had purchased. Pete had done all the footwork in her absence. That was the first day they were together intimately. *Two years ago.*

As she shifted her gaze to the horizon where the Atlantic Ocean met the cloudless sky, her mind became clouded with memories of Ethan. *Oh, Ethan. Why couldn't I have been what you needed? Why couldn't I have shared my life with you when you wanted me to? You never asked much of me. What is the matter with me?*

"Are you awake, luv?" Pete peered around the corner of the open doorway leading from the garden room. He was holding a bouquet of fresh flowers from Rachel's garden.

Startled, she turned and absorbed the picture-perfect scene before her across the room. All thoughts of Ethan were swept from her mind.

"Look at you." She sat up in bed and fluffed her pillows before leaning back on them. "You're up and at 'em awfully early this morning, and you've been out in the garden? Aren't the roses magnificent? Pink and yellow. I just love them. And the purple Iris."

"Yes, I've brought you a bundle of scent, my Luv. Where shall I put them?"

"There's a vase in the cupboard above the fridge. It should do the trick."

"Be right back," he vanished as quickly as he had appeared. He called out to her from the other room, "Would you like a glass of orange juice, I've made it fresh this morning."

"Yes, yes. That would be great. Thanks." She leaned her head back and smiled. *Oh dear. Here Ethan has just died and I'm having a glorious time with Pete. Something is definitely wrong with me.*"

"Here you go, luv," Pete was carrying a tray holding the vase of flowers and a large goblet of orange juice. "To the most fetching lady I've seen this morning."

"Ha! Well, that certainly qualifies the compliment. I don't imagine you've seen any other women this morning." She laughed as she reached for the OJ.

"I beg your pardon. I've been out talking to the neighbors on both sides of you, already today. Both are female and both were admiring your garden. And I glanced down the lane and spied several other creatures of the female species wobbling off to do their morning shopping. So you see, it was a valid comment. An apology is in order, me thinks."

"Thank you for the juice, the flowers and the undeserved compliment. And I do apologize.*"* With eyes smiling at Pete, she gulped the juice. She set the glass back on the tray that he had set on the bedside table and fastened her gaze on him again.

He was leaning against the curtainless window frame, his tall lanky body flanking the window as a drapery would. His eyes were focused on Rachel through his long dark lashes, a serious look had spread across his face. "How do you feel this morning?"

He reached into his shirt pocket for his cigarettes.

"I'm going to get up. Two days in this bed is long enough. I can't do anything about anything from here," she said as she threw back the coverlet. "Let's go out in the garden where I can smell the ocean, and you can smoke. Yes?"

Pete laughed at her observance of his need for a cigarette. "As you wish."

Rachel grabbed her robe from the bedside chair as Pete opened the French doors. He held out his hand to her and they walked down the brick steps to the grass and towards the wrought-iron table and chairs near the cliff. Although her property gave the illusion of dropping off to the sea below, there were other cottages niched in the downward slope to the boats bobbing in the bay. But from Rachel's vantage point, looking straight out, it appeared her cottage was sitting on the edge of the world with nothing but the sea beyond.

She had spent many hours under the Magnolia tree that hovered over the heart-patterned settee which she had found and added to Pete's generous gift. She also added cushions to the chairs and the settee, which made lounging more inviting and comfortable. Of course because of the forever damp atmosphere of Cornwall, she had used a waterproof fabric – a purple, yellow, pink floral and green leafy pattern.

Rachel loved her cottage. She loved her garden. She loved living in Cornwall, in Newlyn. Whenever she sat out under the tree on the bluff, her concerns, worries, fears, and problems seemed to vanish. She could hear the waves rolling in, the baby seagulls screaming at feeding time. She could hear the lines clanking against the masts of the boats below, the boatmen and fishermen giving orders. To the left she could see the town of Penzance. She could see St Michael's Mount - the rock with the castle perched atop. To the right was the winding coastal road that led to Mousehole and its tiny harbor that butted up against the historic village. This was her world. This was all she needed. This was all she wanted.

They sat quietly for a few minutes - Pete smoked a cigarette, Rachel watched a boat making its way to the horizon.

Pete's cell phone rang. He took it from its holder on his belt.

"Hello. Yes . . . no, I hadn't planned on it. Well, yes, next week. Monday. Yes. Of course. I'll get back to you later today. Yes. Talk to you then." He looked pensive as he placed the phone back into its holder.

"A problem?" Rachel asked.

"Just a reminder that I have work to do." He took a long drag on the cigarette.

"When do you have to go?"

"Today." He shut his eyes and sighed. "I have to prepare for the trip to South America next week."

"You're going to South America?" Rachel frowned as she felt a cold, hollowness in the pit of her stomach. "For how long?"

"Two months," he replied quietly as he snuffed the cigarette against the heel of his shoe. "I'll be looking for new plants to add to the project. Something I've been looking forward to doing. The first field trip that I'm in charge."

Rachel turned her face away so he couldn't see the emotion welling up in her eyes. "Two months?"

Pete reached over and turned her face back towards him. They looked into each other's eyes for a moment and then kissed long and hard.

CHAPTER 22

There was a knock on the door. Rachel lifted her head from the sofa pillow, not sure if she had heard it or not. She had been in a half sleep. Now it was a pounding on the door.

"Oh no," she sat up and looked around the room. "What a mess." She got up and quickly grabbed as much of two-week's clutter as she could.

The pounding continued.

"Just a minute!" she called out as she tossed an armload of bills, empty frozen dinner boxes, and a potato chip bag into her bedroom and closed the door.

"Rachel? Open up."

It was Paul. She stood still. *I look like crap.*

"Rachel, open this door right this minute!"

"Okay, okay. Jeez!" She shrugged her shoulders and opened the door. There stood Paul and Dudley.

Paul took one long look at her and knew his suspicions were warranted. "I've come for a cup of tea and brought it with me." He handed a decorative tin of exotic China tea to her.

"And I brought the cups," Dudley said as he held out a wrapped gift box. "You'll like these. Straight from China, too. Tis a Chinese mission we're on today, right mate?" he said as he winked at Paul.

Paul winked back at him and then faced a bewildered Rachel once again. "So, are you going to invite us in, or are you serving our tea to us out here on the doorstep?"

"Oh! I'm sorry. Come in. Here, I'll take those. Sorry about the mess. I've been sort of under the weather." She took the tea and the package and headed for the kitchen. "I'll put the kettle on. Make yourselves comfy."

Paul called after her, "You haven't been to the studio for days and we've been worried about you."

Rachel appeared in the kitchen doorway holding a teakettle. "I've been meaning to call Belinda. She's all right, isn't she?"

"Yes, she's called you several times. Keeps getting the answer machine. She misses you," Paul answered.

"So does Baby Jake," Dudley added. "So, Rachel. How's the book coming along?" He noticed some typed pages lying on the floor near the cocktail table.

Rachel disappeared into the kitchen again. "That, I don't want to discuss, thank you."

Paul raised his eyebrows at Dudley. "Maybe that's the problem."

"No, I think it's about Pete being away."

"You think so?"

"Yes."

"But I thought that had simmered somewhat."

"Blimey, no! Pete's mad about her, couldn't you see it?"

Paul frowned. "I know she had feelings about him at one time. At least it appeared that way."

"Yes, I thought so, too. I don't know what happened. Maybe they both got caught up in their work. She was away quite a bit."

"But he was gone during the week anyway. Was only here on weekends."

"I think what has confused Pete is her reaction to Ethan's death. He told me he thought she might have really loved Ethan, after all. And it hurt him that she had felt that way while they were living together. A blow to his ego, most likely."

"Okay, you two meddling, handsome blokes, you. Here you are. Tea for three." Rachel was smiling, having gathered her wits to put on a happy face. She set the tray on the cocktail table after shoving papers to the floor with her foot.

"You're a rather ambidextrous soul." Dudley chuckled.

"You don't know the half of it."

"Now that's our Rachel," Paul said as he poured the tea into the flowery china cups. "You did good, Dudley. These cups look as if they were made for Rachel's cottage."

"Oh yes, they're delightful, Dudley. Thank you so much. You've brightened my day, you have." She leaned over and gave Dudley a peck on the forehead.

"Hey, what about me? I brought the tea," Paul coyly whined.

Rachel gave him an identical peck on the forehead. As Paul and Dudley chatted back and forth over their cups of tea, Rachel remembered when she had met Paul. *Far from a peck on the forehead*, she recalled as she admired his perfect facial features and long blond hair. *He always looks like he just stepped from the cover of a historic romance novel.* They met in London at Trafalgar Square at the stroke of midnight on a New Year's Eve. He had kissed her. A complete stranger and she kissed him back. She had never felt such a thrill in her life. And it seemed her whole world turned upside down from that moment to this one. What had begun as a sensual kiss had since turned into a simple peck on the forehead. She laughed at herself.

"You're laughing, that's good," Paul said as he poured another round of tea."

"So what do you hear from Pete, Rachel?" Dudley braved the subject.

Paul gave him a discerning look. "Hey, Dudley. We're the men of the house at the moment. Let's talk about us."

"Oh, that's okay, Paul. It's alright. I hear from him every couple days. He calls. He's still in South America and I don't know when he'll be back." Her facial expression became blank once again. "Here, I'll make more tea." She picked up the teapot and hurried into the kitchen.

"See, I told you. That's it. She's pining for Pete. He's a fool to have gone off and left her like this. I'll say it to his face, even if he is my friend."

"Dudley, we don't have any control over this situation. You know that. It'll just have to play out. There's nothing we can do. He has his work, she has hers."

"But she's not working. Look at her."

"Here we go, more of your wonderful tea, Paul."

"Thank you, my dear. It's a pleasure to have such fine tea parties with you in our midst."

"Oh, I think I need to roll up my pant legs on that one," Rachel replied.

They laughed and the mood of the day seemed to relax.

CHAPTER 23

Pete's gone. Ethan's dead. Daddy is dead. Mother is dead. I have no one. She had been lying in bed all morning in a depressed stupor. Rachel shook her head as she jumped up and said aloud. "Oh, for heaven's sake, stop this! Get a grip, girl!"

She put on a pair of jeans and a black turtle-neck sweater. Slipped on a pair of boots and pulled a sock cap down to her ears. She opened the French doors and stepped out onto the brick stoop. A cold wind slapped her in the face and took her breath away. Undaunted and against the wind, she made her way to the edge of the bluff beyond the Magnolia tree. She glanced down at the cottages sloping to the churning water where the boats rocked like toys in a stormy bathtub. She loved the storms on the Cornwall coast. They were magnificent! Merciless! It excited her as she stood looking far out to sea where the sky was becoming blacker by the moment. She watched a sailboat hurrying back to port.

I wonder what it would be like to be in a shipwreck. What if I were drowning? Would I give up and die or would I fight to live?

Her thoughts switched to the heroine in the movie "Titanic." *But she had someone forcing her to hold on, she didn't do it by herself. He saved her.*

She squeezed her eyes shut and thought about being alone, about having no one to force her to survive, about jumping off the grassy edge at her feet and plummeting down the hillside. Her thoughts ran rampant. However, the problem with jumping off the ledge was, she would probably land in a neighbor's yard with only a broken arm or leg at the most. Then she would have to face the embarrassment and the explanations. So, she would have to jump off a cliff that dropped directly into the ocean - a very high one, and with no chance of survival. *No one would miss me.* Suddenly her son's face flashed across her mind's eye and jolted her eyes open. She felt guilty for the feelings that were consuming her. How could she be so selfish and be thinking only of herself. Without hesitation she took a few quick, deep breaths and turned back towards the cottage, wiping her eyes. She raised her voice and yelled to the wind, "Okay! I'm over it. I'm over it! Don't worry about it!"

She had decided to call her son in Denver. When Rachel's father was alive, he was the one she telephoned when she was depressed or at her wit's end.

The phone was already ringing as she entered the cottage.

"Hello."

"Rachel, where were you? The phone rang eight times. And you don't have your answer machine on. What's up?"

"I was in the garden. Sorry. I forgot to turn the machine on."

"Mind if I stop by? Dudley's watching the shop."

"Oh, well . . . sure . . . okay. Where are you?"

"I'm just turning up your lane, almost there."

"Okay, I'll meet you at the door. Bye."

She quickly removed her sock cap and ran a brush through her hair several times. She brushed her teeth and splashed cold water on her face and toweled it briskly before putting on a moisturizer. She heard a car door and hurried to meet Belinda.

Belinda was coming up the walk as Rachel opened the front door. "You're alive," Belinda said as she hugged Rachel.

"Just barely. Come on in."

Belinda followed her into the living room. "I've been worried sick about you."

"Let's go into the kitchen. I feel the need for a big shot of caffeine." Rachel led the way.

The kitchen was a mess. Dirty dishes in the sink, more empty frozen dinner boxes on the table and counter. Candy bar wrappers. Empty Diet Pepsi cans. Empty wine bottles.

"Rachel! What's been going on? Look at this. This isn't like you. You're usually a neatnik!"

"Oh, I'm all right now. I've just been depressed, you see. Have had a difficult time getting through it. But I've made it, got over it just a few minutes ago, as a matter of fact. All of a sudden I emerged from the pit and now I'm okay."

"Why didn't you call me? You know I would have been here for you."

"I couldn't do that. You've had enough on your hands with the new baby coming and all. Where's Baby Jake and Paul?"

Belinda began picking up the trash and removing dirty utensils from the table. "You know Paul, he takes Baby Jake everywhere with him. Today he took a few paintings to St. Ives, to the Tate Gallery. They sold some and wanted more."

"That's fabulous! And how are you feeling?"

"Okay, but feeling a bit tired lately. Which is one reason I've left early today. And then I thought I'd stop by and see how you're doing. I was worried about you."

"I'm sorry. I've just had to get some things straight in my head. I haven't been able to write or do anything. It's been pretty bad, Belinda. I used to be able to get through these depressions much easier and quicker. This one took longer. It must be because I'm getting older." She reached for two clean cups as the coffee was brewing.

"I wish you would have let me know what was happening. Maybe I could have helped. Is it about Ethan?"

"Partly. I feel so bad I let him down like I did. He loved me, Belinda. And I was so into myself I couldn't be there for him," her voice weakened. She looked out the window as she continued, "I feel so guilty because he was coming here to see me. I know him, he was rushing to get here."

"But that's not what happened. It was an aneurysm. Would've happened wherever he was. It had nothing to do with you."

Rachel turned and leaned against the countertop. "But he might have survived if he hadn't crashed the car."

"I don't think so, Rachel. You mustn't think of it that way."

Rachel set the cups on the table and sat in a chair, eyes full of tears. "I can't help it. But I'm going to be all right about that. Really I am. But that's not all."

"There's more?"

Rachel laughed. She looked at Belinda's wide eyes and felt a sudden surge of love for her. Here was a young woman who had been through so much in the past two years and she was sitting here trying to console Rachel.

"Tell me," Belinda pleaded.

"It's Pete."

"I thought so. You know it's going to happen, Rachel. You two were meant for each other."

"He's in South America."

"But he'll be back."

"Not for weeks." She got up to get the coffee pot.

"So, do something for yourself while he's gone. Go on a holiday."

"I need to get back to work."

"So go somewhere and write your novel. Who says you have to write it here? Of course I'll miss you, but you've got to think about yourself and your own health for a change."

Rachel poured the coffee as Belinda's words sunk in.

"You've wanted to spend some time in Paris. So why not do it? I'll take care of the cottage for you. You needn't worry about that."

"Well . . . "

"Do it, Rachel. Just do it."

"I'll think about it."

CHAPTER 24

Belinda got inside the door just in time. She couldn't hold back the pee any longer. It ran down her legs onto the wooden floor as she hurried to the guest toilet nearest the front door. This had been happening a lot lately. She hadn't told anyone, not even Paul. She had managed to keep it from him so far. She figured it was just pressure from the fetus. Although it didn't seem logical because she wasn't that far along and hadn't gained any weight to speak of. She would ask the doctor about it on her next visit, which was in two weeks.

She remained on the toilet after she finished because she felt a little dizzy. She rested her head in her hands with her elbows propped on her knees. "God, please let my baby be healthy. And please let me always be there for him and for Baby Jake." She was wishing for another boy. A son for Paul. His very own son. Although Paul thought of Jake as his own, Belinda still wanted him to experience having one of his own bloodline. She loved Paul so much she wanted to at least give him that. But it had frightened her when she first found out she was pregnant.

The doctors had said she could never carry another baby, that it would be too dangerous. They'd wanted to give her a hysterectomy, but she had refused. The damage done to her had left her innards scarred and fragile, including the bladder and the uterus. There had been considerable damage inflicted by the knife wounds and the brutality of the five men who had raped her. One of those men was the father of her Baby Jake.

She rose from the toilet and felt liquid still running down the inside of her leg. She grabbed some tissue to catch it. It was blood. "No, no! Please, God, don't let this happen." She wadded up a handful of tissue and held it between her legs and hobbled to the phone in the hallway. She dialed Rachel's number.

"Rachel! I'm bleeding . . . no . . . I don't know. I just went to the toilet and found that I am bleeding . . . no . . . not a whole lot . . . just a little . . . it was running down my leg . . . okay. I will." She hung up and went back to the bathroom and grabbed some towels as Rachel had suggested and went to the nearest sofa. She spread one towel over the sofa and stuffed the other between her legs. She positioned herself with a cushion under her knees and leaned back, waiting for Rachel.

Rachel had telephoned the doctor on her way to Belinda's and made arrangements to take her directly to the hospital. Belinda had put up a bit of a ruckus when Rachel told her she was taking her to the hospital, but she finally quit resisting and gave in. Rachel had convinced her that if she wanted the baby to survive, she had to follow doctor's orders and he said she was to go to the hospital right away.

Rachel called Paul and he said he would meet them there; he was on his way back from St. Ives.

After a 24-hour vigilance, it was determined to be less serious than they first thought. She didn't lose the baby. The doctor told her after another 24 hours, she could go home in an ambulance and would be transferred to her bed there. He said she must have complete bed rest for at least two weeks, at which time he would examine her again and make a further determination.

Paul was beside himself. He completely lost it. Rachel tried her best to console him and ended up taking Baby Jake home with her while Belinda remained in the hospital. Paul wouldn't leave Belinda's bedside.

As it turned out, Baby Jake was a handful. Rachel hadn't

been around children in years. Although she was his godmother, she had only played with him at the studio and in their home. She had never babysat him or taken him for any lengthy periods of time. Dudley usually did that. He was Baby Jake's godfather. But Dudley was just as useless as Paul over this. One would think he was the husband as well.

Rachel tucked Baby Jake into the guest bed and kissed his forehead. She had rocked him to sleep and sang to him like she had sung to her own son those many years ago. She hadn't thought of those days in such a long time. But it made her feel good to remember her own child in her arms. Holding Baby Jake made her think about how long it had been since she had seen her son. She would call him tomorrow. She left the small lamp light on and left the door half open. She glanced back at Baby Jake who was sound asleep on his pillow - his bright orange hair was curly and tousled as usual. She smiled at the sweet, endearing image that seemed so out of place in her cottage.

The phone rang. She hurried to pick it up before it awakened Baby Jake.

"Hello?" she whispered. "Oh, Pete. Hold on a minute." She took one last look at Baby Jake and went quickly to her bedroom. "Okay. I just put Baby Jake to bed. He's asleep, thank goodness. Boy, what a handful. Yes, he is spending the night. Belinda's in the hospital for observation, we had a scare, but she's alright now. So, how are you?" She nestled back into her pillows and shut her eyes, listening to Pete's deep, sexy voice tell her his latest news. Suddenly a frown crept up her forehead. She sat up. "You are? When?" She stood up and began pacing. "But you said it'd be for only two months." She walked out of the bedroom down the hall into the kitchen. "So, bottom line, how long?" Her voice sounded cooler. "When will you be going?" She reached for the coffee pot and poured herself a cup of coffee and began sipping. "It sounds like it is." She set the cup on the counter and wiped a tear from the corner of her eye. "Yes, I think it's wonderful for you. Of course. If that's what you want." She put her hand over her mouth to cover the shakiness in her voice. "It sounds exciting." The sobs were coming, they were coming.

"Oh, someone's trying to get through, Pete. It might be the hospital. I'll talk to you tomorrow, okay? Bye."

She couldn't believe it. It had to be because she was in such a fragile state. She couldn't stop crying. Only two other times had she had such an emotional outbreak. When her father died and when her mother died. She had cried when Ethan died, but that was different somehow. *So is this another death? The death of Pete and me?*

Pete had told her his stay in South America was going to be longer than they'd figured, that next he was going to Brazil, and that he probably wouldn't come back to England until sometime late December. He said he was sorry, that he missed her terribly, but he had to finish what he had set out to do and the project depended on him.

Baby Jake's sudden cry took Rachel from hers.

CHAPTER 25

All was back to normal. Belinda was sculpting again in the studio in Mousehole; Paul was in the upstairs loft painting again, Baby Jake was getting into everything including Dudley's gem and lapidary shop next door. It was as if nothing had happened and everyone was breathing easy once again. But this time they were all keeping a watchful eye and were more tuned in to Belinda. Paul insisted she leave the studio every mid-afternoon to go home and nap. He kept Baby Jake with him while he worked so she could at least have that time to herself, to put up her feet and rest. Dudley would pitch in and help with Baby Jake, too. So between the two doting "fathers", Baby Jake had it made.

Rachel even came to the shop and took the child to the park or the beach for a couple hours occasionally. She had become quite fond of him since he had spent those few days and nights with her. She had gotten into the swing of it just about the time he was returned to his father and mother. He was with her for a week, as it turned out.

Pete had telephoned Rachel several times since he told her about his plans to be away till December. She had begun to distance herself from him - a survival mechanism she had mastered very early in life when she felt hurt or disappointed or felt a situation was hopeless.

Rachel opened the "Newland's Near Newlyn" studio door and greeted Belinda, cheerfully. "Hey! That's a beauty you're working on. You've never done fish, have you?"

"This is a first. Thought I'd give it try. So, you like it?"

"Oh yes. It's fabulous! So, where's the Baby Jake?"

"You just missed him. Dudley took him to the park. Said he was tired of sitting in his shop waiting for customers who never came. He's a pill, isn't he?" She wiped her hands with a towel and stood to stretch. "So, why are you here today? I thought you were going to do some serious writing."

Rachel sighed heavily. "I'm having trouble with the story. I'm just not inspired, Belinda. I have my two main characters, but I can't seem to get a grip on the story."

"You need to go to Paris, Rachel."

"I know. I know that would do it. Paris has always inspired me. I don't know why, but it does. Maybe I've lived there in a past life, too. It feels so familiar." She poured a cup of coffee and sat on a stool nearby.

"That could be it, and of course the atmosphere is unsurpassed. The beauty of the parks everywhere you turn, the buildings, the museums and churches. The sidewalk cafes. The shops."

"Yes, it's all of that and more. I find the people so colorful and dramatic. So full of life. The way they dress. It's different to any other place on the planet. The food. The wine."

"I'm sold! When do we leave?" Belinda laughed as she began working again.

"I wish you could go with me on a trip, we'd have a great time." Rachel walked around the shop touching and looking at the sculptures as she sipped her coffee.

"Are any of your sculptures in Paris?"

"Yes, as a matter of fact. In a small gallery in Montmartre."

"No kidding?"

"No kidding."

"But you haven't been there since you've been here, have

you?"

"No, I haven't. Paul made the arrangements and shipped them; they handle his paintings, too." Belinda rubbed the stone eyes of the largest fish with a polishing cloth. "There, that'll do it. My family of fish. What do you think?"

"I think I have to have that piece, I do."

"No, Rachel. You can't keep buying them. I want to sell to other people, too." She swiped the cloth at Rachel. "So, when are you going to Paris?"

Rachel stopped and thought for a few seconds. She looked at Belinda, then turned away and shook her head. "I can't go until your baby's born."

"What? That's ridiculous!"

"No it isn't. I don't want to leave till you have the baby and I know you're both okay."

"Oh, Rachel, you're daft! That makes me feel awful." She reached for Rachel's hand. "Paul's here, Dudley's here. The doc says I'm doing great. Please. Don't do that to me. I want you to go. For you. You need to, for more reasons than one. Please."

"I don't know what to do with myself. I'm eating junk food; drinking too much wine, I flit from one thing to another, can't concentrate or don't want to concentrate on anything. I'm going out of mind thinking about Pete. About Ethan. And I can't clear my head enough to write. I'm a disaster. Men always do this to me. They interfere with my process."

"Your process, you say? Come here." Belinda grabbed her hand and led her to the computer. "We're going to find you a nice studio apartment to rent in Paris, right now. And you're going to book it. I mean it." She connected to the Internet while Rachel stood by with her mouth hanging open.

"Belinda?"

"No, we're going to do it right now. Here. We'll do a search. Studio apartments in Paris. Watch. Look at this. Tons of them. Okay, sit down here and pick one. Try Montmartre first. Come on. Do it Rachel."

Rachel half laughed, half cried, as she sat at the computer. "I could do this at home, you know."

116

"No. I want to see you do it. I don't trust you. Oh look, there's a good one."

"I'd rather stay in a hotel first and look for an apartment when I'm there. That's the best way."

"Okay. Do a Montmartre hotel search," Belinda said as she stood with her hands on her hips.

"All right! Here we go. Yes. Quite a few. That one. Hotel Sacre Coeur, near the church. Looks good. What do you think?"

"I think you should book it. Here's your purse. You want me to take out your credit card for you?"

"I think I can do that myself, Mommy."

"Well, you need a good bit of mommy-ing, if you ask me. Okay, so when are you going? Today's Thursday, how about Sunday? Will you take a train or fly? We can drive you to Newquay, if you want to fly."

"No, I think I'd like to take a train across country and then the train through the chunnel. Trains are relaxing to me. And I haven't been on a good train trip since I came here. I can take a train in Penzance to London. Okay, you win. Sunday, I'm going to Paris."

PART TWO

"I Love Paris"

"I love Paris in the springtime, I love Paris in the fall . . . "

(Song by Cole Porter)

Rebecca Randolph Buckley

CHAPTER 26

Shellie didn't think she would ever get used to the houseboat's rocking each time a boat passed by on the River Seine. Even though the Simpatico was secured tightly to the quay, the movement had kept her awake for the past three hours. She turned out the lights at 11:00 p.m., hoping to get a good night's rest before the first day at her new job. But no, it wasn't happening. It was 2:00 a.m. and it seemed that every time sleep was near, a boat would churn through the waters and the waves would head directly for the Bateau Simpatico and would rock it till it felt to Shellie like it was going to capsize. Bob told her she would get used to it, and that she needn't worry, it wouldn't capsize. But she had been there nearly a month, and she hadn't gotten used to it yet. That was her only complaint about the Simpatico, and a minor one at that. She loved everything else about it.

She threw back the covers, stood and looked out of a porthole. It was a clear, sparkling August night in Paris. The historic and romantic buildings on the Right Bank across the river took her breath away. It was surreal seeing the reflections of the lights rippling across the water towards her. Every day and night she pinched herself, unbelieving that she was actually living in Paris. She turned away from the window and began to walk across the luxurious 800 square-foot living area to the steps that led up to the bathroom. But first she peered through a porthole on the opposite side at the Eiffel Tower looming high into the sky. It was a five minute walk to the tower from the Simpatico. How privileged she felt to be living in such unique quarters, and she was grateful to Bob and to Janet for arranging it. Being in Paris was a dream come true. She pulled herself away from the view, feeling the urgency to get to the bathroom and scurried across the polished wooden planks.

The Simpatico's beautiful interior was inlaid with mahogany and pine, artistically furnished, and pampered by Bob and his team of caretakers. He owned several houseboats along the river, but the Simpatico had been his first love and she was a jewel. She was built in northern Holland in 1916 and had been powered by sail. She carried cargoes of steel, coal and grain throughout the seas and waterways of the Netherlands. Then in the mid-fifties she was outfitted with diesel power and in the seventies, Bob purchased her and converted her to a "living boat". He lived on her for several years before investing in other boats and buying real estate on land.

Bob E. Benton . . . Bob, as his business associates called him . . . was an architect. He had served in the Vietnam War and had never returned to the United States. His family, who had to travel to Paris when they wanted to see him, lived in the Great Lakes region of the U.S. He was an ex-pat who loved living in Europe. He invested in property in the U.S., but had no intention of ever living there again, having never recovered from the political and emotional fallout of the Vietnam War.

During a discussion with a Los Angeles vacationer, who had rented one of his houseboats, Bob Benton was given Janet Corrigan's phone number at Coldwell Banker in Los Angeles to contact for purchasing property in the States.

Janet flew to Paris to meet him after she put together a portfolio for him and they hit it off instantly. But with the time difference and the thousands of miles between them, what began as business dealings, then a hot romance, was soon reduced to daily phone calls, then weekly, then monthly over a year's time.

But when Shellie said she wanted to go to Paris and live, Janet telephoned Bob immediately and set it all up. She sent him signed blank checks and asked him to let Shellie stay as long as she wanted, told him to just fill in the blanks for her monthly expenses and rental amount.

Now Shellie was craving solid land under her feet. She decided to start looking for an apartment in Montmartre where she was hired by Pierre-Louie Beauvais, owner of a historic bistro in the main tourist square on the hill not far from the Sacre Oceur. At first she didn't think anyone would hire her because she couldn't speak French, but Mr. Beauvais was taken in by her petite curvaceousness, her Ava Gardner face and mass of curly hair. She told him she was a singer and was hoping to find a gig somewhere in the evening, hopefully in Montmartre, and that she was also looking to rent a room or studio apartment there.

The Gods had certainly been watching over her that day, because Pierre-Louis hired her, told her she would be helpful to him with the American tourists, and said he would put out the word about a night-time singing job for her. Of course she would have to audition, he told her. But the immediate problem was how he was to pay her. There were certain government guidelines to follow and he would have to look into that in the meantime. He told her not to worry, he'd take care of it; he wanted her to begin on the 25th of August. She was elated, said the 25th was her birthday and what a nice way to celebrate it.

Shellie left the bathroom and returned to the king-sized bed at the other end of the Simpatico's wooden-lined belly, determined to sleep. She had to be at work at 10 a.m. So she needed to be at the train station by 8:00 a.m. That meant she had to get up no later than 7:00 a.m. She went over it in her mind as she closed her eyes and thought about her impending first day at work.

I'll take the RER to the Metro and either get off at the Pigalle station and take the funicular up the hill, or I'll get off at the Abbseses station and walk the rest of the way. It depends on when I reach the foot of Montmartre.

Her thoughts became fragmented as she began to drift off

to sleep.

I hope he has a uniform that fits me . . . . it'll probably rain, must remember to take an umbrella . . . happy birthday to me . . . thank you, God, for watching over me . . .thank you, Janet . . . God, take care of Janet . . . and . . . Jerold . . .

CHAPTER 27

It was early afternoon and Shellie grabbed her purse and umbrella and left the Bistro de les Artistes. She'd been working three hours on her first day and it was time to take a quick lunch break.

The sun was shining the last days of August, as it would into September. Bob had told her the average temperature in early fall was in the upper 70s. July being the hottest month of the year, but by the end of September it would be in the low 70s. Strange as it might seem, August usually had the most rainfall of all the months; cloudbursts appeared as quickly as they disappeared, however, it was wise to always carry an umbrella in August. She was grateful to have Bob watching out for her.

Shellie hummed as she strolled through the old village square outside the bistro. The Place du Tertre was one of the most popular squares in Paris. She loved the quaintness of the winding streets leading from it, the small greenery-filled terraces and the feeling of intimacy that seemed to float in the air. Montmartre exuded romance in spite of the fact that its name was ascribed to the local martyrs who were tortured in Paris in the third century – *mons martyrium*. The butte, as it is sometimes called, became a haven for artists by the end of the 19th century and works of famous 20th century artists are on display in the museums and galleries hidden in the nooks and crannies of the close-knit maze of lanes and alleyways.

She loved browsing through the colorful array of artists displaying their art in the square. And the portraitists were out in full force this afternoon. She'd spied one earlier through the bistro windows as she was serving a table. He'd been sitting off to the right of the square, by himself. He seemed to be the busiest. And there he was, sitting on a wooden stool in the shade of a shop that was overgrown with shrubbery. She casually walked the perimeter of the left side of the square, periodically glancing across to him. She could see patrons stopping to look at his work and talking to him. One young girl sat on the posing stool he provided and he began sketching her. Shellie picked up her pace so she could watch the drawing in process.

"That's it; lower your chin a little, please. Yes, perfect." He spoke English.

Shellie noticed the quick, aggressive movements he made with his charcoal. She stood behind him and watched how the resemblance to his subject was already taking form. *He's good.* She stepped closer to get his perspective on the girl he was drawing. *He's very good.*

"Would you like me to draw you?" The artist said without looking at her, continuing to sketch without pausing.

Shellie was startled. He had to be talking to her because she was the only other person there besides the model.

"No charge," he added. This time he looked up at her and she was startled by his penetrating dark eyes same color as his coal black hair. She'd never seen eyes so dark.

"Oh, no. Thank you, but no. I have to get back to work. I was just noticing how quickly you make the drawing look like her. It's amazing."

"I've had a lot of practice," he said as he continued drawing.

"I wish I could do that."

"I see you're working at the bistro. You started today, right?

"How did you know that?"

"I observe quite a lot sitting here every day."

"Well, I have to go. Have to grab a bite to eat before I go back to work. I'm afraid I've let too much time go by already."

"I have an idea. I have some bread and cheese and sliced cucumbers, and I'm taking a break after this is finished. We can go over to one of the tables and order something to drink and share my lunch. Say yes."

Shellie's first reaction was to say no. But it wouldn't come out of her mouth.

"Now the final touches. A little here . . . a little there."

Shellie was flabbergasted by the speed in which he finished the portrait. "How do you do that so fast without making any mistakes?"

"I'll tell you over lunch. Do I hear a yes?"

After a few moments' hesitation, Shellie answered, "I'll meet you at that table over there. The second one from the door. What would you like to drink? I'll order it."

"A beer. Any beer."

"Okay," she said as she walked away, wondering what had possessed her to say yes. He certainly wasn't French. Sounded more German than French, but looked Italian. She looked at her watch. Just enough time left to have a quick lunch. She chose a vantage point at the table where she could watch the young artist gather his things. She ordered a large coffee and a beer from the waiter.

The artist was walking towards her. *My God, he's huge!* She couldn't believe how tall he was. She hadn't noticed that while he was sitting.

"Let me introduce myself," he said and reached for her hand. "I'm Adrian van Allman. I'm from Switzerland and I've been in Paris for almost a month. And you are?"

"Shellie." She was mesmerized by his eyes and broad smile of perfect teeth.

"You're American? Yes?" He leaned his artist's case against the building and sat across from Shellie.

"Yes, I am."

"I thought so. So you live in Paris?"

127

"Yes. As a matter of fact, I've been here a month, same as you."

The waiter brought the drinks.

"What a coincidence." Adrian reached into a small Thermos carrier and lifted out the cheese and bread and spread a newspaper across the table. "So what made you decide to come live in Paris?" He reached back into the carrier for the sliced cucumbers that were stored in a plastic container.

"Music. Jazz. I'm a singer. And I'd heard that it was easier to make it here than in the U.S. Big fish in a small pond, you know." She laughed.

"Oh yes. I've heard that, too. So where are you singing?" He cut slices of cheese and tore off a hunk of bread for Shellie and placed it on the newspaper in front of her.

"I haven't had a chance to start looking for a gig, yet. All my time has been spent finding a daytime job. I'm so lucky to have found this one. And of all things, my first work day is on my birthday." She took some cheese and bread and began eating.

He lifted his beer, "Happy birthday!"

She clanked her coffee cup to the beer bottle. "Thank you."

"You know, there are quite a few jazz venues in Paris. A couple here in Montmartre, as a matter of fact." He held the container of cucumbers out to her.

She took several slices. "Yes. I know. Pierre-Louie, the owner of the bistro, says he's going to set up an audition for me with one of them this next week. But otherwise I haven't been out looking."

"Where do you live?" he asked as he took a healthy bite of bread and cheese simultaneously.

"On the River Seine, by the Eiffel Tower."

"On the river? You mean next to the river."

She laughed, "On the river. As in houseboat."

"Whatever made you choose a houseboat? Isn't it a bit damp?"

"Not at all. I love it," she felt defensive all of a sudden.

"Wouldn't it make more sense to find a place closer to

128

where you work?"

She was beginning to feel intimidated, too many questions.

"I mean, it would just seem to be more convenient for you to live up here, for instance, since this is where you work."

Who was he to tell her where she should live, even though she was thinking of moving to Montmartre. "I don't mind the commute. I'm from L.A., we're accustomed to long commutes. Doesn't bother me at all." Mentioning L.A. darkened her mood even more. She took a swallow of coffee and gazed across the square.

"I live in my sister's apartment, here on the Butte. It's her holiday flat, she lives in Italy. It was available, so here I am." He noticed the change in Shellie. One moment she was looking into his eyes, now she was looking away and seemed to be somewhere else. "Are you all right?"

She set the cup on the table. "Actually, I've got to get back to work, it's late. Sorry." She stood up and reached into her purse.

"No, no. I have it. Go ahead, wouldn't want you to be late on your first day. Thanks for having lunch with me."

"Thank you for inviting me." She began walking away.

He called out to her, "Let's do it again."

Without looking back she answered, "Sure."

He was stymied. What happened? What did he say? He knew it wasn't time for her to go back. He'd noticed the time when she came out of the bistro for lunch. Something happened. He sipped his beer and re-ran their conversation in his head.

This wasn't the first time he'd seen her. She'd been in the square on several other occasions the past couple weeks. She was so pretty and stood out like a sore thumb. How could he not notice her. And when she arrived this morning in her short, black satin skirt revealing shapely legs and a yellow shirt that didn't reveal, and had knocked on the bistro door, he was hoping she was going to be working there. That meant he'd be able to possibly talk to her, maybe get to know her, if she wasn't married. But now he wasn't so sure.

129

Shellie was surprised to see Adrian standing outside the bistro when she got off work that afternoon. He came towards her as she descended the steps.

"Shellie, I've got a proposition for you," he said. His ebony eyes sparkling in the sunlight.

"Yes, what is it?"

"May I take you to dinner tonight for your birthday? In fact we have time to go to the art museums here in Montmartre, if you'd like. I would love to impress you with my knowledge of the painters and their paintings. And we could stroll through the quaint passageways and maybe take in the Sacre-Coeur and the park if we have time before dinner. That is, unless you have someone to go home to. Do you?"

"No."

"I would love to do this for you." He took a deep breath and held it for a moment. "For your birthday."

"Are you serious?"

"Of course, I'm serious. I've been waiting here to ask you. Please, say yes."

The pleading boy-like expression on his face was too much to resist. "Yes," she giggled. "Has anyone ever told you how persuasive you are?"

"My grandmother and my mother," he reached for her hand. "Come this way." They began walking.

"How old are you?" she asked.

"Thirty-two, almost thirty-three. Why do you ask? Does it matter?"

"Probably not." She wished she hadn't asked. He was ten years her junior.

"You must be in your late twenties, yes?"

"Oh, yes, at least." She laughed hard on that one.

"Why is that so funny?"

"Surely you don't really think I'm in my twenties?"

"Yes, of course, I do." He looked at her quizzically.

"You're serious?"

"Of course, I'm serious. Seems I'm saying this many

times today."

"So where are we going first?'

"First we're going to my apartment so I can shower and change my clothes."

She stopped and withdrew her hand from his. "Excuse me?"

"I would like to shower and change clothes."

"You want me to go to your apartment with you?"

"Of course."

"You're serious."

"Not this serious business, again. What is it? What are you afraid of? I won't hurt you. I won't kidnap you and ravish your body. Although ravishing your body doesn't sound like such a bad idea, yes?" He raised his eyebrows and flashed the most appealing smile she'd ever seen.

"Don't even think about it! So, where's your apartment. I might freshen up a bit too, if you don't mind."

"That's better. It's right down this very romantic cobbled lane."

"Well, don't get any ideas. You're too young for me."

He ignored her comment, took her hand, and they walked away from the square, hand in hand.

CHAPTER 28

Rachel was invigorated. Paris did that to her. She dialed Belinda's telephone number as soon as she got into the hotel room.

"Hi, Belinda."

"You're there?"

"Yes. And it's just what the doctor ordered. Thank you for insisting I do this. I can already feel the difference. I feel like a new person. Haven't given Pete or Ethan a thought since I've been here," She closed her eyes and wrinkled her nose, "Well, maybe just a tiny thought to Pete."

Belinda laughed. "It's okay to think about him, Rachel. So what's the hotel like? When are you going to look for a studio? Have you met any interesting people?"

"My, my, my, we're full of questions, aren't we?" She went to the window to see what was happening on the street below. "I chatted with some wonderful people on the train from London and one of the couples invited me to dinner one night. They live here, had been to London to shop."

"Why would they go to London to shop when they live in Paris, for God's sake."

"I wondered about that, too. Oh, and the taxi driver from the train station was entertaining. A bit demonstrative, but entertaining. He kept swearing and screaming at the other drivers. Amazing. So that's about it so far."

"So get on with it. Hang up and get on with it."

Rachel opened the window to let some fresh air into the room. "All right, I will. I want to go to a jazz club tonight. It's been so long since I've done that. Give the Baby Jake a big kiss for me, and plant a couple of them on Paul and Dudley, too."

"Sounds good to me. I'll tell them you called. Take care. Love you. Bye."

"Love you too. Bye."

Rachel placed the phone on the table and picked up one of the city brochures lying there. She sat at the window and began to read it.

Her cell phone rang.

"Hello?"

"Hello, luv."

Her heart stopped. "Pete! How are you?"

"You're in Paris, I hear."

"Yes, just got here a couple of hours ago. I'm in my hotel, getting ready to unpack."

"I wish I were there with you, doll."

Rachel took a deep breath and didn't respond.

"Rachel?"

"I wish you were, too." She hesitated for a moment, then, "You . . . you could always come join me." It was more of a weak question than a weak statement.

"But I'd spoil all your fun and you wouldn't get much writing done. Belinda told me you were there to write. I'm getting ready to board a puddle jumper to fly further into the interior, luv. We've made some exciting, startling discoveries on this trip already."

This time she was quiet for too many moments.

"Rachel? Hello? Are you there? Did you hear what I said?"

"Yes, I heard you. That's great, just great. I was closing the window; it's raining all of a sudden." She reached up and closed the window to substantiate what she'd just said. She understood what he was doing. He was making excuses for not wanting to be with her. She got it. It was as clear as the rain outside.

"I have to go, Pete. Someone's at the door," she lied. *To hell with truth. I can't take anymore of this.* "Thanks for calling. Bye bye. Have fun." She threw the phone on the bed and plopped down beside it and cried. After a few minutes, she jumped up as if she'd been zapped by a make-it-all-better wand, wiped her eyes and went into the bathroom to run a bath. It'd been a long trip and she wanted to wash off the traveling muck and the muck from her mind.

After she soaked in an oil bath and shampooed her short, chestnut pixie cut, she felt refreshed and revitalized once again. She contemplated not answering calls over the next few days, decided to turn it off. She was determined to focus on Paris and writing. After she dressed she stood for a moment looking at her cell on the table. *I better take it with me just in case of an emergency.* She dropped it into her shoulder bag and opened the door and stepped into what she hoped would become a new adventure. "Okay, wild and beckoning Paris, here I come, ready or not!"

CHAPTER 29

Adrian came out of his bedroom wearing a pair of tan slacks and a sweater draped over his shoulders, the sleeves looped in front of his designer, tan and red print shirt. Italian leathers had replaced his worn loafers, and now he was wearing a gold watch instead of the brown leather banded watch he'd worn earlier. He'd combed his black hair straight back which emphasized his alluring eyes even more.

Shellie did a double take. The contrast between the "beautiful people" look he now possessed compared to the "struggling artist" look he normally portrayed was startling.

"Did you find a jazz club?" he asked as he plopped on the sofa beside her.

She flipped another page in the Paris magazine. "Actually, no. The only one I'd really like to see is here in Montmartre - the Agile."

"Then the Au Lapin Agile it is. Shall we go have a drink somewhere and a tapia, first, since they don't open till later? And people watch?"

"I'd love to do that. But do you think I'm dressed appropriately? You look so elegant, and I'm afraid I'm a bit dowdy after a day at the restaurant."

"You could wear a friar's frock and still look fabulous.

135

But we could take a taxi to your place and you could change if you want. It isn't necessary, but it's up to you."

"I think I would feel better about going out on the town, if I did. But that's so far away, and a taxi would cost a fortune. No, I'll go as I am." She stood up and placed the magazine on the cocktail table. "Do you mind if I freshen up a bit?"

"Of course, go on. There's a clean towel on the rack near the door. Will you need anything else?"

"No, that'll do. Maybe I can adapt my clothing a bit, too, while I'm at it. Would you happen to have a tank top I could borrow? A black one, maybe? And a black belt?"

"As a matter of fact, I do. I'll get them for you." He moved swiftly to his bedroom and came out holding up a tightly ribbed, black tank top and a braided leather black belt. "Will these do the trick?"

"Yes. Perfect." She took them into the bathroom with her and shut the door.

Fifteen minutes later she appeared with the tank top reaching to a couple inches above the hem of her skirt, the belt wrapped twice and hung loosely just below her tiny waist, and her yellow shirt with upturned collar was tied into a knot under her breasts that were revealed above the low, scooped neckline of the tank. A fashionable transition and one that caused a double take by Adrian.

"My god, you are gorgeous! How did you do that?

"Oh, something my best friend taught me. I have the nicest friend in all the world that came to my rescue and taught me a lot in the few weeks I spent with her before coming to Paris. You'd like her."

"What do you mean; she came to your rescue?"

Shellie realized what she'd just said and wished she hadn't. But it was too late to take it back. "Oh, we don't want to get into that right now. Some other time, maybe."

"Okay then, let's go." He guided her from the fourth floor flat to the narrow cobbled street below leading to the Place du Tertre, at the same time wondering from what this adorable, fragile doll had to be rescued.

"We've got just enough time to visit the Musee de Montmartre," he said as he took her hand in his and led her down the lane. "It has a Modigliani and paintings by other famous artists who lived here, as well as some modern day painters. I'd love to have my work hanging in there. I know it's out of the question to be hanging in the Louvre. But one day I would like to have my own gallery here in Paris."

"So you paint, too?"

"Yes, the charcoal and pastel portraits are just for pocket money and to be in touch with the public. I paint oil portraits and landscapes."

"I didn't see any in your apartment?"

"No, there's a studio at the far end, on the other side of my bedroom. I'll show you next time you come up. In fact, I'd like to paint you. Would you sit for me?"

"Me? Why me?"

"Because you have something I can't quite put my finger on. You're exotic, your features are perfect, your hair and eyes are incredible, your figure is sublime—"

"Hey!" She stopped and backed away from him. "That's too much. You're embarrassing me. Stop it."

He grabbed her hand, pulling her along behind him. "I'm only telling the truth."

Her face was radiant. *Who is this guy?*

CHAPTER 30

Rachel walked through the crowded narrow streets, peering in windows, breathing deeply, inhaling the atmosphere she loved so much. She was glad Belinda had persuaded her to come to Paris. It gave her a creative sense of energy. This was something she needed more than anything else. Her passion was writing and she'd veered away from it when she fell for Pete. She had never been able to combine the two – writing and relationships. It was one or the other. Yes, she definitely had needed to get away from her daily reminders of Pete to revitalize her writing and get back on track.

Up ahead of her she could see the awning of the Gallery du Montmartre. She walked faster in excitement. This was where Belinda and Paul's art was being displayed. *It's a superb gallery*, she thought to herself as she entered the double doorway. All the artists that were represented in the gallery were remarkable, she noticed. There was nothing run-of-the-mill in the place. Paul's incredible oversize brightly colored paintings of women with tiny squares of black and white nude drawings in the background covering the canvas from edge to edge were being featured in the center of the gallery. Nine of his paintings were displayed. Belinda's sculptures were individually set on pedestals and placed sporadically throughout Paul's display area. They were billed as husband and wife – Paul and Belinda Newland of Cornwall. Rachel picked up the brochures the gallery had made of their work and beamed with pride over knowing the two featured artists. She couldn't wait to tell them she'd been there.

She purchased one of Paul's paintings and one of Belinda's sculptures and made the arrangements for them to be shipped to her address in Newlyn. Then she returned to her adventurous trek through Montmartre in the 18th Arrondissement, north of downtown Paris.

Rachel was feeling the steepness of the streets as she walked towards the heart of what originally was a small farming community around a hill. She decided to sashay from east to west to east as she traversed the south side of the mount, until she came upon the funicular that would take her up the final steep incline to the church, the Sacre Ochre. While she took the easy ride on the modern cable car, the more ambitious climbed the hundreds of steps alongside, leading up to one of the city's most visited basilicas perched atop martyr's hill.

She had visited the picturesque and historic church before and had enjoyed the expansive mosaic and the monstrous bell in the bell tower – both the mosaic and the bell were considered among the world's largest. But this afternoon her destination was the Place du Tertre. At one time the square had been filled with famous artists who lived in the village, such as Renoir, Monet, Van Gogh, and Picasso. Writers and musicians had gathered in the sidewalk cafes discussing the events of the day. Although those days had come and gone, she still enjoyed sitting at the sidewalk tables, dining and drinking, while the hours lazily passed by. She enjoyed watching portrait artists and talking to budding writers such as herself. On this visit to Paris she'd hoped for inspiration and possibly a story for her next book.

She stepped off the funicular unsure in which direction to go. She'd forgotten. There weren't any signs pointing to the Place du Tertre, so she decided to follow the rest of the people who'd headed to the left up a street that wound up and around the multi-floored houses and apartment buildings. She'd made the right choice. The Place was up ahead. Her adrenaline quickened, she loved the feeling she always had in this part of Paris. She wasn't exactly sure what caused it, but it was certainly thrilling. She also became aware that she was smiling, not at anyone or anything, just smiling. She was happy. She loved her life and loved being here in this spot at this moment in time.

A Frenchman was pulling the arm of and bellowing at a teenager. The victim appeared to be with a group of students, filing through the area with their chaperones or what might be their teachers. Rachel wasn't sure which it was. She couldn't understand the language, but felt the severity of it. Several of the students stepped aside, waiting, obviously friends of the berated one. From what she could gather, the boy either had said something to the man or maybe gestured or maybe lifted something off a sidewalk café table as he passed. It wasn't clear. But whatever it was, none of the chaperones were interfering. They kept walking towards their destination which appeared to be down the other side of the hill. Rachel wondered why they hadn't come to the rescue of one of their fold. And then again, maybe the man was one of the chaperones. Whatever the circumstance, the young man was getting the chiding of his life.

She walked on past the ruckus and entered the central part of the square. Some of the artisans were still there, painting, most likely hoping to sell to the early evening crowds of strollers and diners. Most of the painters were packing up their wares for the day, however.

Cafes lined the perimeter of the Place du Tertre and were also set up in the center of the square under awnings and wrought-iron partitions, creating a corridor around them for the artisans and general public. She hadn't remembered the cafes in the center of the square, only the cafes in the buildings around the perimeter. As she recalled, the center had always been filled with rows and rows of painters and craftsmen. It might be as she had heard, the artisans were becoming less attracted to Montmartre and going elsewhere. But it still was a wonderful place to be. She still felt the excitement and creative spirit in the air as she made straight for the café on the corner at the table she had claimed as her own during past visits. No one was sitting there; she'd timed it just right. In fact it appeared she had arrived between the afternoon tourist swarm and the evening strollers. Only she and the two people sitting next to her table were at the Café CoCo.

She breathed in the warm air and sat on a wrought iron chair at the small round table covered with a white, linen cloth. A single rose was in a colorful, mosaic, glass vase in the center of the table. It felt good to be alive. She closed her eyes and drew in another deep breath while her hair and face sparkled in the lingering sunlight that had appeared after the rain. She was glad she'd worn the simple, green print sundress, a departure from her usual black attire. The darker green scarf she'd draped around her waist would double as a shawl if she needed it during the cooler part of the evening. It was nearly seven in the evening but it seemed like it was in the middle of the day.

As she looked over the menu she became more aware of the young couple sitting next to her and listened to their conversation. Rachel was a proverbial eavesdropper. She could spend hours sitting and listening. This was how she learned to write dialogue – overhearing and paying attention to conversations.

"I loved the Modigliani, what was it called?"

"Portrait of a Woman. Did you notice he painted it in 1918?"

"Yes, I did. I hadn't realized that those famous painters were still alive in the early 20th Century. For some reason I thought they were from the 18th and 19th centuries. I've got a lot of catching up to do in the world of art. My world has been saturated with jazz. I know pretty much anything you'd want to know about jazz. But not art."

"Jazz is art," Adrian said while sipping a glass of red wine.

"Well, you know what I mean."

He laughed and squeezed her hand that had been resting on the table. "Yes, I'm just teasing you."

Rachel felt a pang of longing. Whenever she saw a romantic couple together, it made her want the same. She'd been grateful after the last divorce that she hadn't re-married and felt that was how it was supposed to be for her, but these moments, these romantic moments in exotic places with blissful couples always got to her.

"Good evening, Madam. A tapia and some wine to start?"

"How did you guess?" Rachel said and pointed at the avocado and shrimp salad she'd selected. "And I'll have a glass of Champagne, please. Or do you have a half bottle, a split?"

"No, Madam, either by the glass or the full bottle."

"Oh. Well . . . "

Adrian interfered, "We'd be happy to split a full bottle with you, if you'd like? My lady drinks champagne as you can see, but it's more economical to buy by the bottle than by the glass."

Rachel hesitated for a split second. "Then that's what we'll do. Yes, a full bottle of this one, please," she pointed at the wine menu. "And two glasses."

"Thank you, Madam, I'll return with the Champagne," the young waiter cheerfully walked away.

"What a good idea, thank you." Rachel smiled at Adrian. "He's very attentive, I notice." she said to Shellie.

"Yes, he is."

"You're American?" Rachel replied.

"Yes, from California, but I live here now."

"Are you two married?"

An awkward silence fell over them as Shellie and Adrian stared at Rachel, neither saying anything.

"Oh, well, I thought maybe you— I'm sorry. I just assumed—"

"No problem, miss," Adrian injected, quickly recovering from his first thoughts of being married to Shellie. It sounded heavenly to him. "We've only just met. It's Shellie's birthday and this is our first date."

Shellie didn't know what to say. And she didn't know how she felt about this being a date and about becoming yet another year older when Adrian was obviously much younger, although his size and charm made him appear to be older.

"When the Champagne arrives, we'll toast your birthday. My name is Rachel. Rachel O'Neill."

"I'm Adrian van Allman, from Switzerland, in Paris to break into the art world, and this lovely lady is Shellie Singer, in Paris to break into the jazz world."

"That's wonderful that both of you are creative, too. I write. And I live in England, in Cornwall."

Shellie's eyes widened and she leaned forward and grabbed Adrian's arm, "Oh my god! I know who you are. I saw you on Oprah. You're with WUTAV. That's you, isn't it?"

Rachel laughed and blushed a bit. "Was with WUTAV. I founded the British branch but soon found out I was in over my head. So now I'm just on tap to do talks and appearances whenever they need me."

"What is WUTAV?" Adrian asked.

Shellie quickly responded, "Women united together against violence. It's an anti-abuse foundation."

"I see." Adrian wondered why Shellie would know so much about an anti-abuse program. She'd loosened her grip on his arm and placed her hand on the table, toying with a spoon. He reached over and touched her hand with his, again, thinking there was much more to this little angel than he'd figured. He looked back at Rachel, "Are you an expat, Rachel?"

"No. I have a home in California and a cabin in Montana. I don't go as often as I wish, but I'm still an American citizen and travel to the States a couple times a year. So, where do you hail from in California, Shellie?"

"Los Angeles," she replied quietly and looked down at her empty Champagne flute.

The waiter arrived just at that moment with the bottle of Champagne.

CHAPTER 31

Pete Bell was feeling uneasy on the Cessna 170. "So, how many times have you flown to the Chaco Forest?"

The pilot, dressed in jeans, a tropical print shirt and a Yankees baseball cap, made a sharp turn and slight dive to the right. "A few times. You aren't nervous, are you?"

"I was just wondering. You know your way around, then?"

"Oh, yes. See that? That's the Great Chaco. It covers over one million square kilometers and stretches across Argentina, Paraguay, Bolivia and Brazil."

"I know. It's one of the richest areas of biodiversity on the planet."

"How long have you been working for the Eden Project?"

"Almost two years," Pete replied as he focused his binoculars on the forest below.

"We're coming up to a clearing and you should be able to get a view of some of the Indians. They come out and wave when I fly over. I tip my wings and give them a thrill.

"I understand there are over four million people living in the two forests . . . the Yungas and the Chaco."

"That's true. But deforestation is driving them from their homes. It's a rotten shame what's happening here."

"Not only here, it's happening all over the world. All the more reason to re-create the environment in biodes and transplant the flora in the safe environment like we're doing at Eden."

The plane sputtered.

"What the hell!" Joe began flipping switches on the control panel as the plane trembled and vibrated.

"What is it? What's wrong?" Pete demanded as he tightened his seatbelt and braced himself.

"I don't know. Everything seems to check out." Joe looked out the windows for an emergency landing site. "Dammit, we're too far from the clearing!"

"We're going down?"

"I'm afraid so, we're losing altitude fast," he flipped the radio switch and pushed on the door handle. "Crack your door, it needs to be ajar. Prop it open."

"Oh my God!"

"*Mayday . . . Mayday . . . Mayday . . .*"

CHAPTER 32

Evening shadows enveloped the Place du Tertre and cool breezes whipped through the square. Rachel had gone inside Café CoCo to use the ladies room.

Adrian finished the contents of his wine glass. "Shall we order more, Shellie, or would you like to walk down to the Agile and see what's happening there?"

"Yes, let's do that. Let's ask Rachel to go with us, do you mind?"

"Not at all. She's a lovely lady and she might like to hear some music, too. After all she's all alone in Paris. Ah! Here she is." He pushed his chair back and stood up as Rachel returned to her chair.

"Thank you," she said to Adrian. "I am so happy to have met you two. This has been a very pleasant couple of hours and I feel safe in saying we've solved all the problems of the world. It's just too bad the powers that be don't know it."

They laughed.

Shellie touched Rachel's arm, "Would you like to go with us to the Agile?"

"The Agile?"

"Au Lapin Agile. It's an age-old cabaret just down the hill past the museum," Adrian explained.

146

"Oh, well . . . I don't think so. Not tonight. I've been traveling all day and I'm feeling as if I could go to sleep right here on the spot. Besides this is your birthday date, Shellie. How about a rain check this coming weekend? Friday or Saturday? I know a place in Monparnasse that's fun. Jazz, interesting people."

"Yes, that sounds good," Adrian responded. "So, Shellie, will that work for you? Friday or Saturday?"

"Saturday would be best for me. I don't work on Saturday or Sunday. Yes, that sounds nice. I'd love to."

"All right, here's my card with my cell phone number on it, and could you give me your numbers? I'll call you on Friday and we'll finalize the plans. I met a young couple on the train coming here; I'll invite them, too, if you don't mind. They live in Paris. My email address is on the card, you can email me and I'll add you to my address book."

"This is fabulous!" Shellie took the cards and handed one to Adrian. "I can't believe I've met you. You know, you're one of the reasons I'm here in Paris."

"I am?"

"How is that, Shellie?" Adrian was puzzled by her statement.

"Well, I don't want to go into right now, but hearing what you had to say on television gave me the strength to make some decisions that were best for me. I want to thank you for that."

"I'd love to know what I'm being thanked for," Rachel said as she patted Shellie's hand and gave her a knowing smile.

"We'll talk," Shellie said as she stood and reached for her purse hanging on the back of the chair.

"I want to know, too," Adrian added with his hand on his hip.

Shellie smiled and said, "It's girl talk."

CHAPTER 33

"How could that happen?" Janet began pacing on her patio with the phone pressed to her ear. "When did it happen?"

"An hour ago, m'am," the detective answered.

"So now what? I don't believe this."

"We've got an APB out on him. It shouldn't be difficult to find him. We just thought you should know he's loose."

"How did he get away?"

"He walked. There was a shift change in hospital security and he slipped through. Believe me; heads will roll on this one. But in the meantime, you should probably get away from your house. Is there somewhere safe you can go till we find him?"

"Damn it. I should have killed the sonofabitch when I had the chance!"

"Now, m'am, you can't be talking like that. You need to get your things and hightail it outta there. I've already sent a car over to watch your house. They should be there already."

"All right. I need a vacation, anyway. I'll call you when I get where I'm going." She hung up and quickly packed her cosmetics bag and one carry-on and called Air France from her SUV. They told her there was a direct flight leaving for Paris at 3:30 p.m., she could make that one. She'd fly first class so she wouldn't have to wait in line. When she drove into her bank parking lot in Glendale, she called her office and informed them of the situation and said she'd be checking in periodically; she'd be out of the country till this was all over. She hopped out of the vehicle and hurried into the bank.

After a few minutes she was back on the road again, this time to the airport. She dialed her housekeeper who was married to her gardener, so that call was two birds with one stone. She gave instructions to Nola and told her she'd be in touch with her weekly. And that they could pick up their weekly checks at the bank. She told her who to contact. Next she called Betty, her personal secretary, and asked her to pick up the mail from her home twice a week and sort through it. Anything of any importance she was to put it in a file and Janet would be telephoning her regularly to discuss things. She told her to drop by the bank and sign a signature card; she'd left instructions that she could sign checks for her while she was away. She thanked her and hung up.

I think that's it. What have I forgotten? Thank goodness I don't have any animals. Oh, I need to call Shellie. She should be home by now.

No answer. She called Bob.

He was ecstatic she was coming and said he'd pick her up at the airport. He told her not to worry; he'd watch for Shellie later that night and would let her know that Janet would be there when she got home from work the next day.

Everything was all set. There was just one problem. She hadn't told Shellie what had happened. She hadn't told her that Jerold had come to her house and that she'd shot him. She was afraid she'd come back because Jerold was hurt. Now she had to tell her.

Janet gave a big sigh. She pushed the dread from her mind and began concentrating on her drive to LAX.

Damn it! What about my car? It dawned on her that she couldn't leave her car at the airport; she didn't know how long she'd be gone. She called her secretary again. "Hi, Betty. Hon, could you and your husband pick up my car at the Hacienda Hotel? I should have taken a cab from home. I'll leave it in the parking lot over behind that service station. You know the one. I can catch a cab from there to the airport. Okay? My spare keys are in the broom closet in the service porch. They're marked. I'm in the SUV. Thank you much."

That should do it. I've thought of everything.

CHAPTER 34

Rachel decided to take a cab back to her hotel from the Place du Tertre. She waited near the taxi stand that was just a short distance from the square. Quite a few people were waiting as the sky darkened and she wondered if many cabs came there at that time of night. She knew she could walk the distance if she had to, it wasn't very far, but she wasn't sure how safe it was, although there were quite a number of pedestrians on the streets due to the moderate weather. After waiting thirty minutes, she decided to walk.

This time she took the stairs instead of riding the funicular. The air was cool and crisp so she wrapped the emerald scarf around her shoulders and tied it in a floppy bow. Music was wafting from a nearby window in an apartment building. She heard waves of laughter from the square below that was filled with rows of motorbikes and young people sitting on stone walls and planters. She stopped for a moment and gazed at the cityscape from the steps on the hillside. *I see why they call this the City of Lights. It's magnificent!* In the distance she could see thousands of lights blinking on the Eiffel Tower. She was overcome with joy. She'd never felt better than she felt at that very moment. *This is what it's all about – the beauty of the sights and sounds of life.* She looked up at a star-filled sky and a silver moon lying on its side.

That night she dreamed of Pete. He was standing on the edge of the cliff at her cottage in Cornwall, looking out to sea, his back to her. She called out to him from the cottage. He didn't hear her. She ran towards him, but he disappeared. She stood on the cliff screaming his name until she crumpled to the ground and wept.

The phone was ringing. Rachel stirred, but didn't answer it. *No, no phones this early.* It stopped ringing. Her cell phone began ringing. *Oh dear, maybe it's Belinda. Something might be wrong.* She scrambled for her purse and grabbed the cell.

"Hello?"

"Rachel . . ."

"I thought it might be you. What's wrong?"

"Uh . . . well . . ."

"What is it, Belinda?" She sat in the chair by the window.

"It's Pete."

"What about Pete?"

"His plane crashed."

"What?"

"In South America, his plane went down."

Rachel couldn't move or speak.

"Rachel, say something, please!"

"Is he—" She began to cry. "Did he—"

"We don't know, Rachel. Only the pilot and Pete were in the plane. There was a mayday call and the search parties were out looking till it got dark. So now they have to wait till morning. It's nighttime there now."

"I should go."

"Go where? What can you do? There's nothing there but millions of acres of forest. You stay right where you are in case he needs to get in touch with you. He knows you're in Paris."

"I can't take this again, Belinda. I just can't!"

"Rachel, listen to me. Are you listening?"

"I had a dream last night about him, he—"

"We don't know anything yet. All we know is the plane went down. It was a small plane. Probably landed in the trees.

People in small planes can survive a landing like that. They just glide down most times. So, keep your mobile with you today. I'll call as soon as I find out something. Okay, luv?"

"Okay," her voice wavered. "How are you, Belinda?"

"Don't worry about me. These two guys are driving me bonkers, hovering over me all the time."

"I— I'm going to hang up now."

"Okay, just take it easy. I'll call you."

"Bye." Rachel was numb.

She stared out of the window, seeing nothing. The sun was rising and the morning dew was glistening on the waxy leaves of the Magnolia tree below her window. Ivy that had been climbing the walls for dozens of years peeked through the window panes. The proprietor of the hotel had built window boxes and planted pink geraniums outside every room. They were blooming in full force this morning. A fat bluejay landed on the window box, and it's loud chirping rousted Rachel from her reverie.

All of a sudden she felt the beauty of the view and foliage and the freshness of the day. With her fingers she wiped the tears from her eyes and sighed deeply. The motion sent the bluejay flying. She watched him land on the tree below next to a huge Magnolia blossom. It seemed as if he was looking up at her, trying to tell her something. He was chirping, looking directly at her with his head cocked to the side.

She nodded and smiled. "I hear you, little bird. I hear you. Be safe, my love."

CHAPTER 35

Shellie came out of the shower in a rush. She was running late. By the time she had returned to the boat the night before, it was after midnight. The Au Lapin Agile had been closed and they'd decided to ride the Metro to the Eiffel Tower like tourists, and then Adrian walked her home after they had a late dinner at a café near the tower. Then he took a taxi back to Montmartre, caught it at the nearby Marriott Hotel just a couple blocks from the quay where the Simpatico was docked.

She quickly towel-dried her hair and began dressing when someone knocked on the door. *Oh dear!* She hurried to the door and opened it while buttoning her blouse.

"Bonjour!"

"Oh, Bob, hi. Come in. I'm just getting ready to go to work, I'm running late." She tucked her blouse into her skirt. "Come on in."

He remained on the stairs leading down from the deck, "I just wanted to tell you that Janet will be here, today."

"Janet's coming?"

"She called yesterday before she left the States. I stayed in the forward apartment last night but fell asleep before you got home. I was waiting to tell you, but I didn't hear you come in."

"When will she be here?"

"I'm picking her up at the airport at noon."

"Oh good! She'll be here when I get home."

"Yes. Well, I'll let you finish what you're doing."

"Thank you, Bob," she said as she threw her arms around his neck and planted a kiss on his cheek.

He blushed as he stepped back. "J'espère que tu passes une bonne journée."

"Merci vraiment," she answered.

"That's very good." He smiled and pulled the door shut.

Shellie was ecstatic that Janet was on her way. She sang as she gathered her belongings, left the boat and walked along the quay towards the Eiffel Tower and the Metro.

An elderly man was leaving Maxims, the massive, elegant dinner boat down from the Simpatico. Only a half dozen houseboats were along the dock between the Simpatico and the river cruise boats that lined the river below the Eiffel Tower. The man looked up when he heard Shellie singing. Hidden by a large palm in a wooden planter, he smiled and listened as she walked towards him. She was singing the song, "I Love Paris", in an upbeat version, not caring who heard her, and finished right before she got to him. He applauded. "That was very nice, young lady. Are you a professional singer?"

"Yes, I am. A jazz singer without a place to sing. What could be worse?" she laughed.

"I would like to hear you sing some more. Is it possible that you would join us this evening and audition with the musicians? I'm looking for a singer."

"Omigosh! Are you serious?"

"That I am. What is your name, may I ask?"

"Shellie Singer."

He laughed. "That is your real name?"

"Yes, it is."

"I am very serious about the audition, Miss Singer. Would seven tonight be possible for you?"

"Oh yes! I'll be here at seven sharp! Thank you, thank you so much! I'm sorry, but I have to run, I'm going to be late for work."

"Where is it you work?"

"I waitress in a bistro at Montmartre. Today's my second day."

"Then I mustn't keep you. You promise you will come at seven?"

"Yes. Seven."

"Magnifico! They call me Pepe. Ask for Pepe when you come tonight."

"I will, Pepe. Gotta run. Thank you so much!"

Pepe watched her run to the steps that led up to the boulevard. He couldn't believe such a talent and beauty lived nearby on the Simpatico. He'd seen her come and go from the houseboat many times and had even remarked to others about the pretty young woman that lived there. He was even more astounded that she was an American and could sing. At least he thought she could sing. He'd let his musicians be the judges.

CHAPTER 36

It was nighttime in Glendale. Jerold got out of the cab one street over from Janet's home. He'd been lucky arriving just as one of the gated community residents had activated the gate and driven through. The cab driver followed right behind. Once through the gates he directed the driver past Janet's home, winding around the block to the next street where he'd pretended to live. He paid the driver and began walking towards the front of that house, picked up a newspaper, and glanced back just as the cab had turned the corner and was out of sight. He threw the paper on the lawn and ran back towards Janet's street. He'd seen a car parked near her house further up the road and knew it had to be a cop. But he knew how to get into the back yard easily enough; he remembered the layout from when he was there before. All he wanted to do was find out exactly where Shellie was. He had tried her cell number again as soon as he'd escaped that morning, but it had been disconnected. He'd managed to grab a cab just down from the jail and get to Glendale to a motel without being seen.

There were no lights in Janet's house. He climbed a tree on the neighboring property and jumped down into Janet's back yard. "Stupid cops."

Now he had to figure if there was an alarm or not. Most

likely there was one. But if he could get to the main box, he knew he could disarm it. In the construction business he'd had to disarm a few on remodels. One of his workers was an expert at it, which made him wonder about the guy. Before he'd quit Jerold's crew, he'd taught Jerold a thing or two about breaking and entering. In fact, last Jerold heard, he'd been arrested for burglary.

Yep. She's got one. Dammit! He stood still on the patio for a moment, thinking, as he looked at the tell tale signs of the alarm system. All of a sudden lights came on in the kitchen. He dropped to the flagstone patio and quickly rolled into a nearby shrub.

The draperies were open and he could see into the house. A man and a woman came into the family room. She went to a desk and sat in front of it, looked like she was going through mail, opening envelopes. The man appeared to be searching through the rest of the house, most likely the cop checking to make sure no one else was there.

Jerold's mind was racing. *I need to get inside.* He knew that they had to have disarmed the alarm to be in there. If there was some way he could get inside before they left, he'd have it made. He waited till the cop came back into the family room looking satisfied, said something to the woman and then left. *He's going back to his car. Yes!*

Jerold crawled through the shrubbery below the windows of the adjacent room. He stood up and tried them. Locked. He continued along the outside wall to the next set of windows. Also locked. Next he pushed his way through a tall hedge and there was a redwood lattice enclosure with a hot tub inside. It looked like it was off the master bedroom. French doors opened from the bedroom into the enclosure. There was a small service gate that led from the outside next to the tub into the enclosure. A hook, inside, held it in place. No padlock. He managed to lift the hook and crawl through. He quickly tried the French doors. Unlocked. "Dumb ass cop." he whispered to himself, elated, surprised and amazed.

CHAPTER 37

It was warmer than usual. Adrian had been watching the bistro for any sign of Shellie. He didn't get to the square early enough to see her before she went to work. It seemed as if everything he attempted to do after awakening that morning was in slow motion. He had been in a dream-like state of mind, reliving the past evening with Shellie: the Metro ride, walking under the Eiffel Tower, having a romantic late supper at a coffeehouse a few blocks from the Eiffel, kissing her goodnight on the quay at the entrance of the Simpatico. The river had been very calm and the lights from the Right Bank shimmered across its surface towards them as they had said their goodnight.

The kiss was only a peck, he knew, but it was a soft, tender peck - a meaningful peck. She'd been reluctant to kiss, so he didn't push it. But oh, how he'd longed to take her in his arms and feel her body against his, and feel the wetness and heat of her mouth and tongue seeking his. Just thinking about it aroused him as he sat on the stool, waiting for his next portrait customer. He crossed his legs and rested his chin in his hands, elbows on his knee. *Where is she?* Strain as he might, he still couldn't see very far into the café through the windows. She must be working a different section.

He looked at his watch. He had brought lunch to share

with Shellie and was planning to ask her to go out with him again tonight. He couldn't get enough of her. He lay in bed most of the night thinking about her, wondering about her life up to this point. They'd talked about her music, Jazz, and her alcoholic mother. He could not imagine being raised as she had been. Having the mother she had. He felt very lucky to have the family he dearly loved. He wanted her to meet his mother and sisters. When he asked her if she'd ever been married, she said no. He thought that that was incredible, a girl like Shellie, never married. But then, he'd never married either. It had to be that she'd just never met the right person. He thought about how attractive their children would be - a boy and a girl. It thrilled him so, that he stood up in excitement of the images and thoughts forming in his head, *a girl just like Shellie, a boy just like me, maybe two girls and two boys*. There were twins in the van Allman family. *Oh yes, twins*! He spun around, gleefully.

"Hello."

He turned at the sound of the voice. "Shellie! I didn't see you come out of the café," he exclaimed and reached for her.

She quickly moved to his left and sat on the posing stool. "I came out the back, around the corner."

"You're early for lunch."

"Yes, today is an early day for me. I'll be going home at three."

"Well, then let's have our lunch, shall we?" He began packing up his art supplies. "So that means we can have an early dinner, tonight? Right?" He didn't look at her, continued packing his things.

"Oh, I can't tonight. For two reasons. I'll tell you while we're eating."

His heart did a flip flop. A wave of nausea spread through him. He was afraid of what she was going to tell him. Maybe she was going to say she didn't want to see him anymore. He couldn't bear that. Not now. He loved her. As silly as it seemed, he'd fallen head over heels, upside down, in love with her. Nothing she could say would ever change that. Just like his father had fallen in love with his mother and taken her home to

Gimmelwald.

Adrian's thoughts were jumping all over the place as he closed his artist's case. All of a sudden his art didn't matter anymore. Yes, he'd ask Shellie to marry him and he'd take her back to Gimmelwald. They'd live in his grandmother's house, where he had been born and raised, where their own children would enjoy the free spirited lifestyle he had experienced, away from the cities of the world. He'd work the farm and continue with his art as he had before, painting for the locals. Maybe he'd display his art in his stepfather's gallery. Yes, he could do that. He didn't need to be in Paris. It wasn't that easy to get into a gallery in Paris, there were thousands of other artists trying to make a name for themselves. He would fix up his grandmother's house as a bed and breakfast and they'd live a storybook romance in the Swiss Alps. He could visualize it.

Shellie moved to the same table they'd occupied the day before. She ordered drinks and was waiting for Adrian. As she watched him close up his artist's case and begin to walk towards her with his folding stools and back pack in tow, it warmed her heart to see the loving expression on his face directed at her. There was something about him that made her feel safe and made her feel as if she'd known him for a long time. She felt she could talk to him about anything and he'd listen. But what she was about to tell him would be difficult. She had sensed that he had a crush on her, and as a matter of fact, she had one on him. But she couldn't let that interfere with her plans of becoming a famous jazz singer. She'd dreamed of it her entire life, and now her chances were better than ever before. She had only herself to think of and only herself to answer to. She wanted to keep it that way. But other than the news about the singing audition and Janet arriving today, her thoughts had been of Adrian all night and morning, and she couldn't wait to get to work to see him out in the plaza. And here they were going to have their lunch together again, but she knew she had to tell him about Jerold.

From around the corner, Rachel O'Neill appeared, strolling along at a casual pace, gazing through the bistro's windows.

Adrian saw her first. "Rachel, come join us for lunch."

"Oh, hello, how are you two this morning? Shellie, you look lovely. You know, I think I will have a bite to eat. Thank you." Rachel was happy to see Shellie and Adrian. She needed a diversion from the worrisome thoughts about Pete since there was nothing she could do but wait. And there'd been no additional news. She'd been on the phone all morning trying to find out if he and the pilot had been found.

Although Shellie was overjoyed in seeing Rachel again, she felt trepidation about postponing the heart-to-heart with Adrian. She knew the longer she put it off the more difficult it would be, not only for Adrian, but for her, too.

"So, did you have a good night's rest after you left us last night?" Adrian asked as he leaned his equipment against the wall and pulled up a chair next to Shellie.

"Yes, uh . . . well, sort of. Actually, I didn't, to be perfectly honest. I'm a bit out of sorts this morning; I hope you'll forgive me. I'm so glad I ran into you, it was a rotten night."

"What happened?" Shellie blurted as she motioned for a waiter.

Immediately Adrian saw the puffiness around Rachel eyes when she removed her sunglasses. The rims of her eyes were red. He reached across the table and placed his hand on hers. "Is there some way we can help?"

"No, no. There's nothing anybody can do at this point," she whispered as tears filled her eyes.

"Oh, my goodness. What is it, Rachel? What's wrong?" Shellie questioned.

Her sincere countenance and empathetic expression captivated Rachel's heart. Adrian's warm touch was genuine and made her feel protected. She had felt a kinship to these two young people since the night before. Although they weren't that much younger than she was, maybe ten years or so. She reached for her purse and took out a Kleenex. "I don't mean to burden you two with my problems. We've just met and here I am weeping on your shoulders. I'm so sorry."

Shellie forgot her own predicament, as did Adrian. Their

162

concern shifted to Rachel.

"I should start at the beginning, it might help me to talk about it," Rachel dabbed her eyes and nose with the tissue. "Oh, first I'll order since this fine young man is here to take it."

The waiter took her drink order and returned to the café.

Adrian opened his cooler and spread out the food on a newspaper, enough for all three of them.

"Last night I told you what took me to England, but I didn't tell you much about what's happened since I've been there. I won't bore you with all the details, just that I met Pete, Pete Bell, when I went to Cornwall in search of some answers to some dreams I'd been having. And I went there to concentrate on a novel I was writing. I fell in love with the place and knew that was where I had to live. At first I stayed in a rented cottage, and that's when I met Pete. He owned a pub not far from the cottage near the Newlyn docks. Newlyn has one of the last working fisheries along the coast of England, by the way. There's a Pilcher factory there, have you heard of it?"

"No, I don't know anything about England," Shellie replied as she nibbled on the cheese and bread she'd placed on a napkin in front of her.

"One of my sisters lives in London, but I'm not familiar with the Cornwall region at all," Adrian offered.

"Well, one day I was walking down to the Newlyn docks, I love to go there early every morning. It is so invigorating. The clear, cool air. The sounds of the boats and the birds. The smells of the sea. There's nothing like it. I felt it was where I belonged. Have you ever felt that way about a place?"

"No, I haven't," Shellie replied.

Adrian didn't answer; but was glad to hear Shellie's response as he chomped down on a piece of leftover steak.

"If you ever do feel that way about a place, you'll know what I mean. That particular morning, standing and leaning against the Swordfish Pub, was a tall, ruggedly handsome man, smoking a cigarette. Now I'm not a smoker, mind you, but seeing him standing there all by himself, puffing on that cigarette with the smoker's frown, my heart did a flip flop, which startled me."

They all sighed.

"That was Pete. From that moment on all I thought of was Pete. Over the next few weeks he told me his story, I told him mine, and we became good friends. Just friends. But I carried a secret crush on him," her eyes sparkled as she smiled, remembering how it was. "You see, I was engaged to be married to someone else. And Pete had said he would never commit to another woman after the mistakes he'd made with his ex-wife."

"That must have been hard for you, to have feelings for someone but not able to do anything about it,' Shellie remarked.

"Yes, dear. It was hard. It was hard to look at him everyday and keep my hands off of him," she laughed.

Adrian glanced at Shellie, wondering how he was going to tell her that that's how he felt about her.

Rachel caught his glance and could almost read his mind. "When you love someone, it's sometimes hard to tell them. But I'll tell you this, I wish I would have been more open about my feelings with Pete when I had the chance."

"So, did you finally get together?' Shellie was into the story now.

"It happened after my mother died. I flew back to the States, to Montana, she was Blackfeet Indian and the funeral service was on the reservation. She was an award-winning teacher, had lived on the reservation almost all her life, except when she married my father and I was born. When I was three, she left. My father told me she was dead."

"Oh no! How could he do that?"

"It was just his way. And I believed him until I found her many years later on the Indian reservation. We were lucky to have had a few years of getting to know each other before she died, and my father made amends to me and to her before he died."

"All those years wasted." Shellie thought about her own mother, wondering if she was still alive.

"Yes, many wasted years. I spent a few weeks in the States before returning to England, taking care of my mother's estate which included a log cabin near the reservation. Then I went to my stepmother's home on the coast of California and pulled myself together somewhat. She's always been good for me in that way. And it was during email communications between Pete and I, when I was in California, that we became more familiar and began to feel we loved each other. When he met me at the plane on the return trip, we fell into each other's arms and that was the moment of realization. Oh boy, was it ever!" Rachel smiled and closed her eyes, remembering.

"What about your engagement to the other guy?" Shellie's eyes were wide with anticipation.

Adrian continued to eat and drink, but was hanging on every word he was hearing.

"I made a plane change in Birmingham, which is in northern England, on the way back to Cornwall and met with Ethan at the airport. Ethan Philips was his name, we'd known each other for a long time and although it hurt me to hurt him, I had to tell him. I had to tell him I couldn't go through with the marriage. It was hard, but I had to do it. I'd always felt we were soulmates of a kind, just as I feel Pete and I are soulmates. I believe in past lives, you see, I believe we're all traveling together in groups through our lifetimes, and my only consolation is that I'll meet Ethan in the next, because he was killed in a car crash just before I came here." Rachel stopped talking and squeezed her eyes shut. She covered her face with her hands. Saying the words brought the pain back. "I'm so sorry—"

Adrian moved to her side and placed his arm around her. He had to kneel down to be at her level to hold her tightly. She gave in to the surge of emotions. They all three held on to each other.

After a few moments, Rachel gained her composure. "I can't bear another death of a loved one – first, daddy, then my mother, then Ethan. And now, Pete."

"What do you mean, Pete?" Shellie clutched Rachel's arm.

"He was off to do some work in South America and his plane crashed last night in the jungle. I don't know if he's alive or dead." Rachel's chin was quivering and her fear was evident.

"But you don't know for sure, right?" Adrian asked.

"I've heard nothing more since my friend Belinda called. She said they had to wait till daybreak to continue the search. You know, I've never given my whole heart and self to anyone. I was afraid to totally surrender to Pete, afraid I'd get hurt, and so I put my career first. Now it may be too late."

CHAPTER 38

Bob was waiting at the railing outside the customs area. He perused the assortment of people that had arrived from all parts of the world. He played a mental guessing game of each one's country of origin.

Janet's plane had landed thirty minutes later than scheduled due to the stack-up of planes landing at Charles de Gaulle airport.

How many times over the years had he stood in this airport waiting to pick up visitors? He thought back to when he had first arrived nearly forty years ago. A lot of changes had been made to the airport since then.

A family crowded in front of him. He stepped back willingly, for he could see they were there for the arrival of a loved one. That level of excitement could only be for a rock star or a family member. And since there weren't hoards of fans flooding the area, it had to be an arriving family member. For a brief moment he thought of his own family in the States. He hadn't seen them for quite a while, and was thinking he might call his sister and invite her to come to Paris after the holidays.

His years in the Vietnam War and the aftermath helped make his decision to become an ex-pat. He had a U.S. bank account where his benefits were deposited, but he hadn't set foot on her soil since the late '60s, and he had no intention of doing so. He'd heavily invested in U.S. real estate, however, and had a business manager taking care of his properties.

As he stood in the crowd he thought back to the first time he'd seen Janet. She was a ball-buster. She came on strong and heavy with her language and real estate savvy, but there was something gentle and feminine about her that most people didn't see. He saw it. And he was immediately hooked. Her brashness and loudness didn't bother him at all. In fact, he was amused by it. It made him laugh. The first time she used the F word in general conversation, it shocked him.

She had seen the shock and asked, "So, does my language bother you?"

He told her, "No, it doesn't. I've heard worse. I'm just not accustomed to hearing it from a woman."

"Well, I believe a woman has the right to say anything a man does. And I believe a woman has the right to do anything a man does, except pee standing up. But then I've heard of some women who can do that. But, not me. So you're one ahead of me."

He had laughed so hard his sides ached the entire time she was in Paris on that first visit. She was unabashedly honest and upfront to a painful point.

What began as a business relationship quickly turned into romance. She made the first move and he commenced to wine and dine her. He wooed her as well as he knew how, and then she went back to the U.S.A. Oh, she returned to Paris a few times after that and they had pleasurable and intimate days and nights while they experienced French culture to the hilt, but she always went home, back to California. He never asked her to stay because he hadn't wanted to hear her say no, for he was sure that's what she would say.

And now she was arriving any minute and he was beside himself. That morning when he told Shellie that Janet was coming, he had been thrilled to the core and it had taken all his energy to act nonchalant about it. He could see that Shellie was in a hurry and didn't want to get into it; he had wanted to tell her how excited he was the night before, but he'd fallen asleep after drinking the bottle of wine he'd planned to share with her when she got home.

Bob and Shellie had become close buddies and they'd talk sometimes for hours at a time in the early evening about life and its mishaps, future plans and dreams. But this week Shellie had been busy, no time to talk at all. He missed that. She was a sweet woman and he felt comfortable telling her things he told nobody else. She'd wanted to know all about his Vietnam days, although he drew the line on some of it. He wasn't over it yet and probably never would be. It happened over forty years ago, but felt like it happened a minute ago, and there were still gruesome images and memories he wished he could swipe out of his head. But it was impossible, they were there to stay.

Bob had gone from high school during "American Graffiti" days, the early '60s, to college at UCLA, then to Pensacola, and then smack dab into the right seat of an A-6A Intruder 'til he was released from active duty in '71 and immediately flew to London without stepping foot on U.S. soil again.

He took in a deep breath and shook loose from his thoughts. *There she is.* He saw Janet rounding the corner looking like a movie star. She was beaming. Her shoulder length blond hair was bouncing and sparkling under the florescent lighting. Her make up was flawless. Being a classic movie fan, he felt that her face, curvaceous body, and shapely legs were a reincarnation of Betty Grable. He didn't have to wave because she saw him immediately in the crowd of eyes that were all upon her. She began moving faster towards the opening in the railing that would let her get to him.

"Bobby! I'm so God-damned glad to see you!" She welcomed his warm embrace and they hugged each other tightly, pulling apart for just a moment to lightly kiss.

"How was the flight?"

"Too fuckin' long. This was one time I wanted it to be over in a hurry," she said loudly, as she looked his face over and told herself he was the handsomest man she knew. "You look pretty damn good to me, fella!"

"I know I don't need to tell you how good you look. I'm sure you had all the eyes of the male populace on you the entire trip."

"But I only want your sexy blues on me, Bobby, just yours." She hugged him closer.

"That's an easy request, I can assure you."

He loosened his grip on her. "So what's this about Shellie's husband?"

"I'll tell you all about the damn bastard on our way to the boat. Let's get out of here."

"You only brought one bag?"

"I didn't have time to pack, Bobby. I had to leave in a hurry. So, I figured I'd buy stuff when I got here."

"Works for me. Let's go."

CHAPTER 39

Jerold didn't know what to do with the information he had gleaned from Janet's house. He paced the motel room, running his hands through his hair, swearing through his teeth. He sat at the table and reached for the Starbucks coffee he'd purchased down the street.

Food, he needed food. His stomach was hurting now. That damn Janet had torn him up good when she shot him. If it was the last thing he did he'd get even with her and Shellie. Maybe he'd tie them up and store them away in a basement somewhere and beat the crap out of them till they begged for mercy. Maybe he'd shoot Janet just like she shot him. The Bible says eye for an eye, tooth for a tooth. He wouldn't kill them, he'd maim them. But then again, maybe he would kill them. He'd do it in a way that no one would ever find them and he'd never get caught. He began to feel ashamed for thinking the thoughts he was thinking.

"Shellie, Shellie, Shellie . . . why have you done this to me? I love you, baby. I love you." He covered his face with his hands and began crying like a baby. "I promise I'll never hurt you again, if you'll just come back to me. Please, baby. I need you."

He shook his head and reached for a crumpled paper

napkin that was left over from a previous fast food order from Taco Bell. He wiped his eyes, blew his nose and threw the paper in the trash can across the room.

"Okay, first I have to get a passport." That might be a difficult feat since there was most likely a warrant out for his arrest. However, since it would be a new warrant, maybe he could get around it. If he went back to Kansas City, his chances might be better there to get a quick passport. *That's it! That's what I'll do.*

He placed a call to a cousin that still lived in KC.

"Hey, Billy, how ya doin'? Yes, God dammit, it's been a long time. Are you still working at the phone company? Hey, that's good. Me? I'm still in construction. But I got a job coming up there in KC, and am wondering if I might crash with you for a week or two so I can check it out. Nah, she's staying here because of her job. Yea. If it works out and I like the job, she'll move back to KC, but not till I'm sure. Yea, it's better that way. Yea. Okay. I'm on my way. I'll see ya in a few days."

He felt good. The stomach pain was gone. Luckily he'd been able to get into his apartment before anyone was alerted and get some clothes and his checkbook. His ID and ATM card were at the jail, so he'd get another ID as soon as he got to KC. He'd take a cab back to the Marina, to his own bank, where they knew him, and make a withdrawal. He still felt safe enough to do that. Most likely nobody there had a clue as to what was going on yet. And he knew the tellers, had been banking there for years. He had the credit cards he didn't normally carry, so he could use those later when he had to. He could get a copy of his birth certificate in KC for the passport.

That should do it, he hoped. He called a cab.

CHAPTER 40

"Joe? Are you all right?" Pete was letting water drip from leaves into a Styrofoam cup he'd salvaged from the plane. They'd decided to save the water that was in the plastic containers that had survived the crash until they actually needed it. The rainforest provided plenty of water from its trees and foliage.

"I found an armadillo." Joe appeared from behind the damaged fuselage. "Have you ever eaten one of these creatures?" He was carrying a dead armadillo that didn't look the least bit appetizing.

"God, no!" Pete frowned at the thought. He leaned back against a tree and sipped the water from the cup. Then he began collecting a cup of water for Joe. "How long do you think it'll take them to find us?"

"I'm sure the natives saw us go down. We'll be seeing them appear from the forest, as soon as they feel they can trust us. Remember, there're four million of them out here."

"But are they friendly?" Pete asked, as he handed the cup of water to Joe.

"Most of them are, as far as I know. At least all reports have been positive." He drank the water and then dug a pocket knife out of his pocket to skin the animal. "You know, in some circles, armadillo meat is a treat."

"I don't run in those circles, mate." Pete lit a cigarette.

Joe laughed. "Well, supposedly the meat is sweet. I'm glad you have a lighter; it'll make it easier to build a fire and barbecue the little sucker. How's your leg?"

"Doesn't hurt as much as it did."

They both had been lucky. Joe had a slight cut on his forehead, a gash in his arm; Pete's leg was injured, possibly a torn ligament and a deep cut on his calf. None of the injuries appeared to be life threatening, though. They'd washed the cuts with an antiseptic that Joe carried in a first aid kit and they'd bandaged each other. Joe also had aspirin in the kit and they'd each taken four tablets to prevent inflammation that might set in. So far, so good. At least they'd be alright until they had the proper medical attention.

"I can't believe we weren't hurt more than we were," Pete commented as he fanned the fire.

"The density of the forest saved the day; you can assure yourself of that."

"The worst part was untangling myself and making it safely to the ground."

"And we were always in danger of the fuselage falling on our heads as we climbed down," Joe laughed as he cut the meat in strips.

"It certainly made enough noise when it finally did hit the ground. I would have thought that if anyone were near they would've heard that crash to the earth."

"Just be patient. They're watching us."

"You think so?" Pete puffed on his cigarette, looking around at the jungle, trying to see beyond the perimeter plants. "There aren't any cannibals in this jungle, are there?"

"No. We don't have to worry about that. The jaguar is our worst enemy here."

They were sitting in a small space they had cleared around the parts of the plane that had followed them down from the sky. One wing miraculously held on to the body of the plane. The other wing was hanging in the trees where they first crashed into the forest. They could see it from where they were sitting. The tail had disappeared.

Until the actual collision with the rainforest, in the last moments it felt as if they were gliding. Pete thought it was exhilarating and had remarked how it felt at the time. He lost his fear as they glided and he still wasn't afraid, everything felt as if it would be all right.

"Too bad neither one of us is much of an electronics person," Joe said as he pulled at a piece of metal that was dangling from a tree.

"And too bad the cell phones don't work. Don't imagine there are any cell towers in this neighborhood."

Joe laughed. "We can use this metal to heat the meat on the fire. I'll just put it across here. There we go. That's good. Now I'll put the strips on the metal."

"Looks better not connected to its suit of armor."

"Yes it does. Okay. Dinner's on."

Pete took a deep drag on his cigarette. "If we had to, could we walk out of here?"

"Not likely."

CHAPTER 41

It was four in the afternoon and Shellie walked down to the cabin door of the Simpatico. She stuck her key in the lock and before she could turn it, the door was opened by Janet.

"I'm here!" Janet exclaimed as she stood with arms wide open.

Shellie gladly stepped into them and they both were giddy with delight.

"I've been waiting for you for all afternoon, Shellie. You're a sight for sore eyes. You look good, honey!" She held her at arm's length looking her over. "Come on down here," she said as she guided her into the expansive cabin. I've fixed us a little snack and a drinkie-winkie. Don't you just love Paris? It's the best god-damned city in all the world!"

Shellie smiled at the cheese and bread and the sliced fruit Janet had prepared. "You must've gone to the store. That looks good."

"You just sit down and tell me all about your new job and what's been happening since we last talked. Here, I'll pour you a glass of red wine. Bobby's going to join us in a minute; he had to go make a phone call. He's taking us to dinner tonight, went to make a reservation."

"Oh no. I can't go to dinner tonight. I've got an audition

at Maxim's, the cruise boat."

"The one down the way?"

"Yes, at seven o'clock."

"Well, then, that's where we'll have our dinner. How's that?"

Shellie grinned and shook her head. "You are something else, you know that?"

"It's okay if we go, isn't it?"

"Of course it is. I'd love you both to come. Adrian's going to meet me there, so is Rachel. You'll love her. Rachel O'Neill. I told you about her, remember? The one that's been on all the talk shows speaking about abusive relationships. I met her in Montmartre."

"Rachel O'Neill, the writer? The one who helped convict the Senator?"

"Yes, that's her. Adrian and I met her last night and we had lunch together today. She's coming to Maxim's with Adrian. She's here to regroup, she says, needs rest. She's having a bad time, actually."

"Well, I'll be damned! Rachel O'Neill, here in Paris? Small world, isn't it?"

There was a knock on the door.

"Come on in, Bobby, it's your own fuckin' boat!" Janet called out with a mischievous sparkle in her eyes.

Shellie grinned.

Bob opened the door and entered carrying another wine bottle and a bouquet of flowers. "I thought you might need some more wine and some fresh flowers for this little party."

Janet took them from him, "Aren't you the most charming man on the face of the river. I poured you a glass, hon, pull up a chair. Wait'll you hear what's happened to Shellie."

"Oh?" He looked at Shellie.

"Well, when I left here this morning, Pepe, the man at Maxims . . . you know, you've seen him out there . . ." Shellie hesitated.

"Yes, I know Pepe."

"Well, he stopped me when he heard me singing this

morning on the way to work and asked me if I'd like to audition on the boat tonight."

"You're kidding?"

"Do you think he meant it?" Janet asked.

"Of course, he meant it. He's the owner. That's incredible! What time tonight?"

"At seven," Shellie answered.

Janet leaned over and put her arm across Bob's shoulders, "So I thought we could go there and have dinner. What do think?"

"Absolutely! I'll call."

"Here, use my cell," Shellie offered.

He took it with him to the desk and looked up Maxim's number.

Shellie sipped her wine. "So what made you decide to come to Paris, Janet?"

Janet raised her eyebrows and darted a look at Bob. He had dialed the number and was waiting for an answer. He lifted his hand gesturing that she wait till he finished.

"I'll tell you when Bobby gets off the phone. Want some more wine?"

"One more, please."

"Is Pepe there? May I speak with him, please?" He put his hand over the mouthpiece. "Good, he's there. Hello, Pepe. It's Bob Benton, on the Simpatico. Yes. I hear you're auditioning Shellie Singer tonight. Yes. I'd like to make reservations for dinner, if I may. Three of us."

Shellie motioned quickly at him, "Five!"

Bob was puzzled. "Make it five, Pepe. Yes. Five for dinner at 6:30. Thank you. In my name. All right. Bye." He walked back to the table and stood, reaching for his glass. "Five?"

"Yes, Adrian and Rachel are coming. We met Rachel last night. She's a writer and we had lunch with her today. So when I told her about the audition she said she wanted to come to give me support."

"Isn't this fun already?" Janet put her arm around Bob

and lifted her glass. "A toast to Shellie, our darling little Shellie Singer, breaking into the Paris jazz scene!"

Bob lifted his glass towards Shellie and slipped his arm around Janet's waist, "May you melt their hearts with song."

Shellie blushed. She felt such kinship to these two loving people standing before her. She felt blessed. Here she was in Paris, happier than she'd ever been in her life, and about to sing jazz on a dinner boat on the Seine. It couldn't get any better than it was at that very moment.

CHAPTER 42

Rachel dialed Belinda's number. She was dressed and waiting for Adrian, they were taking a taxi together to Maxim's on the Seine. She'd dressed in a pair of black satin, brocade pants and black spiked heels, and a black silk shirt. Try as she might, she found it difficult to wear color. Even when she forced herself to do it, she felt uncomfortable. So tonight she was going to be comfortable and wear all black.

"Belinda. Oh good, I'm glad you're there. Have you heard anything? No, I haven't either. I'm so scared. If he were alive he would have called me. Okay. I'll think positive. Yes, I promise. What about you? You're kidding? How far apart are they? Then I'll call the hospital in a couple hours if I don't hear from you. I'm on my way to hear a new friend audition at Maxim's. It's a river cruise boat. Down by the Eiffel Tower. Yes, I will. All right. I love you, Belinda. Let me talk to Paul."

There was a knock at the door. Rachel opened it. Adrian was standing there wearing a black linen embroidered shirt hanging out over black jeans and black tasseled loafers without socks. Along with his thick, ebony hair and smooth, olive complexion, he was star-quality breathtaking.

"Come in, Adrian, just need to finish this call."

He stepped into the room and closed the door.

"Paul. Hi. How is she really? Is everything normal? All right. I'll have my cell phone on, so call me if anything happens. Yes. No matter what time it is. Promise? Okay, Paul. I'm here if you need me. Love you. Bye." She stuck her phone in her purse and for a moment was in deep thought, forgetting that Adrian was in the room.

"You all right, Rachel?"

"Oh, I'm sorry, Adrian. Yes, I'm fine. Let's go, shall we? I'll tell you all about it in the taxi."

Adrian opened the door and Rachel exited. He followed.

In the cab, she explained that her friend Belinda was in early labor with her second child. She told him the story about Belinda's brutal rape and about Baby Jake, her godson. "I'm so worried, Adrian. If anything were to happen to her, it would destroy Paul. I don't even like to think about it."

"Then don't think about it. Push the thoughts from your mind. You look very lovely tonight, Rachel."

"You do, too. Shellie will think we planned our outfits to match."

It was three minutes to seven when they arrived at Maxim's. Adrian paid the cab and they hurried onto the boat.

Pepe was introducing Shellie to the audience as Adrian and Rachel were seated at the table with Bob and Janet. A spotlight shined on the combo and Shellie.

She was wearing a short, strapless, black cocktail dress that had a flowing, metallic gold organza sash tied into a poof in the small of her back. The dress fit her like a second skin and revealed her perfectly shaped body. Gold four-inch heels completed the ensemble. Janet had talked her into wearing the outfit. At first she wanted to wear something less revealing, but now she was glad she had listened to Janet.

The piano player began the intro of "I Can't Get Started", a Frank Sinatra favorite. Shellie loved Sinatra songs and sang most of his - even his "One For My Baby" and "My Way" which were among the seven songs she'd planned to sing. She selected numbers that would show off her range and style. And she knew most people around the world could relate to Sinatra songs.

As she captivated the audience with her perfect pitch and bold melodic sounds, her friends were spellbound. They hadn't heard her before, didn't know the level of her talent. Adrian beamed. The applause was overwhelming as she finished the first song.

Next she sang an upbeat "Falling In Love With Love" and "I've Got A Crush On You", then "Just One Of those Things." After that the band did a few numbers while she took a break and joined her friends at their table.

Pepe met her at the table with a waiter carrying two bottles of Champagne. "My dear young lady, you are superb! It is my pleasure to invite you to sing three nights a week - Thursday, Friday, Saturday – for my patrons. We can talk about the money tomorrow. Yes?"

Shellie was ecstatic! She couldn't believe her ears. He was hiring her. "The band is terrific; they make me sound better than I am."

"I think you make them sound better than they are," Pepe said with a smile. The rest of the group chimed in agreement. "I must go now, but you will meet with me tomorrow, yes?"

"Yes, I can do that. I have two days off; I can come meet you at ten in the morning."

"Perfect. And the meal is on the house for you and your friends tonight. Bon appetite." He bowed slightly and walked away.

"Oh my goodness, can you believe that?" Shellie said to Janet as she sat in the chair next to her. "This is too much; I don't think I can stand it."

"Honey, you can stand it. It's high time some good things happened to you. You deserve it. And you are a helluva singer, Shellie. You didn't tell me how good you are."

"Thank you." Shellie looked at Adrian who was sitting to her left. "I was afraid you weren't coming."

"It's my fault we were late," Rachel interjected. "I had a phone call right before we left. Sorry."

"Oh, where are my manners. This is Rachel O'Neill,"

Shellie said to Janet and Bob.

"We're a step ahead of you, Shellie, we've all met." Bob announced as he lifted the glass the waiter had just filled with champagne. "I'd like to make a toast, if I may."

Shellie raised her glass, holding it out with the others as they waited.

"To the toast of Paris on this exciting first night performance, and to a most charming and talented chanteuse - may all her dreams and wishes come true."

"Hear, hear!" Adrian and Rachel chimed in.

Shellie was gleeful as she sipped her champagne and listened to her newfound friends getting to know one another. Her thoughts drifted to Jerold and she felt sad that he could not be part of her happiness, sad that he was caught up in his own fury.

Janet had told her what had happened and why she'd suddenly come to Paris. At first Shellie was terrified that Jerold might find out where they were. But Janet had assured her there was no way he could know where either of them was. Told her they were safe as long as they were in Paris and that she'd stay there till he was found. Bob also assured them both that they would be safe in Paris.

He'd already decided to install an alarm system on the Simpatico and he'd made a call to a fellow Vietnam vet friend of his that was living in Paris and owned a private security company. Rudy Galende provided body guards and security for politicians and notables. Most of Rudy's employees were ex-pats like himself and Bob. In fact before and during the time Bob had attended university in Paris to become the architect that he had become, he had worked for Rudy. His knowledge of martial arts and firearms had come in handy on many occasions.

So, he would make damn sure the girls would be safe.

Shellie and Adrian were walking ahead of the others towards the Simpatico. It was midnight and Shellie was still bubbling with energy and excitement. Adrian adored her and he was happy for her, but at that same time sad for himself. For now he knew she would never want to go to Switzerland and live as his wife. It would be much too dull for her on a farm high up in the Alps. What had he been thinking? He had been ready to chuck it all and forget about his art and take Shellie back to Gimmelwald with him.

He'd always dreamed of being in Paris, studying the masters, becoming the world-renown artist everyone told him he could be. In the past few weeks, though, he had begun to see the futility of it all. There were scores of artists in Paris, in Montmartre, in the galleries, displaying in the squares and on sidewalks - hundreds, maybe thousands – all trying to make their mark in the art world.

Rachel had told him about the gallery in Montmartre that handled her friends' work from Cornwall. She said she would talk to Paul Newland and the next time he was in Paris maybe he could meet up with Adrian and work out something at the gallery. But Adrian didn't feel he had gallery quality paintings. He'd been spending most of his time dabbling, experimenting, and searching for a significant difference of style. Most of his paintings were unfinished, most were merely drawings and etchings. If he were to do some paintings for Paul to see, then he'd have to buckle down and concentrate on nothing else. But he wasn't up to it right now. All he could think of was Shellie.

"Well, here we are," Shellie said, taking a deep breath as if she were inhaling all of Paris. "You are coming in for a while, aren't you? Everyone else is."

"Of course, I'd love to see your house on the river." He stepped across the watery gap between the boat and the quay, then reached back for Shellie. "Jump, I'll catch you."

She took off her shoes and jumped across the void into Adrian's arms. He held her body against his until she gained her balance and pulled away, laughing.

Janet went to the gangway. "Damned if I'm going to jump and fall between the boat and the damn pier."

Bob was right behind her, laughing, "Hardly a pier."

"Well, you know what I mean. Come this way, Rachel. You don't want to fall in the water. That's too dangerous doing what those kids just did."

"It's only a two-foot gap, Janet," Bob added. "Just two feet, 24 inches."

"Looks more like a yard to me, don't it, Rachel?"

Rachel laughed. She had been amused at Janet all night and was glad she'd met these people. They were taking her mind off what was happening in her own small world. It was good to be out of hers and in someone else's. It felt good.

"Take your shoes off, honey. You might trip on that damn mat," Janet called out to Rachel.

Bob held Rachel's elbow as she lifted one foot and then the other to remove her spike heels before boarding the boat. "I have some slippers you can wear while you're on the boat." He helped her across the gang plank and went to the small cabin where he stored gear and sometimes slept. Although he lived on the "Patriot", two boats up, he sometimes rented it out and slept in the small cabin on the Simpatico.

It was nearly two in the morning and after many laughs and a few bottles of wine, the party was obviously coming to an end.

"I hate to say this, but I've got to get back to the hotel. I'm really tired," Rachel said as she reached for her purse. "Adrian, you don't have to go yet, I can get a cab."

"I'll walk with you," Bob said. "We'll have to go up to the Marriott for one. It's not far." He stood and drank the last drop of wine in his glass.

"I want to go, too," Janet said. "And Shellie, I'm staying with Bobby on his boat, so I'll see you in the morning. Good night, honey."

After they closed the door and could be heard walking along the deck to the gangplank, Adrian stood and poured himself another glass of wine. "Would you like another, Shellie?"

"Yes, I would, as a matter of fact. I'm glad you stayed. I don't think I can go to sleep yet. I'm really revved."

"I thought you might be. And I'm not ready to leave you

yet."

"Adrian, there was something I wanted to tell you today at lunch, remember?"

"Yes, I've been wondering what it was." He handed her the glass of wine and sat beside her on the leather love seat. She was wrapped in an rose-colored afghan that Bob had taken from the linen closet for her. Adrian had been smitten by the soft, cozy picture in front of him for the past two hours. He'd embedded it in his mind and was going to do a drawing of her from memory as she was at that moment, and then a painting.

"Well, I don't know how to begin." She looked up at him with her big green eyes and he melted.

"Just tell me the gist of it in one sentence. That's what my father used to tell my mother when she was having trouble telling him something." He smiled as he rested his arm on the back of the sofa and gently touched her bare shoulder with his fingers as he sipped his wine.

"I'm married."

He choked on the wine.

"You said to say it in one sentence."

"I'm listening." He quickly stood and went into the kitchen to get a paper towel to wipe his mouth where he'd sputtered the red liquid. "Go ahead." He couldn't look her in the face. He needed a couple more minutes to hide his hurt and disappointment. "I can hear you from here."

"No, I'll wait till you come back."

All of a sudden he staggered and plopped down on the floor in the kitchen. Shellie couldn't believe what she was seeing. "Adrian? Are you all right?" She stood up. "Adrian, what's the matter?" She hurried to him. He was sitting on the floor, leaning back against the kitchen cabinets staring straight ahead, not seeming to hear her. "Adrian? What is it? " She knelt down in front of him and it appeared that he was catatonic. Some saliva had gathered at the corners of his mouth. "Adrian!" She didn't know what to do. She felt his forehead; it was cool to the touch. He was pale, almost gray. She waved her hand in front of his face, he didn't respond. "Oh, Adrian, I don't know what to do.

Please, say something. Please!" She hurried to the sofa and grabbed the Afghan and took it back and wrapped it around him. His back was against the cabinet, his legs out in front of him. He was still staring straight ahead with saliva drooling to his chest. She dampened a cloth and wiped his mouth and chin. Then she held the cloth to his forehead, all the while talking to him - trying to get a response. She thought she should call for help and reached for her cell phone, but before she could dial, he began to come back around.

"Shellie?"

"I'm here, Adrian. I'm right here. Are you all right?"

"Shellie." He turned towards her.

"You were catatonic; you didn't see or hear me."

"Drink of water . . . please."

"Okay, sweetheart. Hold on." She quickly poured a glass of water and lifted it to his lips. "Here you go."

He lifted his hand to hers and sipped from the glass she was holding.

"Epilepsy. Sorry."

"Don't be sorry. It isn't your fault. You just scared me. I didn't know what had happened. Should I call a doctor?"

"No. It's over now. I'll just sit here a little longer."

"So will I. I'll just get my glass of wine and we'll sit here on the kitchen floor together. How's that?" She gave him one of her most charming smiles.

He loved this woman and she would be the only one he would ever love. But she was married. His heart sank even lower.

CHAPTER 43

It was nighttime in the Brazilian jungle. Two days had come and gone and still no sight or sound of any rescuers nearing the scene of the plane crash. Pete Bell had busied himself exploring the nearby foliage and preserving cuttings of plants and collecting seeds. He'd appointed himself the designated food gatherer and since jungle fruits and plants were plentiful, he had managed to acquire an abundance of edible sustenance.

Neither of the two men had been thrilled over the taste of the Armadillo and hadn't had any since the first day. Regardless of not having meat in their diet, they were thankful they had survived the crash with only minor scrapes and scratches that were healing and showing no signs of infection. Battling insect bites was the worst of the experience now. Luckily they had packed repellent and all of their medical supplies and equipment had survived the fall through the trees.

They hadn't seen any animals other than a few noisy monkeys and the armadillos. The dangerous animals, mostly Jaguars, stayed in the tops of the trees during the day and roamed the forest floor at night.

Joe had been busy trying to fix the radio that hadn't been as lucky as the rest of the equipment. They'd built a makeshift dwelling inside the fuselage for their protection at night.

Being the official fire monitor, Pete had discovered which leaves billowed white smoke when burned and had hoped the smoke would spiral up from the jungle floor as an alert to the rescue planes.

"Come have a bite to eat, Joe. Lunch is on." Pete lifted some wilted greens from a piece of metal that had been situated over the fire and put them on another piece of metal that already contained fruit. There were samplings of mango and passion fruit and assorted palm nuts all over the ground that continually dropped from trees. He reached over and scooped water from a leaf-lined hole he'd dug under dew-laden plant leaves that were dripping into the receptacle.

Joe lifted his book of maps and carried it with him to one of the mounds of scrap salvaged from the crash. They'd created seating mounds to protect themselves from the armies of gigantic ants that feasted on leafy plants and bit humans for sport.

"You know, I figure we're probably 200 kilometers south of Tefe and the Amazon River. And probably the same distance from villages to the west, south and east. But I believe our best bet is to get to a river that runs north to the Amazon. Once we reach the Amazon we'll find civilization of some sort and can make our way to Tefe. There are villages all along the river."

"So you think we should go?" Pete lifted a glob of spinach-like substance to his mouth.

"I think we might stay one or two more days and if no one shows, we should break camp and go north. Thank God we have a compass. There's also the possibility we might run across some natives who could help us. Worst case scenario, we might run into flooded forest floor. But I think that likelihood would be closer to the mouth of the river, more to the east and north of the Amazon." Joe munched on the fruit. "This tastes pretty good, Pete. What is it?"

"It looks like guava, has the texture of it, but I'm not sure. Could be a strain of mango."

"You don't think it will poison us?"

Pete laughed heartily, "I think we're safe." He took a bite of his fruit. "So, if we hit a flooded forest, then what?"

189

"We'll have to go around it. I don't particularly care to tackle what might be lurking beneath jungle water, do you?"

"We could construct a canoe of sorts." Pete's eyes twinkled as if he were a boy once again planning a simple excursion in a neighborhood canal in his childhood Wales.

"What was that?" Joe snapped around towards an unmistakable sound that he was hoping was his imagination.

Through the foliage a large spotted Jaguar appeared and in a flash it crouched and leapt towards Joe, landing full force, sprawling on top of him.

After the initial shock of what had just happened, Pete jumped to his feet and grabbed glowing embers from the fire with his bare hands and threw them in the Jaguar's face.

The Jaguar rolled off Joe, violently shaking his head, pawing at his eyes and screaming in pain as he retreated into the forest.

Joe miraculously sat up, pale, bleeding and in shock. His arms had serious gashes where he'd protected his face and head, and there were deep scratches from the animal's claws on other parts of his body, his flesh and clothing were torn.

Pete immediately grabbed a container and scooped up water and set it on the remaining embers that were still burning in the fire pit. Then he took off his shirt and tore strips from its tail for tourniquets to tie off two major wounds on Joe's forearms that were bleeding profusely as if he'd slashed his wrists in a suicide attempt. He helped Joe to the shelter of the fuselage, still not a word exchanged between them. Joe was in a stupor.

After bathing Joe's open wounds with hot water and applying antiseptic from the first aid kit, Pete finally said, "Well, that was a bit of excitement we hadn't planned on, wasn't it, mate?"

Joe looked up at him and nodded and closed his eyes.

Until that moment, Pete hadn't given his own hands a second thought much less a first one. Now they were burning like hell.

CHAPTER 44

Shellie lifted the Simpatico hatch and stepped out onto the deck. She waved at Bob and Janet who were sitting on the deck of the Patriot having their breakfast.

"Come join us," Janet called out to her.

"I'm having lunch at the Louvre with Adrian. I'll see you later," she answered as she closed the hatch door.

"We plan to come hear you sing tonight at Maxims. Invite Adrian."

"I will." But Shellie had no intention of inviting Adrian. She was going to tell him today that it would be better if they didn't see each other any more. She knew he was falling for her, and she was falling for him. She didn't want a relationship. She had so much to do still, she wanted a career, didn't need another man in her life to control her and tell her what she could or could not do. She was on the brink of making it in the music world and she didn't want to spoil what she'd started.

The week before, at Shellie's insistence, Adrian had spent the night on the boat after his epileptic spell. He'd fallen asleep soon after she'd situated him on the day bed, still a bit groggy from the incident. The next morning she had made breakfast for him and they rode together on the Metro to Montmartre: Shellie to work, Adrian to his flat to change and then to the square to draw. She'd avoided him at lunch that day, didn't go out, and he was nowhere to be seen when she got off work that afternoon. He did show up at Maxim's later that night, however, and on one of her breaks, he asked her to have lunch the following Saturday at the Louvre. She told him she would and after performing one of the songs in the following set, she watched him get up and leave. She wondered if she was making a mistake in saying she would meet him at the Louvre that next week. She had been thinking about quitting her job at the Bistro in Montmartre, so they wouldn't be seeing each other every day. She had to discourage him; there was no other way to handle it.

Now a week had passed and it was a lovely Saturday, so Shellie decided to walk to the Louvre, not knowing just how long it would take or the route she'd take. She knew it was a bit further than the Hotel Des Invalides to the Place du Palais Bourbon. Then across the river on the Pont de la Concorde and voila! just a short trek to the Louvre. Another afternoon she'd walked to Invalides hospital from the Eiffel Tower. There were some lovely apartment buildings in that area that she'd thought she might look into when the time came, if they weren't too expensive.

She loved the Trocadero district, too, on the Right Bank which was straight across the river over the Pont d'Iena from the Eiffel. She usually shopped in the Trocadero, a ten-minute walk from the boat, and had an occasional meal in one of the sidewalk cafes that bordered the square facing the Palais Chaillot with its arching fountains and spectacular setting for three museums. The view from the Palais to the Eiffel was breathtaking at night. Something was always happening below the Palais, on a grand scale, whether it was a concert or a celebration or a political rally. Many weekends, Shellie would fall asleep in the wee hours of the morning with the sounds still echoing from across the river.

She looked across the river at the Palais de Chaillot as she headed for the steps taking her up from the quay to the Eiffel. Something was going on as usual. Crowds of people were cheering and music was playing on loud speakers. Situated on the plateau above the river, long low buildings curved out from two multi-floored duplicate castle-like structures that were separated by a square where people would congregate for the view over the fountains back across the river at the Eiffel. Very impressive, she thought to herself and then turned to face the horrendous traffic on the Left Bank boulevard she had to cross.

While watching Shellie disappear from sight beyond the steps leading to the boulevard, Janet whispered, "Isn't she the most striking creature you've ever seen?"

"The second most striking," Bob answered as he reached across the table and took her hand. "I'm glad you're here, for whatever the reason."

"I am too, actually. It really feels good this time. I mean, well, it's been awhile since I've been ravaged by such a goddamned animal!"

"Me? An animal? What do you mean by that?" His response was mischievously calm and quiet in contrast to her loud brashness. He continued to sip his Mimosa.

"You are a tiger, fella. That's what you are. A goddamned tiger!"

In his raspy, whispery voice he replied, "How could I not be a tiger when I look at you and those voluptuous breasts that are staring at me across the table right this very moment inviting me to suck them."

"Well, I think that's a damn good idea." She stood and lifted the pitcher of Mimosa mixture and headed for the raised hatch with both pitcher and glass in her hands. She looked back over her shoulder, 'C'mon, baby boy, come to mama," and disappeared down the stairs. Bob was right behind her.

In the middle of the spacious heart of the boat, Bob took the pitcher and glass from Janet's hands and refilled both their glasses, then set the pitcher on a nearby table.

She removed her silk robe and dropped it right where she was standing. She'd been wearing it over a matching pink night gown and now she boldly let it fall from her shoulders, exposing her body to the waist.

Bob handed her a flute of the champagne and orange juice and as they both sipped and looked into each other's eyes, he reached out and gently squeezed and massaged one of her breasts.

"Ohhhh, don't ever stop doing that, Baby, it feels so good," she whispered. After a few moments, still standing, still sipping, eyes closed, she took his hand and moved it, "Now do the other one."

He did as he was told, gladly.

She slipped her free hand through the front opening of his silk pajama bottoms and enclosed her soft, smooth fingers around the hard, elongated protuberance awaiting her.

It had been this way with them since their first encounter. Bob had never met a woman like Janet. He wasn't worldly in the sexual sense; he'd been reserve and selective with his favors throughout his life, even when he was in the military. Through college he was a serious student, not participating in the usual sexual exploration and parties that took place in the fraternity house communities. He'd never been engaged, never been married. Education and Vietnam absorbed his first 27 years, then after Vietnam he withdrew even more than before. He'd had a relationship with a Vietnamese woman for ten years in Paris but it had finally ended. He still cared for her; they had dinner together on occasion. But he'd wondered if all along he was just trying to make up to her for what he'd done to her people and homeland. He wouldn't accept the fact that war begets death and the fatalities were not his personal responsibility. He knew he had done what all troops before him had done since the beginning of time, obeyed orders. But it didn't help to try to rationalize the horror that way. The visions and nightmares still came. Not as often and not as long, but at any given moment he could close his eyes and still see the anguish and devastation as if it were happening all over again.

He'd slightly opened up to Janet about it after their first intimacy. A woman like Janet, who was sensitive, sexual, smart, and sweet – 4S, he tagged it – was hard to come by. And not only was she 4S, she was as tough as his flying buddies. She could handle firearms, she knew martial arts, she could swear like the vilest, and she was the most honest person he knew. To top it off, she was Betty Grable beautiful. What more could he want in a woman? He had to have her. He loved her and he wanted to marry her. But he didn't know how to pull that off. She had her own money, was quite wealthy in fact, so he couldn't buy his way into her heart. He had to find a way to make her stay.

Janet opened her eyes after a brief nap. They'd both fallen asleep, but Bob was smiling at her curiously when their eyes met. "What?" She asked as she lazily reached over and laid her hand on his bare chest. "What is it?"

"I'm just watching you sleep."

"I hope I didn't snore."

"You didn't. Shall we get dressed and take a walk?"

She threw back the sheet and jumped up, her naked body tan and glowing. She faced him in a sexy stance, "I'm gonna take a shower, wanna come?"

"If I do, we'll never see the light of day," he said as he got out of bed and slapped her on the backside. "You go ahead. I've got some calls to make, and then I'll shower."

"All right, but I do give good soap," she teased as she headed for the shower.

He laughed, "Yes, you do. You definitely do."

CHAPTER 45

He was waiting for her near the entrance of the pyramid, sitting on the ledge by one of the fountains. It'd taken Shellie almost two hours to walk to the Louvre and she looked like she was definitely ready to sit and relax over lunch.

"I'm glad you made it," Adrian said shyly. He felt as if he hardly knew her now, as if they hadn't spent any time together the past week. Telling him she was married had changed it all. He was confused.

"I wouldn't miss it. I have been looking forward to seeing the Louvre with you, Adrian."

They walked through the glass doors and took the escalator down into the expansive foyer where the guarded entrances led to the various sections of the Mussee du Louvre and its different periods of works by International artists - the Mona Lisa painting by Leonardo da Vinci and the statue of Aphrodite known as the Venus de Milo being the two most famous.

"I'll buy the tickets first, and then we'll go up to my favorite lunch place which is down the corridor from the Mona Lisa. I want you to see her first after lunch. I don't go to the food court out in the mall. You know there's an underground mall, don't you?"

"No, I didn't."

"If you take the Metro and get off at the Louvre station it's right there, and you can get to it from the outside as well. It's too hot and full of people. I prefer the museum cafes. They're on the stair landings between floors. You wait here. I'll be right back." He was chattering non-stop and hated himself for doing it, but he felt off kilter now. It wasn't the same. He didn't know how to act or what to say. His mind kept repeating, *she's married . . . she's married . . . she's married!*

Shellie watched Adrian go to one of the ticket booths. Her heart had warmed at the sight of him waiting for her at the entrance of the world-renown museum. She had wished she could just fall into his arms and they could run off together and never have to think about anything else, not about her career, and most of all, not about Jerold. She immediately pushed those thoughts from her mind, knowing it was impossible not to think of her singing career, and especially impossible not to think about her marriage to Jerold. True, she wanted a divorce, but she was in Paris now. She'd have to go back home to get a divorce and the thought of doing that sickened her. No, she'd just not have a relationship with anyone, not even with Adrian, no matter how much she thought about it. She had to tell Adrian during lunch. She'd felt his withdrawal from her. So, maybe it wouldn't be necessary to talk about it much. Then again, maybe she should wait till after they left the Louvre. She didn't want to spoil the Louvre experience.

"Okay, we're all set. Shall we? He held the tickets and gestured toward a security entrance and they both walked towards it, him being a little ahead of her, not reaching for her hand as he usually did.

Shellie was disappointed he hadn't taken her hand. But she had no right to be, she knew that. She was not a free woman. Nevertheless, she missed his loving, protective touch. All of a sudden, she felt empty and lonely.

"We'll take the stairway up to the left to the café. The Mona Lisa is on that floor. Come along." He led the way to the landing café and they sat at a table against the railing where they could see the French sculptures on the floor below and the grand rooms of giant paintings ahead of them and the door that led to the room that held the Mona Lisa.

An hour later Shellie wiped her mouth and placed her napkin on the table. "I love this, Adrian. Lunch in the Louvre. It's fantastic! I never dreamed this could happen. I feel so— so— well, I'm speechless. I don't know how to describe what I feel. It's breathtaking, as if I'm in a dream and I'll wake up any moment and it'll all be gone. Those marble sculptures and statues are incredible. Can we go in there first?"

"Yes, we can do that. Then we'll go into the gallery of huge paintings. Here, this is where we are and where the Mona Lisa is." He pointed to the schematic on the brochure he'd handed her when they first sat at the table. "We'll see as much as we can today. But it will take days, weeks, even months to see everything in this museum."

"I can't believe this was once a palace."

"George V turned it into a palace in the fourteenth century. It was originally a fortress built a couple centuries earlier to protect Paris from the Viking raids. It has quite a history. Have you been to Versailles, the extravagant palace that Louis XIV built and where Marie Antoinette lived when she was queen?"

"No, I haven't."

"You have to see it. That's a must." He quickly reached for his cup of coffee and took a sip. He wanted to offer to take Shellie to the palace and gardens of Versailles, but held himself in check. He had to back off. As much as it hurt, he had to distance himself from her. There was no future in it. He felt depressed.

Shellie watched the change come over Adrian's face. The atmosphere between them had become even more awkward. It was on the tip of her tongue to ask him to take her to Versailles. *Why would it hurt to be friends? We could do things together.*

He started to say something, but didn't. He continued looking at his cup.

"Adrian, I have something to say to you."

His heart quickened as he continued to sip. "Go on."

"Well, this isn't what I'd planned to say to you today. Not at all. But what I'm thinking, Adrian, is maybe it would work out for us if we could just be friends. Can we do that? Can we keep seeing each other and go to all the tourist places and enjoy them together? I would rather have you than anybody else take me around Paris. I'd share expenses with you, I don't mean for you to pay for it all. Can we do that, Adrian? Just be friends?"

Adrian blinked the tears back as he looked across the table at Shellie, wanting to crush her to him and never let go. "Yes, we can do that."

CHAPTER 46

Rachel rested her head against the curtain bordering the café window that looked out into Trocadero square and the Palais Royal across the way. In the distance she could see the Eiffel Tower looming high above the city. She loved Paris. Even at her most stressful times she'd lose herself in its captivating excitement and would always emerge with renewed spirit and heart.

The reports she'd received that morning about Pete were discouraging, the wreckage and the two men still hadn't been found. It had been explained to her when she finally got through to one of the rescue efforts - a telephone number and name Paul Newland had given her - that they could still be alive. Two weeks had passed since the plane went down and still no sign of them. As close as it could be figured they were somewhere south of the Amazon River in the middle of the densest part of the Amazon jungle. Natives from surrounding villages and government rescue teams were searching from dawn till dark.

She saw the two women immediately as they appeared in the courtyard of the Palais Royal. They stood out from the Parisians and tourists, Janet with her bright blond hair and red jogging suit, Shellie in her Kelly green sweater and matching slacks. Christmas ornaments came to Rachel's mind - red and green. She chuckled at the vision. Rachel had become quite attached to these two women in the short time they'd known each other. She was feeling more and more like a protector towards Shellie, and Janet was a kindred spirit fashioned after her own heart. Rachel hoped their friendship would continue long after she left Paris.

The only other women who Rachel considered as close friends were Belinda and Margaret back in England. Both had been in her life for almost two years – she'd met Belinda first, then Margaret. She'd never had gal pals before, had always been a loner, never trusted anyone well enough to let them get close to her. And now she was feeling that same closeness to Shellie and Janet.

"Hey, Rachel!" Janet called out as the two of them stepped through the doorway of the sidewalk café, one of many Parisian cafes that edged every square. "How come you don't want to sit outside?"

"I thought it would be cozier if we sat in here away from the noise and all the other diners." Rachel moved her purse from the chair next to her. "Sit here, Shellie."

"Any word about Pete?" Shellie asked as she sat where Rachel had indicated.

"Nope. Nothing. You both look fantastic. You're lovely in green, Shellie, and Janet, red is definitely your color."

"I like red, lifts my spirits. You're looking much better today, Rachel. You slept better last night?"

"Yes, as a matter of fact, I did. Finally. Didn't wake up once. I think our two bottles of wine last night did the trick."

"That was so much fun, Rachel. I have never had a night out with girls in my entire life. And that café is now on my favorites' list. I hadn't been to Montparnasse before," Janet said.

Rachel signaled for the waiter. "I go there a few times every time I'm in Paris. Great place for people-watching. And we do tend to frequent our favorites, I find."

Janet unzipped her jacket, revealing a matching red knit tank top, cleavage spilling up over its edge. "God Dammit," she said as she shoved her breasts down into her bra, trying to eliminate some of the spillover. "I wish I had B cups instead of

D's. No matter how much weight I lose, these puppies keep thinking they're Goodyear blimps trying to lift off."

They laughed heartily and began looking at the menu.

After the scrumptious luncheon salads and an abundance of mineral water and coffee, all three women were satiated. The waiter had just opened a bottle of champagne that Rachel had ordered, and poured three glasses full to the brims.

"Anyway, the guy says he can get me a gig during the week in a club in the Latin Quarter. Isn't that exciting?"

Rachel carefully lifted her champagne glass trying not to spill a drop, "It most certainly is, Shellie."

Janet squeezed Shellie's hand, "Honey, I knew you'd take Paris by storm. I'm so happy for you. Let's make a toast to Shellie and her career."

"Yes, and I'd also like to toast our friendship and please say you'll both come visit me in my cottage on the hill in Cornwall. Please say you will."

"Oh, I want to, Rachel," Shellie quickly responded. "I've never been to England."

"You can bet your bottom dollar I'll come visit you, and I'll bring Shellie when I do," Janet added before gulping the drink.

"I'm so happy," Shellie said as she set the glass on the table. "I didn't tell you last night, but Adrian and I came to an understanding that first day we had lunch at the Louvre. We've been back there twice since, by the way. Anyway, we're going to be friends, just friends. Nothing more than that. I was going to tell him I couldn't see him anymore, but I just couldn't do it. So just being friends would be all right, don't you think?"

Janet rested her hand on Shellie's. "Honey, you can be more than friends, there's nothing wrong with that. I don't see anything wrong with it, do you, Rachel? That boy is downright handsome and sexy, how can you resist him?"

"We know how Adrian feels about you, Shellie. He looks at you like a love-sick puppy," Rachel added.

"And you haven't had a loving relationship in years,

honey. You don't have to worry about that dang Jerold anymore. I'm hoping the sick bastard drops off the face of the earth, I really am. Besides, you gotta do whatever your heart tells you to do, especially here in Paris. It's the city of love, honey. Do what you damn well please!"

"I do like him a lot, but I'm afraid. I loved Jerold at the beginning, too, and look what happened. How do I know that won't happen with Adrian? And how can I fall in love with Adrian when I'm married to someone else? I don't have the right. Even if we did fall in love with each other, what about my career? I've always wanted a singing career. Shouldn't I focus on that first?"

Rachel took a deep breath and leaned back in her chair. "Well, I can't help you there. I'm having my own tug of war between career and Pete. Of course he may not be alive." Sadness flooded her face.

Janet reached across the table and grasped her arm. "Rachel, he's going to be all right. You must believe that. He'll survive."

"And if he does, what then? My first thought is to chuck everything and run to him and beg him to marry me and go home with me and live happy ever after. But I know that's a silly school girl's dream. He has a life of his own that takes him all over the world, too. He's totally immersed in this environmental cause of his, working for the Eden Project. He loves it. He doesn't need me. So where does that leave me? Alone in my cottage on the hill."

Shellie listened with wide eyes, taking it all in. "But you have so much going for you, Rachel. You have a writing career. You travel."

"I know. I have plenty to do when he's away. It's not the end of the world. Yes, I know. And I do love being alone most of the time, being able to do what I want, when I want, with whom I want. But, something's nagging at me, deep inside. Something's missing, something's not right. I want to love Pete and I want to be loved by him, but even if we married, it probably wouldn't work. I'm afraid it would end up in another divorce. I just don't know what I'm supposed to do. I thought I knew. I even thought I'd found my purpose. But now I'm not even sure about that anymore. It's all too perplexing." She sighed and reached for lipstick in her purse.

"Now that's a good one. Finding one's purpose. I've asked myself that question millions of time. What the hell am I on this earth for? Why am I here? Is it just to make money, which I most certainly do, let me tell you. But surely that's not all there is? And I'm afraid, too. So I should talk. I'm afraid to have a permanent relationship. You know, I just adore the socks off Bobby. He is terrific! I could put my shoes under his bed anytime he asks. That man is so sexy! But I'm afraid of him. My history with men hasn't been even close to good. It seems like the men I fall for are downright mean or crazy."

Shellie smiled at Janet, "Bob isn't mean or crazy, Janet. He's the kindest man I've ever met. And I can tell you that he's nuts about you. He talks about you all the time. You shouldn't be afraid of Bob."

"I think you're right. I don't see him being any other way than how he is. He's something else, isn't he, honey?"

"He's right up there with the best, Janet." Rachel took another sip of champagne.

Janet gulped hers and poured more. "The only thing is, he was in the Vietnam War and I hear about how some of those guys are emotionally crippled by what they saw and did. They never get over it."

"Like abused women who are crippled emotionally. It's the same with war vets. Those emotional scars are not easy to heal, Janet. Since I've worked with WUTAV, I've learned so much about how love and patience heals the emotionally wounded. It just boggles my mind. Sometimes I miss being as involved as I was. At first I thought that was my purpose in life, to work with WUTAV and help others. I really did. And so did my friend Belinda. And maybe it was for a while, but neither of us felt committed and equipped enough for it. Writing is my passion."

"So maybe writing is your purpose, Rachel," Janet added.

"A vehicle to help mankind. At least you've got that. What can I do as a real estate agent for the good of mankind? Not take commissions?"

Shellie frowned, "So you believe a person's life purpose is to help mankind in some way?"

Janet smiled at Shellie, "Yes, I think it is, hon, now that we're talking about it. Even though I'm not a religious person, I'm thinking maybe our purpose in life is to help others."

"But it doesn't have to be in a big way, do you think?" Rachel asked.

"No, probably not," Janet answered. "But then it sure is better if it is in a big way. I like to do things in a big way." She laughed. "Hell, if you don't get noticed for your deeds then what's the use of doin' them? Just kidding, of course. I don't really mean that."

"We know you don't," Shellie said as she reached for the Champagne bottle to pour the remains in the three glasses. "I just love our conversations. You know I grew up without having conversations with anyone. My mother never would talk to me. Then I married Jerold and he never talked to me. I didn't have any friends. So, this is good. It is. I never want it to end. I never want to leave Paris and Janet you can't ever go home and neither can you, Rachel. We have to all three live the rest of our lives right here in Paris."

"You'd love my Cornwall. Both of you would."

"Well, by God, I certainly want to take you up on the invite. And like I said, I'll bring Shellie when I come," Janet said as she lifted the glass Shellie topped off. "I don't know how long I'll be in Paris, though. It depends on whether or not they find that God-damned prick, the dirty bastard! How could they let that cock-sucker escape?" She took another big gulp of bubbly. "Sorry, Shellie. I just get all worked up when I think of the rotten scum-butt. Honey, I don't know how you stayed with him as long as you did."

"I don't either." Shellie lifted the flute to her lips and gazed out the window at the beauty of a sunny autumn day in Paris.

CHAPTER 47

Jerold parked his truck next to his cousin's in back of the farm house in Kansas. He was tired, and the excitement of opening up the envelope containing his passport had added to the lack of energy he was now feeling.

The thoughts of finally going to Paris to find Shellie were also wearing him down. He'd never traveled out of the United States; he'd never flown on a plane. He was a good ol' boy from farm country and he'd never had any desire to fly or travel anywhere. The only reason he moved to Los Angeles was because Shellie had wanted to go there after they were married. Now he had no reason to be in California. When he brought her back from Paris, it would be to Kansas. There would be no more city living. She would live where he wanted to live come hell or high water, even if he had to lock her up.

"You look ragged, Jerold," Billy said when he looked up from the newspaper as his cousin came through the screened door.

"Yea, I'm tired today. I had no idea bartending would be more tiring than pounding a hammer." He walked on through the kitchen and up the stairs to his bedroom. For a moment he stood looking at the familiar furniture that had once belonged to his Aunt Cecelia. This had been her room. He loved it here. He spent many nights with his aunt when his father was at his worst. If it hadn't been for Aunt Cecelia he and his brother wouldn't have survived their youth. His brother was living in Canada now. And Jerold had thought that maybe he'd take Shellie up there when he found her. It was a possibility. Either Kansas or Canada. They could start a new life together.

Billy called up the stairs, "You comin' back down, Jerold?"

"Yea, I'll be down in a minute." He sat on the bed and looked at the passport again. It was worth sending the $179 for fast service to get it. He'd found the service online and all he had to do was go to the courthouse and have the form stamped along with a copy of his birth certificate and his new Kansas driver's license. It worked out just as he had planned. Now all he had to do was go. But when? He'd have to quit his job, of course. But then what? He needed to plan it all out carefully - what he'd do for a living wherever he took Shellie, whether it was here in Kansas or in Canada. It hadn't been as easy as he thought it would be to find work in construction; that's why he was bartending. But then the bartending job wasn't all that bad. He liked it, actually. He liked the people he worked with, Carole especially. He could hear the ringing downstairs.

"Jerold, it's for you."

"I'll be right down." He put the passport in the nightstand drawer and went downstairs. "Who is it?"

"Carole."

"Oh." He took the receiver and sat at the kitchen table. "Hi, girl. What's up? No, we're just sitting here. I'm about to have a beer, just got home. I guess so. Sure, if you want. Alright. See you." He hung up and went to the refrigerator for a beer. "Carole's coming over. Says she needs to get away from the house for a little while, her kids are driving her crazy."

"Didn't she work tonight?"

"No, she was off. Took three days off, her sister's visiting her from Oklahoma."

"What do you hear from Shellie?"

"Got a letter from her today. Says she misses me, but she

doesn't want to come till I have a good job. These God-damn women are fuckin' undependable, you know. You ought to be glad you didn't ever get married."

"I am glad. So what's going on between you and Carole?"

"Not a god-damned thing. She's just a friend. I feel sorry for her having to work and raise those kids all by herself. She's a damn good cocktail waitress and can handle herself pretty good warding off the drunks.

"She's big and tough enough to ward off a dozen bulls in a small bull pen."

Jerold laughed. "She's tall, not big. She's got a good shape, muscle, not fat. We laugh a lot. Remember her sense of humor when we were in high school?"

"Hell yes! She was one funny tough bird even then. Too bad she settled for that ass-hole Gary Bolen who knocked her up three times. What a jerk he turned out to be. Left her and the kids and went off to Wyoming with another woman."

"So that's what happened. I wondered. Well, anyway, she's a bright spot in my life right now. She helps keep my mind off my troubles."

"Troubles? You got troubles?"

"Well, you know. Deciding on a future, Shellie's and mine."

"Seems to me if Shellie wanted to come here, she would have come when you came."

They both heard a car in the driveway.

"That was quick." Jerold grabbed two bottles of beer from the refrigerator and went out into the night air to greet Carole.

CHAPTER 48

Pete finished packing up the utensils and equipment they would take with them. They'd decided it was time to head towards the Amazon River or to whatever village crossed their path on the way.

"Okay, Joe. You ready, mate?"

Joe rose from the mound where he'd been resting and answered, "Not really, but what the hell." His forearms were wrapped with washed and dried gauze while cuts on other parts of his body were bared and scabbed over. His arms were the worry and both men knew he needed to get more extensive medical care as soon as possible. Inflammation had set in, a reddened area about an inch wide surrounded the gaping wounds, and green puss mixed with blood had been oozing. Every time Pete changed the dressings he had to use all his inner strength to keep from reacting to the smell and the look of Joe's arms.

Pete shouldered his backpack and slipped Joe's machete under the strap across his chest at his waist, pointing downward. Then he adjusted a smaller pack on Joe's back, first gently slipping Joe's arms through the straps. He didn't think the pack would be too taxing for Joe, for he knew he'd need all his strength just to make his way through the jungle. Their water and food supply would be collected from the forest as they went along. They'd carry enough with them till they camped each evening, when they'd gather more. Or rather, when Pete would gather more. Joe still wasn't able to do much. Pete was worried. They both knew it would be slow going and that was all right. At least they'd be moving towards help rather than sitting where help might not come. Their biggest hope was that they would come across one of the many villages that dotted the Amazonian Jungle and its rivers that branched south from the Amazon.

Pete had left a written message in the plane about what had happened and that they would be traveling north by compass to the Amazon River. He wrote that he would notch trees with the machete along their route. Wrote that Joe had been mauled by a Jaguar and it was imperative they get to a doctor quickly.

"Come along, my friend. Let's go home." Pete led the way, stopping every few steps to look back to see how Joe was doing. "You all right?"

"I can see my wife and children standing on the porch waiting for me," Joe said. "I'll make it."

Thoughts of Rachel flashed through Pete's mind again, one of hundreds of times since the crash. He'd dreamed of her again the previous night. Dreamed they were together in her cottage on the bluff in Newlyn overlooking the Atlantic. Oh, how he wished he were in Paris with her that very minute. So much time had been wasted. He'd come to realize how life can be snuffed away without a moment's notice. And waiting for the right time, day, week or year might not ever come. If there was any chance at all, he had to go for it. And he was going to do just that as soon as he got to an airport where he could make haste to Paris. He'd convince Rachel to marry him if it was the last thing he'd ever do.

CHAPTER 49

It was the middle of September. Adrian donned a sport coat and reached for his comb. He was satisfied with how he looked in the new jacket his mother had brought to him from London. She and her new husband, George Schmidt, had arrived early that afternoon after taking the EuroStar from London through the chunnel to Paris. Adrian was thrilled to see his mother who he hadn't seen since he had left by train from Interlaken earlier in the summer. *They look happy*, he thought to himself as he stuffed his comb in the inside pocket of the new grey blazer. He'd chosen black slacks and a dark red turtle neck sweater to wear with the grey and as usual appeared to have just stepped out of the latest fashion magazine.

"Are you ready, Adrian?" Gina was tapping on his bedroom door, eager to see her son again. The half hour he'd spent getting dressed was far too long to be separate from him. She'd missed her only son more than she'd expected. All the changes that had suddenly taken place when she married George – the death of Mama Anna and Adrian moving to Paris, as well as her own move to Interlaken from the Van Allman farm in Gimmelwald to live with her new husband – were almost too much for her - too much all at once. But George had been loving and patient and seemed to be sensitive to her need for coddling

211

and pampering through this most difficult time in her life, and she appreciated him even more for that.

"Coming, Mama." Adrian opened the door and beamed at the vision of his mother standing there in her lavender wool suit. Her hair was pulled up on top of her head and she was the most elegant woman he'd ever seen. "Mother, you are gorgeous!"

"I miss your generous compliments, darling, and your coat is lovely. You're such a handsome man." She looked at George, dapper in black and silver tie, waiting at the end of the hall near one of the other four bedrooms on the second floor of the extravagant apartment. "The grey is perfect, George darling. You were right. He looks fabulous."

Adrian stepped forward and hugged his mother. "I love you, Mama. And I've missed you so much."

"I've missed you, too. When are you coming to visit us? Soon, I hope." She gave Adrian's face a squeeze and stepped back.

They walked towards George as he descended the stairs to the living area.

"I would like to come home for Christmas, Mama, if that is all right with you. We've always been together at Christmas and I'd like to ask Shellie to come with me."

George turned at the bottom of the stairs and looked up at Adrian with a wide smile on his face. "So does this mean we will soon be having another wedding in Interlaken?"

"Oh no. No, no. She's just a friend. A very good friend. Although I must admit, I do wish it could be otherwise. But I'm afraid that's impossible."

Gina went to George and took his arm. "Why is it impossible?"

"I'd rather not go into it right now, if you don't mind. Shall we go? The taxi should be waiting." He ushered them out of the room, locked the door to the flat and they took the lift to the ground floor. "Our dinner reservation is at seven. Shellie goes on at eight, so I've asked her to join us till then. I hope you like her. In fact, I'm sure you will. You are going to be surprised. "

Shellie was waiting near the boat ramp when they arrived at Maxim's.

Adrian thought his heart would burst out of his chest when he saw her standing there. His first thought was to run to her, throw her over his shoulders and carry her away from everyone else and make love to her till morning. He'd dreamed of doing that every time they were together, but had honored her request and kept his distance. He didn't know how he would get through the evening without grabbing her and kissing every inch of her delectable face and body. She was tearing him apart, standing there in a strapless short, fitted, green sequin dress. Her shimmering white skin and thick curly hair was driving him mad. As he crossed the gangplank his heart was pounding. *I've got to get control of myself.* But he was finding that more and more difficult each time he saw her.

"I'm so glad you came, Adrian," Shellie said as she reached for him and they kissed each other's cheeks as is the European custom.

"You are gorgeous, Shellie. You take my breath away."

"Thank you."

"Uh, this is my mother, Gina, and her husband George Schmidt. This is Shellie Singer."

"Now I understand what you were saying, Adrian. You're lovely, my dear." Gina greeted Shellie in the same manner as her son.

"We're happy to meet you, Miss Singer." George followed suit.

"Please call me Shellie. Come this way, your table is ready. Janet and Bob will be here around 7:30, Adrian. Rachel said she'd be here a little later."

They followed Shellie and were seated at an elegantly laid table near a window adjacent to where Shellie would be singing.

"This is lovely," Gina said as she perused the dining room and the lights skimming the river towards the opposite bank. "I've never been here. Have you, George?"

"No, I haven't, as a matter of fact. I've seen the Eiffel

213

Tower many times, have dined there, but never here on the Seine. Thank you, Shellie, for suggesting it to Adrian."

Adrian couldn't take his eyes off Shellie as he spoke "It was my idea, actually. I let Shellie know this morning that we were coming."

"Yes, it was a pleasant surprise. I didn't think I'd be seeing him tonight."

"So, you live near here, I'm told," Gina questioned.

"Just down the quay. A few boats down or up, I get confused about that. Whether it's up or down river. I guess it really doesn't matter, does it?"

Adrian laughed, "No, it doesn't matter."

George was intrigued with the obvious spark he saw in Adrian's eyes and that he couldn't take his eyes off Shellie. "How long have you been in Paris, Shellie?"

"Oh, about four months, I think. About the same length of time Adrian's been here," she replied.

"We met during our first month here and we've been seeing each other ever since," Adrian added.

"But we're just friends," Shellie said. "Very good friends. Oh, here comes two more of my very good friends. Bob and Janet are here."

Adrian stood up and turned towards the couple. Bob was wearing a silk gray suit with silver tie over a black shirt and Janet was decked to the nines in long flowing, layered red chiffon with a skin-tight bodice showing off her ample bosoms. The two of them were striking and all heads turned as they entered and walked towards the table.

"You are magnificent, Janet," Adrian said as he kissed Janet's cheeks. "So are you, Bob."

"I think you were right the first time. Janet's the magnificent one." Bob pulled a chair back for Janet.

Shellie squeezed Janet's arm and beamed.

"I'll introduce you," Adrian announced. "Janet, Bob, this is my mother, Gina, and her bridegroom, George. They arrived today from London and are staying a week with me in the apartment. They live in Switzerland."

"Hello, Gina, George." Bob reached across the table and shook their hands as they nodded back at him.

"My Lord, will you look at the handsome people around this table? I never saw so many good-looking men and women at one table in my life. And Shellie, honey, you top us all. You are the most beautiful girl in the world. You know that don't you, honey? That dress must be all of a half a yard of material. It's the same size as a napkin, don't you think, Adrian?"

Adrian laughed and leaned over and gave Janet a hug. "What would we do without your humor, Janet Corrigan?"

Bob took Janet's hand in his. "She's kept me laughing for days. I'm not going to let her go home."

"Oh?" Janet seemed startled. "This is the first I've heard about that, Bobby Benton. And just how do you expect to keep me here?"

Bob had a mischievous look in his eyes. "Oh, I'll think of something."

Janet continued looking at him quizzically, speechless.

"What are you all doing for Christmas?" Adrian blurted.

"Christmas? I really hadn't thought about it," Shellie answered.

"If Janet's still here, which I hope she will be, I'd like to take her to one of my favorite places for the holidays."

"And where would that be, pray tell, Bobby Boy?" Janet asked.

"Vietnam."

Janet sputtered and the rest of them looked on with widened eyes. "Vietnam? Are you crazy? Why would we go there with all the other places in the world to choose from. You gotta be crazy, Bobby."

"When you see it, you'll understand. I go back every year," he signaled the waiter, felt it was time to have a Scotch.

Adrian looked at Shellie, then at his mother. "I've never been away from my family at Christmas. My sisters and I have cousins and aunts and uncles who live in the Bernese Oberland and most of them are in Gimmelwald. Christmastime in Switzerland is like being in a dreamland. The villages are festive,

215

families gather together for the Christmas feast."

Shellie was watching him intently as he spoke.

"I would like you to go home with me for Christmas week, Shellie."

She was surprised at what he said and started to say something.

"Before you answer, let me say this. You would be a guest, would have your own room. We'd love to have her come, wouldn't we, Mama?"

"You'd be most welcome, dear." Gina turned towards Shellie and rested her hand on the back of Shellie's chair. "Have you been to Switzerland?"

"No, I haven't. I'm sure it is beautiful, but I don't know if I can do that, Adrian. I don't know what my schedule will be. It's something I haven't even thought about. Christmas hasn't been on my priority list, you know. It's always been a sad time for me. And I have another gig that may be starting up, anyway, three nights during the week. So I don't know. But thank you for asking me. I appreciate it. I really do." She lifted the wine glass that the waiter had poured for her after filling the other glasses as well. "May I give a toast before I leave to join the band?"

Adrian sat sadly, slow to pick up his glass.

"Go on, Shellie, make a toast. You're on!" Janet said as the rest of them chimed in with "yes, please do", etc.

"I'd just like to say that I appreciate you all being here to support me. I love music, I love to sing. This is my life. And you are my closest and dearest friends in the entire world. My only friends, as a matter of fact," she laughed self-consciously. "So, I drink to you."

Adrian picked up his glass and sipped while his and Shellie's eyes met over the tops of their glasses.

The looks of longing weren't missed by Gina; she recognized the mood of the moment and wondered how she could help her son realize his dream that seemed to have shifted from wanting to be a world-renown artist to wanting this dazzling, tiny woman. She remembered when she had met Adrian's father as if it were yesterday. They had fallen in love at a ski resort in the Italian Alps and that was that. She had dropped her own fledgling fashion design career in Italy and went home with Henri Van Allman as his bride to live in Gimmelwald, a farming village with only a cog train as transportation up and down the mountain, no automobiles, and no roads, no shops. How more isolated can one be, she remembered questioning herself several times over the years. But she had loved Adrian's father and she loved her three children. And now her life was different with George. He was metropolitan, like her. They were very happy. She felt lucky to have had two husbands who adored her and who she cherished.

"Okay, I must be off. Do you have any requests for me to sing? I sing ballads, mostly, Gina. I hope you don't mind if I call you Gina."

"I don't mind at all."

"She sings Frank Sinatra songs, Mama. You love those."

"Oh yes. One of our favorites is 'Our Love is Here to Stay'. Do you know that one, dear?" Gina reached for George's hand and smiled warmly to his affectionate glance.

"Yes, I do. I love that one, too. How about you, Janet?"

"Do you know 'You Picked a Fine Time to Leave Me, Lucille?'"

They all laughed heartily.

"Actually, I love the way you sing 'Ain't Misbehavin', will you do it for me again, Shellie?"

"Sure will, Janet. How about you, Bob?"

"'Someone to Watch Over Me' will do the trick."

"Perfect. Adrian?" She touched his face, bringing light into his eyes once again.

Without hesitation he answered, "The Very Thought of You."

"I knew you'd say that." She gave him a kiss on the cheek and left the table.

It was nearly midnight. Shellie was eager to greet Rachel who'd arrived during her last set. After she and Rachel had exchanged waves, Adrian introduced Rachel to Gina and George before Shellie's final song of the night.

Gina, Janet, and Rachel exchanged knowing glances as Shellie sang 'The Very Thought of You' to Adrian. It was as if she meant every word of it and Adrian felt every word of it.

A tear rolled down his cheek before he could prevent it and he rapidly ducked his head and tried to wipe it away before anyone could see it.

But it wasn't lost on the three women whose female antennae were working overtime. They continued to glance at each other several times during the song, and it was as if a bond had formed between them. They all three cared for these two kids. Each one of the doting women was looking at the prospective relationship from different perspectives, each with different knowledge of Shellie and Adrian, each having racing thoughts of playing cupid.

The applause was overwhelming and Shellie was embarrassed that it continued as she joined her friends at their table. It was obvious she didn't realize how good she was.

"You were fantastic, Shellie," Rachel said as she stood and hugged her. "Sorry I was late."

"I'm so glad you could come. How's Belinda?" She sat on the chair Adrian had placed between him and Rachel, anticipating that she might want to talk to her."

"Mother and baby are doing well. He's a preemie, though. Of course Baby Jake doesn't know what to think of another boy in the family. They say they're letting him hold Paul Junior, that's what they call him, and he thinks he's a toy. I miss them so much. And I feel guilty I didn't go after the baby was born. But Belinda wouldn't have it. She said she's doing great and wants me to stay here till I do what I came to do. Whatever that is. But that's enough about me. You look adorable tonight, Shellie. Doesn't she, Adrian? And, Adrian, you are the handsomest man in the room. I mean, well, Bob, you're not so bad yourself. And of course George is quite distinguished looking. My, what a group of handsome people you are, and I don't know why I'm rambling on so much. Sorry."

Janet laughed and put her free hand on Bob's thigh. "I

just love your outfit, Rachel. Let me feel that sweater. Oh, my gawd! It's cashmere. And your pants are fabulous. That's embroidery, isn't it?"

"Yes it is. They were made in Italy. Every time I go shopping, anything black catches my eye. I can't buy colorful clothing. I'd love to be able to wear colors, but almost everything in my closet is black. I don't know why that is, I've been that way for years. Makes for easy traveling, though. I can mix and match everything, don't have to take as much."

"So, what have you heard about Pete, Rachel? Any news?"

"Nothing, Adrian. Nothing at all. That's why I was late tonight. I was talking to search and rescue in Brazil. They said they had reports of some debris spotted about 150 miles south of the Amazon, right in the heart of the remotest jungle and it's going to take time to get there. No roads. Just jungle to cut through. I'm trying to stay positive about it, but I don't think there's any chance of finding them alive after all this time. It just doesn't seem possible. Anyway, I don't want to think about it tonight."

George beckoned their waiter that was standing nearby, "May we have two more bottles of the same wine, please?" Then he stood and walked around the table to pour the remaining wine from the last bottle into Rachel's glass. "I understand you are a writer, Rachel. What do you write?"

"Romance novels. Although they could be classified as women's fiction, not just romance - romantic suspense, literary fiction.

"And she's part of WUTAV," Shellie piped in. "Women United Together Against Violence. That's how I first heard of her. I saw her on Oprah one day when I was at home sick from work. When I lived in Los Angeles. If it weren't for her, I would probably still be there."

Janet chimed in, "Yes, taking the beatings from that rotten son of a bitch'n husband of hers."

Shellie's face and body froze. She couldn't believe what had just been said. It wasn't Janet's fault. It was hers for bringing it up.

Gina shot a glance at Adrian.

Adrian was frowning, his eyes lowered. This was the first he'd heard of Shellie being beaten. She hadn't told him anything about her marriage, just that she was married. He suddenly felt overcome with compassion for Shellie and when he lifted his eyes that were brimming with love, it was too late. She was on her way out the exit. "Excuse me," he said as he stood and went after her.

"Oh, my." Gina straightened up in her chair and looked at George with raised eyebrows.

Janet took a big gulp of wine and leaned back in her chair and told them the entire story, as she knew it, about Shellie and Jerold.

CHAPTER 50

"Shellie! Wait!" Adrian sped up as he saw she wasn't about to stop for him or anyone. She was heading for the Simpatico and refuge.

At the boat ramp she stopped. "What do you want, Adrian? Didn't you hear enough back there to make you never want to see me again? What's the matter with you? Are you a glutton for punishment?"

Adrian was panting as he stood with his hands on his hips in front of the small, wounded figure before him. "There's only one person that I know of who needs punishment and it isn't you or me. Why didn't you tell me that you'd left your husband? Why didn't you tell me that he hurt you?"

"I'm just not ready to deal with it, Adrian, and I wanted to keep our relationship at a friendship level."

He stepped closer and grasped her shoulders. "You're supposed to talk to a friend, Shellie, don't you know that? You should have been able to tell me anything. What are you afraid of?"

"I don't know, Adrian. I don't know." She began to cry.

"Come on, let's go inside."

Adrian lifted the hatch and followed Shellie down into the boat.

She wiped her eyes with tissue and was still a little shaky as she turned on the lamps. She put on a Frank Sinatra CD. "I play his music to make me relax. I hope you don't mind."

"I love his music almost as much as I love yours. You were fabulous tonight. My mother thought you were better than the female recording stars she hears on the radio. You're going to be a star, Shellie. There's no doubt about it. No doubt . . ." His voice trailed off. The thought of her becoming famous saddened him because he knew when it happened she'd be out of his life. She'd be off on tours playing the famous person she had dreamed of being. No, there wouldn't be any room for him in her life when stardom came her way. He flopped down on the love seat, depressed.

"Would you like a glass of wine? I'm going to have one,"

"Yes, I believe I would, thank you," he said.

"Are you all right?" She hesitated. "It's getting to you, isn't it? Me being married and abused. It is, isn't it? It's too abstract for you and your traditional family."

"Abstract? You're embarrassed because of my family?"

"Well, you're from a close-knit, loving family, who has holidays together, you work together on farms, live together, and have been doing it for centuries. All nice and cozy. So what do I have? Nothing. I didn't know my father. My mother was a prostitute and a drunk. I went right from her to Jerold. And now after all those horrible years, I've escaped and left all of it behind. I'll never go back. I have no family." She handed Adrian a drink and sat next to him on the loveseat. "But Jerold is coming after me. You can bet on it. I know he is. He's not going to let me go that easy. I'm afraid, Adrian. Not only for myself, but I'm afraid he'll hurt anyone who is near me when he finds me."

"Darling," he set his drink on the cocktail table and leaned nearer her. "I will not let anything happen to you. I love you."

Shellie abruptly stood and walked away. "You can't love me, Adrian. You can't. I have plans. I can't be—"

He quickly rushed to her, took her drink and set it on the dining table and turned her around facing him. "Shellie, listen to me. I won't interfere with your plans. I know I can't have you. But please, let me love you. Let me love you for now. I won't make any demands on you, I promise. You must believe me. I'm in love with you, I would never hurt you."

Shellie looked up into his eyes and saw the desire and love he felt. She reached up and caressed his face. "Oh, Adrian."

He couldn't stand it a moment longer. He uncontrollably kissed her hard and furiously all over her face, her lips, and her neck. He lifted her and carried her to the bed. She didn't resist when he undressed her. She wanted him as much as he wanted her.

CHAPTER 51

A slight breeze was working the leaves loose from twigs on the trees lining the Seine. Janet stood still on the boat deck, watching the falling leaves, taking it all in. She breathed in the cool air slowly and stretched her arms up and out, feeling better than she ever had. A few boat-owners were hosing down their boats, others tinkering with this or that.

She walked over to the hatch and called down to Bob. "I'm going over to check on Shellie. Be back in a minute."

She walked across the short gang plank onto the cobbled walk that bordered the river. *What a life! I could live like this.* But then her thoughts traveled back to the States to her work and home. She loved her home in Glendale. She'd built that house, hired an architect to draw the plans to her specifications. It was something she'd always wanted, along with the respect of the wealthy gated community members. As a child she lived "across the tracks." Her parents had been hard-working, but were poor. She didn't starve, far from it, and her parents doted on her. She never had what most girls in school had. She wore used clothing her mother would buy from Salvation Army and thrift stores. Until she got married, she never had anything new of her very own, never had anything that hadn't been worn by someone else, never had a new pair of shoes. She was smart, an "A" student, but always an outcast because of her financial status. The middle and upper class kids were cliquish in elementary and junior high, and she was too shy to work her way into them. But in high school she developed a loud-mouth crassness that competed with the bawdiest of the bawdy. She got their attention. And as her body developed into the epitome of soft, feminine curvaceousness, what spewed from her mouth remained hard, foul and brash - a combination to reckon with. Even as she walked towards the Simpatico, men were gawking at her from the street above, leaning against the concrete banisters. Passersby turned heads in admiration, but she was oblivious to it all.

Up ahead she saw Shellie lift the hatch and come up the stairwell.

"Good morning, Sunshine! Or is it afternoon?"

Shellie waved. "It's still morning, almost noon. Want to go up and across the street and have some coffee and a croissant?"

"I'd love to. Wait right there, I'll tell Bobby where we're going." She hurried back to the Patriot and quickly boarded and climbed down into the hull of the boat. She emerged just moments later with a jacket and her purse slung over her shoulder.

Shellie was waiting at the bottom of the incline that led up to the street above the quay. "You're looking chipper this morning."

"I am chipper. Don't you just love Paris?" She caught up with Shellie who had already begun the trek up the short cobbled street.

"I can't imagine living anywhere else. Janet, I'm sorry for leaving like I did last night. That was rude, I'm sorry."

"Honey, I understand you more than you think. And no one was offended by it. Everyone was fine. We had a good time afterwards, we took Gina and George to the Patriot since we saw that you and Adrian were busy busy busy on the Simpatico."

"What do you mean you saw?"

"No, honey. We didn't actually see. Relax. But we knew something was up . . . uh . . . well, it was, wasn't it? Up, I mean?"

225

Shellie burst out laughing when she saw the mischievous look on Janet's face. "Yes, as a matter of fact, it was certainly up, as you put it."

Janet gleefully hugged Shellie and gave her a kiss on the cheek. "It's about time!"

They both giggled the rest of the way up to the boulevard.

"I'll have another coffee, please," Janet asked the waiter as she picked up the second half of a croissant and broke off a small piece. She leaned back in her chair from the sidewalk table and squinted at Shellie. "So, how did he get back home? When did he leave?"

"I don't know. He said not to worry. So I didn't." She giggled like a child. "He's definitely a big boy."

"Oh, is he? Tell me, how big?" Janet's eyes were teasing.

"Janet!"

"I was just curious." She continued munching her pastry, still waiting for an answer. "So?"

"So, what about Bob?"

"Shellie! I'm not going to tell you that."

"Same here." They both laughed loudly.

Janet coughed, choking on her coffee and still laughing. "Have you ever heard about the thumb rule?"

Giggling, Shellie answered, "No. What is the thumb rule?"

"It's—" She couldn't stop giggling. "Did you know that you can guess the size of a man's prick by the size of his thumb?"

"You mean it's the size of his thumb?"

"No silly. If a man has a big thumb, well, you can just about bet he has a big . . ." She couldn't finish. The look of astonishment on Shellie's face threw her into a fit of laughter.

They both held their hands over their mouths and were unable to stop laughing. They began glancing at the thumbs of male patrons and waiters and would give thumbs-up or thumbs-down gestures to each other in response to what they saw. They were out of control. People around them had begun to chuckle, not aware of the cause of the two crazy Americans' laughter. It was contagious nevertheless.

Finally they paid their tab and began to walk down the boulevard towards the Eiffel Tower.

"Adrian told me he loves me."

"That's no surprise."

"You knew it?"

"Of course, honey. It's obvious."

"I don't know what to do about it."

"Why do you have to do anything? Just enjoy it."

They passed the Marriott Hotel nearing the Eiffel. The crowds were already at the tower snapping photos and riding up and down the elevators to the different levels to view the city.

"Now, I would say that's an imposing erection," Janet commented glancing up at the Eiffel Tower.

Shellie laughed, "You've got a one-track mind today."

"Well, honey, it's been a long time for me, and I'm just enjoying it all. That thing is 1052 feet high, did you know that?"

"No kidding?"

"Yes, it was the tallest structure in the world till the Empire State Building was built."

"Janet, what'll I do if Jerold comes after me?"

"He doesn't know where you are, honey. Don't worry about him. He's out of your life forever. Forget about him. Act like you never knew him. You can do that, can't you?"

"I wish I could."

"Just do it."

"What about you? You know Bob adores you. He wants you to stay here. Not go back to the States."

"I wish I could stay. But I can't."

"Why not?"

"I have my work, my home."

"You can sell real estate anywhere. You can sell your house and buy one here."

Janet stopped and looked at Shellie in a new way. "How did you get so smart?"

Shellie took Janet's arm and pulled her onward, "I have a

good teacher."

CHAPTER 52

It was nightfall and they had camped again along the stream. They'd been lucky to finally stumble upon the waterway on their trek northward. Joe's spirits had risen at the sight of the tributary, he had felt that at any moment they'd surely come upon a village or native hunters. Where there was water, there were people. He'd lost track of the number of days that had passed and they hadn't seen another human being.

Joe was weaker. His wounds were taking their toll. The inflammation had decreased on most of them, but it had begun to flare up again on one of his arms - the arm that had been gashed the deepest. The Jaguar had taken out huge chunks of flesh on both arms, so the cavities that were left had been literally open to the bone, no skin or flesh to close. It left gaping rawness to heal from within.

The antibiotics and topical antiseptics were almost gone. Pete had rationed them, had cut down the dosage and figured that was probably why the inflammation had started up again. At least it was affecting just the one arm. That day Joe's temperature had risen.

What had started out as an adventure was now just another day in hell. At first Pete had enjoyed living off the jungle; it was exciting to him, even though Joe was injured.

Collecting plant life and soil samples as they made their way through the jungle forest, stopping to admire clumps of butterflies that appeared to be colorful blossoms perched on gigantic leaves, listening to the soothing forest noises at night, the monkey chatter, the exotic birds, discovering something new every day . . . that was all well and good for the first few days, but now all he wanted was to get out of the damn jungle. He'd had dysentery for four days, horrible stomach cramps, was craving food that he couldn't have, didn't want to eat another piece of fruit, leaf or root for the rest of his life - which he was thinking might soon be over.

"This paradise is hell," he said aloud as an intestinal cramp overtook his senses. He was leaning against a tree next to Joe, both of them sitting up. "You asleep, Joe?"

"No."

"Try to sleep."

"I'm afraid to sleep, might not wake up."

"You're not that sick, you'll wake up."

"What was my temperature?"

"101."

"Oh."

"So, go to sleep." Pete had lied. Joe's temperature was 104. He'd made cool compresses of grass and mud from the stream and had given Joe all but three of the aspirin. Only three left. He had wanted to take them himself for a terrific headache he'd had all day, but didn't do it because Joe would need them in the morning.

God, help us! Get us out of here! Pete put his hand over his mouth, afraid Joe would hear the sob that was rising in his throat. His head hurt, his belly hurt, he was covered with itchy bug bites. He still felt the burns on his hands and could still visualize the beast attacking Joe. He was afraid Joe was going to die from infection or his arm would go gangrene. It was already looking suspicious. The thought of cutting Joe's arm off was tearing at him. If he had to do it, there would be nothing to keep that wound from getting infected. He could cauterize it with fire, but would that take care of it? He'd never been this afraid in his entire life. This was not how he wanted to die, alone in a jungle in South America.

They both knew there had to be other Jaguars nearby. They could hear them at night. So they took turns sleeping because one of them had to be awake to keep a fire burning – not easy in a dark, damp jungle. His thoughts flipped flopped from fear to Rachel then back to fear again.

CHAPTER 53

"I'm going to Brazil!"

"You can't do that. What are you going to do, parachute into the jungle?" Paul couldn't believe what Rachel was saying. "Hold on a minute, will you?"

"All right, but I'm going."

"No you're not. Stay there, I'll be right back." He put his hand over the mouthpiece and called out to Belinda.

Belinda gently laid Paul Junior in the crib and hurried from the room. "What is it, Paul? You sound frantic."

Paul met her in the hall that led from the stairway he'd just traversed, three steps at a time. "It's Rachel. She's losing it. She says she's going to the Amazon to find Pete. Here, tell her she's being mental." He handed the phone to Belinda.

"Rachel? What is this Paul tells me?"

"I'm going to Brazil. It's been a month and I can't stand the wait, not knowing if he's dead or alive. I just can't do it anymore. You understand that, don't you?" Rachel was falling apart, sitting in a glass alcove in the apartment she'd rented in Montmartre, down the lane from Adrian's flat.

"Oh, Rachel, I wish I were there with you. You must get hold of yourself. You must. Nothing will be served with you going to the Amazon. It's a vast area, thousands of miles of forest

232

and jungle. That's why it's taking so long to find him. They have experts searching for him. What could you do? Paul just talked to the head of one of the crews this morning. He and Dudley talk to them almost every day. You must be calm and not let this destroy you. For Pete, for me, for your godchildren, you have to have a stiff upper lip."

Rachel laughed. "A stiff upper lip? Now that is British through and through."

"Well, I'm British," Belinda nodded her head at Paul. "Here's another one . . . now that's a good girl."

"I miss you and Paul so much. Maybe I should come home for a few days. I need to hold the babies. I haven't even seen Paul Junior." She reached for the tissue box. "How are you doing? Are you healing all right?"

"Yes, I am. The doctor said this has been a miracle. He said I shouldn't have been able to have another baby. And Paul and I have decided that there won't be any more, we feel we've pushed it at far as we can. I'd love to have a little girl, but I'm having my tubes tied when I'm better. We can always adopt."

Rachel sighed in relief.

"Rachel, are you alright?"

"Yes, I am now, but I'm coming home to see you. I'll take the train Sunday to Penzance. All right?"

"We'll pick you up at the station."

"I'll call you with the schedule. Thanks, Belinda. And thank Paul for lending his ear. I love you both, you know."

"And we love you, and want you to be happy."

"Well, I'm trying. Anyway, I've got to go now, I'm meeting three women this afternoon for lunch at the Louvre. I do love Paris, you know."

"I know you do. And all the more reason to do what you have to do while you're there. How's the book coming along?"

"Great. I'm half way through it."

"That's fabulous, Rachel!"

"Yes, it is. I've got to go, Belinda. Love you."

"Love you, too. Bye."

Rachel took a deep breath and ran her hands through her

hair. She looked around the charming apartment with its lace curtains and rosebud wallpaper that complimented the furnished antiques and smiled. She knew she had to go on with her life, no matter what happened to Pete. She was without him most of the time anyway. "So, why all the grief?" she said aloud. She continued to talk to herself as she went to her bathroom to freshen up. "You're never here, anyway, you know. So, what's the difference? You want to go and traipse around the world and take risks, so go ahead and put yourself in danger. I can't stop you. I don't want to stop you. I have my own life and I'm going to live it, damn it!" She was doing what she had always done, bury the hurt deep within and cover it over with life. "When will I ever learn? I don't need a man in my life to distract me and mess me up."

CHAPTER 54

"I've never had lunch at the Louvre," Gina said as she looked at the limited menu the waiter handed her. She was a vision of old-world elegance with her hair pulled straight back and clasped at the back of her neck. "What a lovely idea, Shellie."

"Adrian and I come here at least once a week. I've come to look forward to our lunches. We talk about all that's going on in our lives. He talks about art, I talk about music."

Janet listened as she looked over the menu. She was glad that Gina liked Shellie. She had been worried that Shellie being married and dating her son might offend her. But it hadn't seemed to make a difference.

"I do hope you'll consider Adrian's invitation to come to Gimmelwald for Christmas, Shellie. He's homesick and I know he would love to have you there with him over the holiday. The farmhouse is just as it was when he left, it belongs to him. It's a big house, lots of nooks and crannies. My husband loved to build. He added several rooms over the years. Henri was born in that house, it belonged to his mother and father and theirs before them."

"It sounds fantastic, doesn't it, Shellie?" Janet closed the menu and placed it next to her napkin. "I've never been to

Switzerland, either, Gina."

"You must come and visit us in Interlaken one day."

"I'll do that. Yes, I'll do that." She glanced at Shellie and saw a worried look on her face. She knew that Shellie was wrestling with her feelings and decided to let it go, not to say any more about it. "So, when are you leaving, Gina, to go back to Switzerland?"

"On Sunday. We hate to leave, but George must get back to the shop." Gina waved at Rachel who was coming up the stairs towards them. "Rachel's here. She's such a lovely woman, isn't she?"

Janet and Shellie turned and greeted her.

Rachel hugged them all, and sat between Gina and Janet. "I was afraid I was going to be late. Had to take care of some errands on the way and got caught up in the beauty of Paris. Have you seen the flower market, Shellie?

"Yes, I have. Adrian and I explored it thoroughly one day after lunch. It's fabulous, isn't it? I can't wait to get my own place and flood it with flowers. How do you like your apartment, Rachel?"

"It's very Parisian and cozy. Just perfect. You'll have to come visit me. I'm almost next door to Adrian."

"That's what he said."

"So how long are you going to stay in Paris, Rachel?"

"I don't know, Janet. I'm thinking about buying a flat here, I love it so much. I want my own place so I can come to it whenever I want. Just a small apartment. I don't need anything elaborate."

"What a great idea! Maybe Shellie could live there, too," Janet said. "She could take care of it for you when you're not here."

Shellie darted a harsh look at Janet.

"It's okay, honey," she patted Shellie's hand. "Bear with me. Rachel, Shellie needs her own nest. She needs a home of her own. I'd be willing to go in halves with you on a nice house. I love this girl, and I want to see her happy. She's like a daughter to me. At least I feel like she is, even though I've never had a daughter."

"You don't have to buy me a house. You've done so much for me already. I'll never be able to repay you."

"I'm not asking to be paid back, honey. Family doesn't loan money, family gives money. Maybe you're my purpose in life, hHon. Remember what we were talking about? About finding our purpose? Well, I'm thinking you're my purpose. So let me do my purpose. Okay?"

Rachel nodded at Shellie. "She's smart. You should listen to her."

"Since the beginning I've listened to her." Shellie laughed.

"Then what do you say, Rachel? Want to go 50/50 with me? I'll find a house that has enough bedrooms to accommodate me too when I come to visit, although Bobby might fight me on that one. He'll want me to stay with him. But you know, I can only take so much of that boat swaying and tossing all night, creaking and smelling damp. I need a Jacuzzi bath tub, a wardrobe with mirrors, a bedroom to die for with fluffy carpet and full of antiques and white on white all over the place. How do you girls feel about that? You like that kinda stuff?"

The waiter interrupted and took their orders.

Janet ordered a bottle of Champagne for them to share then looked back at her newfound friends. "So, what do you think about the house?"

Rachel answered, "Sounds good to me. But in my bedroom and bath I'd like it to be a bit more old fashioned. I like birds and flowers. I saw some fabulous wallpaper with birds and flowers in a shop. I'd love to find out where I can get some rolls of it. That will be the theme of my bedroom and bath, and I'll need an alcove for writing. And I must have a window seat with a view of the hustle bustle, preferable on a square. We have such expensive tastes." She laughed. This is going to cost a fortune."

"Just leave the looking to me. That's my business, real estate. So what do you like, Shellie?

Shellie sat silent for a moment, watching the waiter pour the champagne. "I would like a simple bedroom and bath, but nice. Fluffy carpet is nice, Janet. I liked your guestroom in Glendale. Something like that would be perfect."

"And we'll have a big living room, with a grand piano so that Shellie can entertain at our parties. Oh, this is so exciting! I feel like I want to get out there and start looking right now." Janet lifted her glass and held it out to the others. "Here's to our new home in Paris."

Gina was dazzled by the three women. "You all seem to enjoy life. This is a blessing, you know. To be happy under any circumstance. I admire all of you. At one point in my life I was sorry I hadn't pursued my career in Italy, sorry that I'd fallen in love with Adrian's father and had given up my dream. But now that I look back, and even then I knew it in my heart, I made the right choice. But as I listen to the three of you, so independent and strong, so sure of yourselves, I wonder if I had been more like you if I would have been swept away to Gimmelwald. I wonder what my life would have been as a designer in Rome. That's what I wanted, you know, to be a fashion designer. But I was a painter, too, and now Adrian is trying to carry on that legacy. But I'm not sure that's what he truly wants."

Shellie was puzzled by what Gina had said. "You don't think he wants to be an artist?"

"I'm hoping his desire has not been a reflection of my desire that I'm sure he felt from me as he was growing up. He's talented, oh yes. That he is. But he also loves the farm and family. And I think he's beginning to feel the void, although he isn't aware of it yet. He used to say over and over that he couldn't wait to go find a wife and bring her back to Gimmelwald like his father did."

Janet and Rachel smiled at Gina over their wine glasses. Gina winked at them. All three were on the same wave length.

PART THREE

"Will You Still Love Me Tomorrow"

"Tonight you're mine completely . . ."

(Song by Gerry Goffin and Carole King)

239

CHAPTER 55

The Newlands were waiting at the Penzance station for Rachel. Baby Jake was rambunctious, his wild orange hair attracting attention from those around them. Paul Junior was asleep in the baby carrier next to Belinda on the station bench. He was bundled in blue and white blankets and wore a blue knitted cap with ear flaps that tied under the soft chubby folds of his chin. Belinda's hand was resting on his swaddled form. Paul was looking after Baby Jake, following him wherever he toddled. Since he'd begun walking he investigated everything he saw and was quick as lightening.

Paul loved his children. He couldn't believe how much his life had changed since he fell in love with Belinda. The years before were a convoluted nightmare – his cocaine addiction nearly killed him, his perverse sexual habits almost destroyed him. Belinda's brutal rape changed his course immediately. Now his adopted son Jake and little Paul were treasures he lived and worked for. He wanted them to have a life he never had. He and Belinda could give that to them. He wanted them to see what a loving relationship was and to learn how to treat a woman. His womanizing dad had been his teacher and example. How he wished it would have been different. But that was all behind him, now he must make sure his sons lived through a better example.

241

"Here she comes," Belinda said as she stood watching the approaching train. "Here comes Aunt Rachel, Baby Jake. See the train?"

Baby Jake ran towards the train track. Paul quickly caught up with him and picked him up in his arms.

Rachel stepped off the train further down the track and immediately saw the excited family waving at her. She was happy she'd come home for a few days. She needed the closeness and familiarity of her dearest friends and her own home.

"Thank you so much, for picking me up," she said as they entered her cottage.

"Our pleasure," Paul said as he carried the travel bag into her bedroom.

"How long are you staying, Rachel?" Belinda set the carrier with the sleeping baby near the sofa and sat down. Baby Jake ran after his dad.

Rachel pulled the draperies open, and opened a window to let in the cool breeze. "Maybe a week. I'll probably go back next Sunday. The Sunday train seems to be best to take to London, and then it's a quick trip to Paris. I may fly this time from London to Paris, though." She continued going through the cottage, opening curtains and draperies.

Paul returned to the living room. "Would you like me to make some tea, Rachel?"

"Would you please, Paul? That would be great," she called out from the guest room.

"You got it." He went into the kitchen.

"It just warms my heart to see you two and the children," Rachel said as she returned and sat next to Belinda. They hugged. "I've missed you."

"I've missed you, too. I miss our chats at the studio. You coming down tomorrow morning?"

"I wouldn't miss it. Is Dudley in town?"

"Oh yes. He wanted to come with us, but we wouldn't have had enough room with the kids and all. We didn't know how much luggage you'd have. So he said he'd see you tomorrow."

"I'll be there bright and early."

"Tom says to tell you hello. He and Peter are throwing a welcome back party for you tomorrow night, I hope you don't mind? They won't take no for an answer, you know how they are."

Rachel laughed. "I think that's so nice of them. I wish Pete—" She stopped abruptly.

"Are you all right, Rachel?" Paul had been standing in the doorway listening, waiting for the tea kettle to boil.

"Yes, I am. I truly am. Really. So, did my packages come from Paris? Did you see who shipped them?"

"Yes, you've been off buying our works, haven't you? Where are you going to put it all?" Paul turned in response to the kettle and went back into the kitchen.

"Well, you aren't going to believe this, I'm going to buy a place in Paris. You know Janet, the new friend I told you about, the gal who has a mouth that won't quit, the one who helped Shellie? She's so funny, keeps us all laughing. She wants to invest in a house and asked me if I'd go in with her. Then when she comes to Paris, she'll have a place to stay, and Shellie can live there and take care of it for both of us."

"That sounds marvelous, Rachel," Belinda reacted. When is this going to happen?"

"Right away. Yesterday she found a beautiful, cozy house in Montmartre that looks over the main square. It wasn't on the market yet. It's furnished, has four floors, an unbelievable price. She's good, Janet is. She can wheel and deal with anybody. I can see why she's so successful. It's unoccupied and we can rent it till escrow closes. We can move in any time. Isn't that incredible?"

"Oh my goodness!" Belinda frowned. "Does that mean we're going to lose you to Paris, permanently?"

"Never. England is where I feel the best. I'll never leave Cornwall. Paris will be my get-away place, same as my mother's cabin in Montana, although I haven't been back since she died, and my father's home in Brentwood. His house comes in handy

243

when I'm in L.A. to meet with my agent and doing promos. So, Paris will just be another get-away spot. And you know, you can use any of them any time you want. You know that, don't you? Now you'll have a place to stay when you're in Paris, Paul, showing at the gallery."

"In a house with three women? I don't think so," he laughed and winked at Belinda as he sat down across from them and poured tea. "I'll stay at my usual hotel, thank you very much. But I'll certainly take you all to dinner when I'm there. How's that?"

"How about when you bring Belinda and the children, you can all stay with us? There's plenty of room. You'll love Shellie. And wait till you hear her sing. She's amazing."

Paul grinned, "You got a deal."

CHAPTER 56

It was over. Pete was deathly ill. He figured it was from one of the hundreds of insect bites. He was covered with them. And the ants had been crawling all over them for the past hour, stinging the shit out of them. He didn't have the energy to swipe them off. Joe had been unconscious all night, so he couldn't feel the ants and bugs that were crawling on him.

The stream had widened and was running fuller now. That was a good sign, meant they were closer to the Amazon. But there was no way in hell they had traveled 200 miles. They would have been lucky if they had hiked 60 miles in Pete's estimation. They were both going to die in this godforsaken, bug infested jungle. He knew it and there was nothing he could do about it. He lay his head back against the tree and shut his eyes. At that point he didn't care if a Jaguar attacked and tore him to shreds. He'd rather be killed by a Jaguar than be eaten alive by friggin' bugs. He was sick and he was tired. He welcomed death. Joe was almost dead anyway. The infection had to be throughout his body by now and his arm was swollen twice the size of the other. Pete didn't have the strength to cut off Joe's arm, even if he wanted to. This was to be their last day alive.

As Pete passed in and out of involuntary sleep he could hear Rachel's voice. He could feel her body against him. She was whispering in his ear.

"Pete, wake up, Pete. Can you hear me, Pete? Wake up."

He could feel her touching his arm and caressing his face like she did when they made love together. He loved that. No one had ever done that to him. "Rachel . . . Rachel . . ."

"That's it, wake up, c'mon, open your eyes, old chap."

That wasn't Rachel's voice. Pete opened his eyes and saw the face of Rupert Gooding - his coworker and counterpart in Brazil. "Rupert . . ." He tried to get up but couldn't.

"Take it easy. We're here. You're going home, Mate. You're going home. Here, drink this." He lifted a water bag to Pete's lips. And then put a tablet on Pete's tongue. "Swallow again; you need to swallow the pill." He lifted the water bag to him again.

There were six natives with Rupert and two other Brits - a paramedic and a guide. They gave shots to both of them and tended to Joe's wounds, although they were sure he was going to lose his arm. They assembled two stretchers and after an hour they were on their way up the river's tributary to the boat that had brought them that far. They would be in Manaus before nightfall where they would fly out to Belem and civilization.

Rachel woke up early. The sun was shining and she felt better than she had in weeks. Paris was invigorating and inspiring, but Cornwall and the sea soothed Rachel's soul. She opened the French doors that led from her bedroom to the veranda and walked barefoot across the lawn to the edge of the bluff. She could see all the way to Penzance and to St. Micheal's Mount. It was breathtaking.

"I wish you were here, Pete. It's one of those mornings." She sighed deeply, shook her head and hurried back into her cozy cottage. The cold had finally caught up with her. Her feet were frozen.

Her cell rang. She couldn't remember where she'd put it. It wasn't in the bedroom. It was on the cocktail table in the living room. She ran for it and caught it on a ring.

"Hello? Yes, this is she. Yes? Oh my god! Where is he?

Yes, I'll have my phone with me all the time. Yes, please. Oh, thank you so much. I can't thank you enough. Thank you, Rupert. Thank you, thank you. Bye."

She immediately dialed Belinda. "Have you heard? Yes, Rupert just called here, too. Isn't that fantastic? He said they were getting medical attention right now, and Pete was too weak to talk but he is going to be all right. They're taking them to Belem by helicopter to a hospital. He's alive, Belinda! He's alive. Yes! I'm so happy! I'll get dressed and come to the shop. Okay, see you in a minute. Put the coffee on. Love you, sweetie. I'm so happy!"

CHAPTER 57

Shellie and Janet loved the house in Montmartre and were standing in the middle of the ground floor parlor when Bob arrived.

"How are you two gorgeous women?" he asked as he entered the open doorway. "This is terrific!" He couldn't believe Janet had signed a deal for such a low amount. "You stole this property, Janet. Admit it."

"Don't you just love it? We're going to move into it starting tomorrow. Shellie's taking the first floor, go on up the stairway. Take a look."

He started for the stairs.

"We each have a floor. I'm on the second floor, Rachel wants the third one. The ground floor will be our common area. Can you believe this? Five bedrooms and four baths. One bath on each level. Wait! Come here and look at this kitchen." She took his hand and led him towards the modern kitchen off the corridor across from a spare room near the large bathroom. "Look at this. It's brand new. They just remodeled it. All new appliances. Everything's modern."

"Wow! Plenty of space to entertain. You might consider cutting a pass-through or a walk-through in that wall that leads into the living area; it'll make it more convenient to serve in the dining area and for parties."

"Hey, why do you think I asked you to meet us here? You're the architect in this family. So, please, by all means, we're open to whatever you think. And I think that's a fabulous idea. Write that down. Now come on, I want to ask you about something across the hall."

They left the kitchen and went into another room.

"See that wall?" She was pointing to the windowless wall that faced the back garden. We have a private yard on the other side of that wall and I'd like to put in some windows and French doors opening onto a patio and fill the yard with lots of flowers and plants. We'll call this our garden room. Can you do that?"

"It depends on where the weight-bearing beams are."

"Write that down, too. Here, let me get you a pad to write on. I have one in my purse." She went back in the living room and dug through her bag and retrieved two pocket notebooks. "Shellie and I already talked about all this, didn't we, honey?"

"Yes, and don't forget the opening into the big room from the garden room."

"Oh yes. Bobby, we want to be able to open up the garden room to the main living room, too, when we have a crowd. Not open all the time, just when we need to. How do we do that?'

"Folding shutter doors. No problem. Again, I'll check for support walls."

"Great. Okay, come with us upstairs." She nearly ran up the winding staircase. "Isn't this the grandest staircase you've ever seen?"

"Like I said, you stole this house for the price you're paying."

"This is Shellie's floor. Honey, you tell him what you want."

"Well, the bathroom is perfect. But I've always liked glass brick. Can we change that wall next to the tub to glass brick? That way no one can see in, but I'll have lots of light in there. Right now it's too dark for me."

"Sure." Bob wrote it in his borrowed note book.

"And I'd like to have a window seat looking out over the city, on that back wall in the adjoining room. I know Rachel wants a window seat looking on to the square, but I'd like mine to look out the other direction. Isn't this beautiful?"

"Yes it is."

"I'd love to have an archway between the two rooms. It would make it more spacious and would feel like a bedroom and sitting room combined. That's all I want, everything else is fine."

Janet hugged Shellie. "We're going to recover the furniture in her favorite colors and change the wallpaper. This is going to be fun, isn't it, honey?"

"I still can't believe all that's happening. I keep pinching myself, trying to wake up."

"It's happening, honey. You can bet your life, it's happening." She walked over to Bob and looked at the notes he'd written. "The other two floors are laid out the same as this one. This was a B & B and they rented out each floor. So that makes it perfect for us, doesn't it? I want a window seat, too, facing the city. Women love window seats, you know. It's romantic. Like Shellie said, Rachel wants hers on the street side. She likes to watch people. She said that's the only change she wants. In my bathroom, I'd like a huge stained glass window above the bath. And that's it. You want to look at that now?"

"Yes, may as well take it all in and get started on it. I can have my guys here tomorrow to measure and work up an estimate of the changes."

"That's perfect. Rachel will be back at the end of the week. So if she has any other changes she wants to make, you can talk to her about them. She might have some second thoughts about what she wants. Oh, I'm so excited about all this!" She gave Bob a bear hug and he laughed as he held on to her to keep his balance.

"So, does this mean you've moving here - lock, stock and barrel?"

Janet pulled back and hesitated to answer.

"Does it?" he asked again.

"Well, no. I mean, well, it means I'm investing in a house

and I'll stay here when I'm here. My home is in the States, Bobby. My work is there, my house is there. This will be my holiday home."

Bob turned and walked towards the doorway without looking back. "I'll see you tonight. I have to meet with a client near here in fifteen minutes." He continued down the stairs.

Janet stared after him. She heard him open the front door and close it. He walked out into the square and disappeared around the corner. She looked at Shellie, "What just happened?"

"He loves you, Janet."

"But why did he just walk out like that?"

"He wants you to move to Paris."

"That's silly! I can't do that!"

"Why not?"

"Because I worked years to get where I am. I'd have to start all over if I moved here. I'd have to give up everything including my client list. No, I can't do that. I won't."

CHAPTER 58

Bells were ringing and Pete could hear the fireworks that marked the festival to the Virgin of Nazareth – Cirio de Nazare, Brazil's largest religious festival. It was the second Sunday in October, the annual celebration in Belem, 60 miles up the Amazon River from the Atlantic.

He sat up on the edge of the hospital bed and set his feet on the floor, determined to walk without any help. He was going to find a telephone to call Rachel. Rupert had told him that he had talked to her and had also talked to Paul and Dudley, so he was relieved that they all knew he was alive.

It had been a week since Rupert had found them. During that week, Joe's arm had been amputated and he almost died. Pete had been in such a weakened state, there had been some concern about his survival, too. But they were both getting stronger every day and were being treated by some of the best doctors in Brazil. The insect bites had filled their bodies with venom and the infection from scratching the bites all over their bodies had been one of the most difficult to deal with. Mega doses of antibiotics had been shot into them every day since they were found.

"There he is," Rupert greeted Pete as he came into the room. "Have you been up, today?"

"I was just about to do that, thank you. I need to get to a phone." He tried to stand and lost his balance.

Rupert grabbed him before he fell. "You've got to take it easy just a bit longer, old chap. No sense in falling and injuring yourself even more. The lady knows you'll be calling. You've lost 45 pounds, they're telling me."

"Then it's true. If you eat only fruit and greens, you'll lose weight." Pete laughed as he lay back in the bed and Rupert covered him with the sheet.

"Nothing to worry about, mate, I suspect you'll be gaining your weight back as soon as you can have meat and potatoes again. A few good Sunday lunches and you'll be fit as a fiddle."

"Yes, roast beef sounds good to me right now, but the doc says no. Says my stomach won't take it yet. So what's he saying to you, Rupert? When will I be able to get out of here?"

Rupert sat in the bedside chair. "It's going to be at least another week, Pete. Maybe longer."

"How is Joe?"

"Too bad about his arm, poor boy."

"I should have done something."

"What could you have done? You used up all the medication you had. You nearly died, Pete. There's nothing you could have done. So don't be feeling you're responsible for his losing his arm."

"I can't help it." He closed his eyes and placed his hand on his forehead. "It all seems like a sodden nightmare. When can I see him?"

"Not yet. He's still in isolation. Infection, you know. He's not out of the woods, yet."

"Oh, God, no. You mean he could die?"

"I'm afraid so."

"Have you contacted his wife?"

"She's here. Came immediately."

"I'm going to finish my mission, Rupert. I'm not going to have all this happen for nothing."

"No, Pete. You should go home when you're well

enough. You needn't stay and carry on. There'll be time enough for that, later."

"I have to finish what I started out to do. You have the samples I collected?"

"Yes, they're on their way to Eden."

"Good. I've decided to explore the river's mouth. I'll stay here, in Belem."

"I wish you would reconsider," Rupert said as he stood up to leave.

"No, I've made up my mind."

CHAPTER 59

Yes, Rachel loved her cottage on the edge of the world. She was sitting in her study, peering out the window at the sea that stretched to the horizon. It was warm for October. She'd opened all her windows to let the fresh air flow from room to room.

The phone rang.

"Hello?"

"Hello, doll."

"Pete! Is it really you? Are you all right?" She jumped up in excitement.

"Yes, I'm much better. Almost able to leave the hospital. I've missed you, Rachel."

"Oh I've missed you, too, Pete. When are you coming home? "

"Well, that's just it, doll, I'm going to stay and finish what I came here to do. You understand, don't you?"

Rachel was silent.

Pete could sense her disappointment. "I've come this far, I can't quit now. I'll join you in Paris when I finish. When are you going back to Paris?"

"Next Sunday. I've been home for a month, much longer

than I'd planned.

"How long will you be in Paris?"

"Till Christmas," she said quietly, almost a whisper.

"Are you all right?"

"Yes, why?" *No, I'm not all right!*

"You sound different." Pete lit up the one cigarette he'd borrowed from an aide before he dialed her number at the payphone on the patio outside the hospital cafeteria.

"I'm just thinking about getting back to Paris. I bought a house in Montmartre."

"You what?"

"I bought a house in Montmartre. Went in with a friend from the U.S. We bought it and we're moving into it right away." She wiped her eyes that were tearing up.

"Male or female?"

"What do you think?"

"Then I'll come there when I finish here. I won't be going to Africa."

"So when do you think that'll be?" She began to perk up again.

"I don't know exactly, a lot depends on when I'm back on my feet and can get back to work. I'd like to spend at least a month exploring the river-sea, as they call it. The Amazon Delta is the largest in the world, full of swamp forests, floating meadows and mudflats. It's incredible. I'll be safe, Rachel. You needn't worry. The vegetation is abundant for now, but not for long because of the deforestation that's going on. So, I must get my specimens while I can, before they're extinct." His eyes began to sparkle with anticipation at the thought of getting back to work.

"Well, I know you love what you do. I understand your wanting to finish. I do, Pete. I'm just as passionate about writing." She sat at the window again and reached for her cup of coffee.

"Thank you, doll. Just be patient a while longer and I'll join you in Paris before I go back to Eden."

"I'll look forward to that."

"When they rescued us, I was so glad to get out of the jungle I swore I'd leave at the first chance. But now that I'm feeling better, I have to stay. It's beautiful, Rachel. South America is a treasure."

"Brazil is known for its beautiful women, too."

"Aw, now. Don't you be concerned about that, doll. I could say the same about Paris and the Frenchmen," he laughed.

"Ha! I don't think so. Most of them are such small men. Not to my liking, thank you. I'll take a big man any day over a little man regardless of where he was born. You fit the bill quite nicely."

"I'm a bag of bones, actually. I have lost 50 pounds, so you might not want me."

"You haven't lost your height. That's what I like. Height." she laughed.

"I love your laugh, Rachel. I miss you."

"I miss you, too."

CHAPTER 60

The house was full of carpenters and plasterers, windows were being carried upstairs. Bob and Janet were looking at architectural drawings spread on the dining room table.

"I like the way you've cut out the walls and designed the window seats upstairs. Mine especially. I'm afraid I'll never want to leave my floor." Janet's eyes were beaming and her excitement was glowing as she watched Bob.

"Maybe you'll never want to leave Paris," he said as he continued to make notes on a pad for his workers.

Janet hesitated, deciding whether or not to respond to Bob's indirect question. Maybe she should just play along and not answer one way or another. She knew he was not going to give up on trying to persuade her to live in Paris fulltime. Maybe if she just playfully teased and danced around it, he'd accept that and would quit pressuring her. It wasn't as if he was pressuring her strongly, it was just that the question or mention of it here and there was irritating her. Why couldn't he be happy with her being there just a couple of months at a time? She could easily do that – six months at home in California, two months in Paris and then repeat the process. She'd worked hard to become the independent woman she had become, finally able to call her own shots. It'd taken years to reach this point in her life. She was able to buy houses anywhere in the world, go anywhere she wanted; pick up on a moment's notice like she had this time. Besides, she didn't know if it would be a good thing to be around Bob all the time. She might fall for him. She didn't want that, didn't want a man to rule her, tell her what to do. That's what happened when she married both times, and Bob might want to get married. Her experience with marriage had been chaotic and crazy; it had nearly killed her the last time. No. She needed to keep the relationship simple, just fun and games. She didn't need a 24-hour, 7 days a week, 52 weeks a year man. That would drive her insane. She knew it would. "Well, who knows what might happen. You never can tell," she finally answered as she reached for a bottle of spring water and walked into the garden room to join Shellie.

"Don't you just love this, Janet?" Shellie was standing on the threshold of the new French doors. "This patio is heaven. When Rachel gets back, we'll have our first lunch out here. When did you say the plants would be delivered?"

"This afternoon sometime. They could arrive any minute, actually. And they're already planted and potted for us to place wherever we want them. Isn't this exciting?"

"Oh I've never been so excited in my life. I never dreamed of living in such a palace. That's what this is, you know, a palace. And my floor is beyond anything I've ever hoped for, Janet. Thank you so much. I hope you'll never sell this house. As soon as I can, I'll pay rent. That, I promise."

"Oh no you're not! You're not paying rent. You'll be managing the place while Rachel and I are away. Neither one of us will be here all the time. So you will be the one to take care of it. And besides, I would never ask you to pay rent. No way. You're like a daughter to me; you don't take rent from a daughter, hon."

Shellie became quiet as she stepped back into the room and closed the French doors. She turned away from Janet and sighed.

"What's the matter, hon?"

Shellie's eyes were full of tears when she looked back at

259

Janet. "Oh, I was just wondering about my mother. Wondering what she would say about me being here in all this beauty. She never had anything like this. She never saw anything like this."

"Oh honey," Janet reached for her and put her arms around her. "I'm sure she would be happy for you, just as I am."

"I wonder where she is, if she's still alive."

"Do you ever think about looking for her?"

"No. Our life together was so horrible I never wanted to find her. She's probably dead anyway. Last time I saw her she was in a drug stupor, had been passed out for two days. Hadn't eaten, there was no food in the house. I was fourteen when Social Services rescued me and was in a foster home until Jerold and I got married. I just think of her sometimes and feel sad."

"Well, you have a new life now, hon. A very promising life. Your career is off and running, you're in beautiful surroundings in the most romantic city in the world, nothing better than that."

"Yes, I guess you're right."

Janet leaned back at arms length, "So, let's go have lunch shall we? Let's go out into the square and sit at one of our very own sidewalk cafes. It's our square, you know."

They joyfully left the room arm in arm.

CHAPTER 61

Jerold stared up at the glass-canopied walkway as he made his way from the gate to the customs area. He was carrying a shopping bag with one change of clothing in it. The airline had advised him about items not accepted in a carry-on, and so not wanting to check any bags, he had decided to buy whatever he needed once he got to Paris.

He hadn't made any hotel reservations because he wasn't sure where he'd be staying. First thing he was going to do was find the houseboat where Shellie was living. The phone number he'd taken from Janet's desk the first time he was at her house wasn't working anymore, but he had the address and name of the houseboat and knew it was near the Eiffel Tower. It shouldn't be difficult to find.

He'd had plenty of time to plan how he would approach Shellie. It could go two ways. She would come home with him, willingly, or against her will. Either way, he was prepared.

In the cab from the airport his thoughts drifted back to Kansas City and to Carole. *She's a tough broad*, he thought to himself, smiling. *Not feminine like Shellie, but yet, feminine in her own way.* He laughed to himself at the thought of Carole chasing her old man out of the house, swinging a baseball bat at him. He knew she would take no guff off any man and he liked that about her. No man in his right mind would go up against Carole. They'd spent many hours sitting around talking about how her husband had beaten her time and time again until the day she fought back and ran him off. In fact he'd begun to see how Shellie must have felt with him treating her like he did. He and Carole talked about it. He told Carole the truth about why he was in KC. Told her he always knew he was doing Shellie wrong, losing his temper and lashing out at her like he did. Said she never did anything wrong enough to warrant his behavior, but he didn't know how to stop himself. He hated being like his dad, and that was what it had boiled down to. He'd made up his mind he was going to promise Shellie he would get counseling. He would change for her. That would make her want to come back with him. Why wouldn't it?

He remembered the night before he left for Paris. Carole and he were out on the porch of his cousin's house talking and drinking beer.

"What are you going to do, if she doesn't want to come back?" Carole asked.

"She'll come back. We're married."

"But she left you. Technically, you're separated."

Jerold looked at Carole for a moment and then took another swig of beer. "She'll come back."

"Well, you have to be prepared that she might not."

"I already bought her plane ticket."

"That doesn't make it so, you know."

"Whose side are you on, anyway?" He leaned back and took a long hard look at the woman sitting next to him.

"Yours, of course. I just don't want you to get yourself hurt none."

"I ain't gonna get hurt, you can bet on that." He took another swig.

"Well, you know what I mean. I don't want you to do anything that might get yourself in jail, Jerold."

"I ain't going to jail."

"I hope not." She put her hand on his knee. "I like you a lot, Jerold. A whole lot. Don't do something you'll be sorry for."

Her touch sent a thrill through his body. It startled him.

"I mean it. I like you a whole lot," Carole repeated as she leaned towards him.

He let her kiss him.

"Here's the Eiffel Tower." The Arab cab driver spoke fluent English, jerking Jerold from his thoughts. "You can take the stairs to the left of the bridge down to the quay."

It took Jerold a few moments to get back to the present, "How much do I owe you?"

"30 Euros."

He paid the driver then stepped out onto the busy sidewalk. Hoards of tourists flooded the area to see the historic Eiffel Tower looming above. He stood for a moment staring up at the gigantic landmark in total awe. He thought of Carole again, thinking how she'd love to see Paris. She'd never been anywhere either. He looked across the street at the bridge and all the buildings that stretched along the opposite bank of the Seine. One of them looked like a palace. *A far cry from Los Angeles and Kansas City*, he thought to himself when he crossed on the green light. The sun was going down and window lights were coming on making the scene more unbelievable by the moment. He stood at the top of the concrete and stone stairs and gazed off in the direction of where he thought the Simpatico might be docked. There were party boats and river cruise boats lining the bank before the long line of houseboats began. He was glad he'd Googled the houseboat name. It had appeared instantly and was listed as a rental. He figured Janet must have rented it for Shellie, because he knew Shellie didn't have the money.

As he walked slowly along the sides of the boats, half enjoying the excitement of the city on each side of the river, half focused on why he was in Paris in the first place, he was wishing he was there under different circumstances. Shellie never said she wanted to come to Paris. He was in such deep thought he didn't see the Simpatico until it was right in front of him. He stopped and stared at the name painted on the front of the boat. After a moment he turned and looked back to see how far he'd come from the bridge. There was a man on the boat next to the

Simpatico, watching him.

"Can I help you?" the man called out.

"I was just looking at the boats. They're great." He quickly headed for the short street that led back up to the boulevard and hopefully to a hotel.

Bob watched him go and had a gut feeling that Jerold Singer had arrived. He fit Janet's description.

CHAPTER 62

"So when will he get here?" Shellie called out to Rachel in the kitchen. She set the flower arrangement on the dining table and took one last look at the dinnerware Janet had purchased that afternoon for their first dinner party in their new house.

"Around seven. He's coming right from the gallery. Walking." Rachel stood at the doorway. "Oh, Shellie, those are beautiful. You're not only a terrific singer, you can arrange flowers."

"All from our garden. Roses, lots of roses."

"You'll love my garden in Cornwall, too."

"So do Paul and Belinda live near you?"

"Just down the road. They live about half way between Newlyn and Penzance. You should see their house. A seaside mansion. Paul got it for an incredible price. Bought it from a friend whose mother had died. She had houses all over the world and his friend didn't want to keep that one. Worked out great, the timing was perfect. He and Belinda had just met and were falling in love. You want a glass of wine, Shellie?"

"I'd love one. Red." She went into the garden room and brought back another arrangement to put on the mantle between the crystal candlesticks she'd found earlier that day in one of the antique shops. Then she stood back and admired her work. She

265

went to the front door and turned around as if she was just coming into the room. "Oh, Rachel. I just want to stand here and look at our pretty house forever."

"I don't blame you, sweetie." Rachel carried two glasses of wine from the kitchen. "Paul will be impressed at the painting I bought from the gallery, and the sculpture of Belinda's. They fit perfectly on that wall, don't they?"

"Oh yes. Perfectly."

The door opened and Janet burst in carrying packages. "I'm back! What a mess out there! You'd think everyone would go home when it got dark. But no. Oh! The table's gorgeous! Who did that?"

"I did the flowers, Rachel set the table."

"It's fit for a king. Three kings as a matter of fact. And three queens. Hell, queens are more important."

They all laughed.

"You want a glass?" Rachel headed for the kitchen.

"Damn right, I want a glass. Champagne for me, hon." Janet set the packages on and around an easy chair near the corridor that led past the garden room and bath to the back door. "You know, we need to buy a bar for this wall here. I saw an antique one today, almost got it. But I thought we might all three go look at it first. Tomorrow, maybe? What do you think?"

Rachel called out, "Okay with me."

Shellie looked into her glass for a moment and then took a sip, not saying anything.

"What's a matter, hon?'

"Nothing."

"Yes there is, now come on, tell me what's wrong. You were bubbling over a minute ago. What is it?"

Shellie's big eyes were filled with tears as she looked up at the two women standing there waiting for an answer. "It's just that—it's just—oh, I wish I could help with the expenses and buying all these beautiful things. You shouldn't have to be doing it all. I should be helping."

"Hey, little girl, you are who I'm doing it for. I wouldn't be here if it weren't for you. You just get over that now, okay?

266

One of these days you'll be making money out your ears, singing on records and all that stuff. So you just be happy. That's all I want from you."

Rachel chimed in, "And I'm grateful to both of you. I'm thrilled to have a place like this in Paris. Shellie, your contribution is as much as ours. Maybe not in cash, but in other ways. You give a tremendous amount of you. So, I agree with Janet, that's all I want from you, too."

The doorbell rang.

"Oh! Our first visitor!" Janet screamed. "Who do you think it is? Let's bet."

"Five Euros, it's Adrian," Rachel whispered.

Shellie smiled and wiped her eyes. "Five Euros, it's Paul."

"I bet it's Bobby," Janet added. "Okay, here we go." She opened the door.

CHAPTER 63

Jerold sat in the rental car in the parking lot a short distance from the Simpatico. He'd been sitting there for two hours. He watched the man leave the boat next door, go to his car and drive up the short cobbled lane to the Pont de Bir-Hakeim and the boulevard that ran along the front of the Eiffel Tower. There hadn't been any sign of life on the Simpatico. Now that the man was gone he thought it might be safe to go and knock on Shellie's door. He hadn't wanted to risk being seen again, so he hadn't tried it yet.

He got out of the car and took the walkway alongside the boats. Maxim's was a busy place he'd noticed. He peered through the windows as he passed, thinking it would be a good place to take Shellie to dinner. Carole would like it, too.

He wasn't angry with Shellie anymore, he'd decided. It wasn't her fault she'd run away. Carole had made him see that. But he was still pissed at Janet for shooting him. She didn't have to do that. So he was going to win Shellie back and then he was going to tell her she could never see Janet again. In fact, he'd make it easy for her, because they were going to live in Kansas City or go to Canada where his brother lived. In fact he was thinking they could have Thanksgiving with his brother. That gave him a couple more weeks to get everything situated with

Shellie.

He stopped at the Simpatico and then glanced in both directions along the quay before stepping onto the boat. It was easy, for the gap between it and the walkway wasn't much. The boat was dark inside, but he knocked anyway. There was no answer. "Dammit!" He hit the top of the cabin with his hand and leapt back across the gap and stomped off to his car.

Leaning against trees on the bluff above at the train station, were two men dressed in black, smoking cigarettes, nonchalantly watching Jerold. They were there until Jerold drove up the lane to the boulevard back to the Marriot, where two other black-clad men took over the watch.

Jerold dialed Carole's number in Kansas.

"Hey, Carole!"

"I was wondering when you were going to call. Where are you, hon?" Carole asked.

"At the Marriot, close to the Eiffel Tower and the boats."

"Have you found Shellie's boat?"

"Yes, it was easy. But I haven't seen her. I've been watching for three days now, nothing."

"Maybe she moved."

"I don't know. There's a guy that lives next door on another boat, if I have to, I'll ask him. You'd like this place, Carole. Too bad you didn't come with me."

"Are you kidding? Now just how would that look? How would you explain bringing a woman along when you're there to win your wife back. I don't think so."

"Well, I'm just saying, I think you'd like it here. You ought to come here when you can."

"Sure. Like I make that kinda money that I can go to Paris."

Jerold was quiet. He was confused about his feelings for Carole. How could he be feeling closer to Carole than he felt to Shellie? Why was he wanting Carole there with him?

"Hello? You there?" Carole interrupted his thoughts.

"Hold on a minute, will you?" He went across the room to get his cigarettes. As he lit one and puffed it, he closed his eyes

269

and remembered the kiss Carole had given him just a few nights ago. He remembered how they lost control of themselves and made love right on the back porch of his cousin's place in the moonlight. It was something he'd never forget. Never. No matter what happened. He picked up the phone. "So how is work? You getting along okay with Scooter?"

"That jerk doesn't know his ass from a turnip field," she said as she laughed. "It isn't the same without you bartending. I hate going to work."

Jerold smiled and listened to her booming voice as he smoked the cigarette.

"Carlos came in and started another fight last night. I had to yank the sucker clear out the front door. He was drunker than he's ever been, Jerold. That bully ain't gonna live much longer, you just wait and see. If the booze don't get him, somebody's knife will."

"Yea. He's definitely on his way out. How's your mom?"

"Oh, she's better. She comes home tomorrow. I'll take care of her till she gets back on her feet. She's a tough ol' bird."

"Same as her daughter." Jerold stood up. "Well, I should get something to eat before everything closes. There's a place down the street that stays open late. They have sandwiches and beer. Wish you were here." It slipped out of his mouth before he could stop it. "I mean—"

"I know what you mean. Don't worry about it. You just take care of yourself and don't get in any trouble, okay? I'm afraid you're gonna do something that'll land you in the pokey over there. Please, be careful, Jerold. If she doesn't want to come back, then she doesn't want to come back. There's nothing you can do about it."

Jerold sat on the bed and leaned back into the pillows. He closed his eyes; put his hand on his brow.

"So, if you don't find her in the next couple days, then come on back home. You've got a life here, you know that. You shouldn't have to go half way around the world chasing after someone who doesn't want you."

"Yea." He felt all alone.

270

"Okay, just get some rest and call me tomorrow, okay?"

"All right. Bye." He hung up before she could add anything else. He felt horrible, turned and buried his face in the pillow.

CHAPTER 64

"I have to say it again, that was a fabulous dinner, ladies," Paul said. He went to the kitchen for the wine he'd brought that hadn't been opened yet. "Better than any restaurant I've ever been to."

Rachel was right behind him. "Well, how could we miss? We each prepared our most famous epicurean delight and with the addition of a few of the locals' dishes, Voila! A feast for kings!"

"And queens!" Janet called out from the living room as she snuggled in Bob's arms on the overstuffed sofa.

"Come along, Adrian. I want to show you what I bought today." Shellie pulled him up the stairs behind her. "We'll be right back, just want to show him the painting."

"Take your time, hon, we ain't goin' anywhere." Janet planted a happy kiss on Bob's cheek. "We're too full anyway." She felt more comfortable at that moment than she had ever felt with a man. And it wasn't just the man; it was the house and the city. Everything about Paris was incredible, she'd decided. That afternoon she'd been shopping for the dinner party, going from shop to shop - all within walking distance. That couldn't happen in her neighborhood in L.A. And she couldn't go for midnight walks or be able to see the romantic sites that one sees in Paris -

all within a few blocks of home. "I love your Paris, Bobby. I really do."

Rachel and Paul came back into the living room, carrying full glasses and the newly opened bottle of wine.

"Here you go," Paul said as he reached to pour more wine in Bob's glass. "Or would you rather have a clean glass?"

"Pour away," Bob answered.

"I'll have some, too, Paul. In this glass."

Rachel sat on the arm of the sofa. "I feel so good here with you, my dear friends. Whether you know it or not, you've helped me through a very trying time, mourning the loss of a dear friend and then waiting for news that Pete was okay. It's been a tough time for me. I want to thank, you." She looked at Shellie and Adrian who had crossed the room and sat in the love seat adjacent to the sofa. "And to you two, you're such a delight."

Shellie smiled, "Well, you're one of my idols, Rachel. If it hadn't been for you on television that day to kick my butt, and you, Janet, to kick my butt again, this wouldn't have been possible. I wouldn't be here in this heavenly city and living in a home like this and wouldn't be singing on a boat under the Eiffel Tower and—"

"Hey, what about me?" Adrian interrupted.

"I was just getting to you . . . and I wouldn't have met Adrian, who I adore very much."

"That's better," he laughed.

"To all of us," Paul lifted his glass.

They all chimed in, "To all of us!"

"So, Paul," Shellie asked, "how does it feel to be the father of two children and be married to one of the most talented sculptors in England?"

"It feels splendid."

Bob questioned Rachel, "You and Paul met in Trafalgar Square?"

"You might say that," she laughed, blushing at the same time.

"You might say our lips met in Trafalgar Square," Paul said as he lowered his eyes. "Then after three more sightings, we met officially in Cornwall, on the walk between Newlyn and Penzance. I was with Belinda."

"Then he literally saved my life when I was attacked by a murdering scumbag in California."

"I told Bobby all about that, Rachel," Janet added.

Shellie eyes widened. "That was you, Paul? That's when I first heard of Rachel; it was all over the news."

"Yes, I just happened to have been with her earlier that night and she left her purse in the cab. I went back to give it to her and in the meantime that asshole was waiting for her. She was set to testify against him, and he was going to make sure she didn't."

"I'd rather not think about all that, if you don't mind. It still frightens me to the core to think about what that man did to me and other women, even though I was one of the luckier ones. I lived, unscarred . . . outwardly."

"I'm so sorry, Rachel, that it happened to you." Shellie went to her and hugged her. "There is nothing more frightening than the fear of death by the hand of another."

The others exchanged uncomfortable glances between them.

Shellie picked up on it. "Did I say something I shouldn't have?

Janet stood up and went to her. "No, hon. There's just something we need to tell you. We should tell her, don't you think?"

Heavy sighs and shoulder shrugs prevailed.

"Tell me what?"

Rachel reached for Shellie's hand and squeezed it. "Jerold is in Paris."

Shellie was terrified and searched the faces of those before her. "How could he—how do you know? Did you know this, Adrian?"

"Yes, I just found out from Bob. He's been at the boat looking for you."

"How could he know about the boat? What am I going to do? He'll kill me. I know he will!" She became hysterical.

Bob reached for her and put his arms around her, holding her close. "Shellie, he won't get near you. Take a deep breath and let's talk about this. Sit down. Pour her a glass of wine, Adrian."

Adrian reached for one of the bottles on the dining table and poured a glass and handed it to her as she sat between Janet and Bob on the sofa.

"Okay," Bob spoke gently, "here's what has happened. He's been watching the boat for several days now. He's staying at the Marriot hotel and we know where he is every minute of the day and night."

"But I go to work tomorrow night at Maxim's."

"I'm going with you, Shellie." Adrian said as he took her hand, kneeling on the floor in front of her.

"We're all going, sweetheart," Rachel added.

"Who is Jerold?" Paul asked.

A few hours later that evening, Rachel and Paul were alone in the living room. Candlelight was casting flickering shadows on the surrounding walls and artifacts. They were listening to music, sipping wine, feeling mellow in the cozy atmosphere of the romantic 19th century house atop Montmartre.

"We've come a long way since that kiss in Trafalgar," Paul whispered hoarsely. He cleared his throat. "Sorry, lost my voice for a minute."

Rachel continued to stare into the fireplace. "It seems like it's been years since then, doesn't it? So much has happened. To both of us."

"Yes, to both of us." He took another sip, glancing at her softness which was glowing from the flames of the fire that made her eyes glisten. He remembered that kiss and how he had been smitten by her. But he still wondered if those feelings were just another byproduct and triggered by the addictions with sex, alcohol, and cocaine he was immersed in at the time. He'd fought hard since he fell in love with Belinda to heal himself of his life threatening sicknesses. The heart attack was the biggest nudge. He was grateful that intense therapy and Belinda took all the rest away. He didn't have the same neurotic and uncontrollable desires he had before. In those days he'd fuck anyone and everyone. He'd combine whiskey and cocaine to maintain a sexual high for hours. He was a disgusting mess and the women told him so. So, no, he didn't believe the feeling he'd had for Rachel all evening and the strong attraction he had felt for her before Belinda were drug and psychosomatic induced yearnings.

"Paul, do you ever think about who we were in our past lives? We haven't talked about that in months."

"Well, don't take me wrong, but I believe we might have been lovers in a past life. I have such strong feelings for you, Rachel. And the way we met and kept running into each other—" He smiled as he continued to speak to her. "We've definitely been traveling through lives together."

Rachel looked at him with gentle, caring eyes, "Yes, I feel that, too. I feel very close to you, like I've known you for centuries. And I take comfort in that. Belinda's lucky to have you."

"I'm lucky to have Belinda."

"Yes." She stood and walked towards the window looking out on the square. "You know, I don't know what to feel about Pete."

"He's crazy about you."

"What makes you think that?"

"It's obvious."

"I don't know that. Sometimes I feel like I want him with me all the time, then other times I just want to be by myself. Then there are times I don't want to have to deal with another person's life and needs. I have my own career to think of and I told him that."

"Yes, that's what he said."

"He told you?"

"Of course. We're buddies. He said he doesn't want to put pressure on you to spend more time with him, because he knows how you'd react to it. He does love you, Rachel. He's just afraid he'll lose you if he tells you how much."

"That's silly."

"Not really. What would you do if he asked you to marry

him?'"

"Well, I don't know. I don't know how we'd do that."

"What do you mean?"

"He's gone all the time.'

"You're away as much as he is."

"Well, that's different."

"Why is it different?'

"Well, I—I don't know, it just is."

Paul leaned back into the sofa and chuckled.

"Just like right now, he's hurt and needs to mend. So what does he do? Instead of coming here to mend, to be with me, he's going to stay in South America and he's going to finish what he went there to do. Why couldn't he come here on R & R and then go back?"

"Maybe he doesn't want you to see him like he is. He told me he's still weak and has a long way to go before he's back to normal."

She turned and gave Paul a cold stare. Then she sighed and plopped down on the sofa next to him. "Why didn't he tell me that?"

"He doesn't want you to worry. He's not out of the woods."

She looked at Paul and frowned like a little girl, then leaned her head on his shoulder. "Or out of the jungle."

Paul laughed and put his arm around Rachel and drew her close in a brotherly way.

The warmth of his body warmed hers. She reached up and placed her hand on his chest next to her cheek and breathed in his aroma. She closed her eyes.

Paul lightly nuzzled her hair. His heart was beating fast.

She could hear it, feel it.

He lifted her chin to his, their eyes met, they kissed. It was as thrilling as their kiss on New Year's Eve at Trafalgar Square nearly two years before. They lingered with their lips caressing, letting the temporary pleasure affect them.

Paul pulled back and whispered, "A remembrance of a past life."

Rachel nodded and burrowed her face into the comfort of his shoulder.

CHAPTER 65

Shellie bounded down the stairs at daybreak. She put the coffee on and cleared away the remains of the dinner party, removed empty bottles, washed and dried wine glasses and champagne flutes, put them away. She sang as she worked.

Adrian sleepily appeared in the doorway. He watched her buzz around the spacious kitchen. "You're a natural born homemaker."

"I love mornings. I love making coffee and going outside and breathing in the fresh air. Sometimes I go to one of the cafes for coffee. We'll have the coffee in the garden, is that okay with you?"

"It's a bit chilly out there this morning. There's frost on the ground."

"We can wrap up in blankets."

Laughing, he grabbed Shellie as she flitted by and pulled her to him. "You can keep me warm."

"We'll keep each other warm."

He smiled, wondering how he could be so lucky. He released her and turned to go down the hall. "Where's my coat?"

"It's in the closet at the end of the hall, beyond the garden room. Same side. Would you rather we have our coffee in the garden room, Adrian?"

279

He opened the closet door and stood looking at his and Bob's coats. "So Bob stayed here last night, too? What kind of place is this?" He laughed.

Shellie came out of the kitchen carrying two mugs of coffee. "It's a house of love. Let's go in here." She turned into the garden room, set the mugs of coffee on the glass and wrought iron table and opened the floral chintz curtains covering the windows and French doors to reveal the garden. "Isn't this fabulous? I love this room."

"Sounds like you love everything."

"I do."

"Do you love me?"

Shellie stood motionless for a moment, then turned and joined him at the table. "I adore you, Adrian. See, I'm learning the French way to express myself. They adore everything."

"But that's not what I asked. Do you love me?"

"Oh, Adrian. Please. Let's not get into this conversation again. Can't you just be happy that I adore you? You're the most important person in my life. You and Janet and Rachel. And Bob. I'm so grateful to you all. I feel like I'm in a dream world. If you could have seen me just a few months ago you wouldn't believe the dramatic change in my life." She sighed and dropped into a sad silence. "But now it might all change, again."

"It's not going to change. I told you not to worry about Jerold. I'm not going to let you out of my sight until he's gone back to the States. You're stuck with me till then, Shellie."

She sipped her coffee, not saying anything.

"You're safe, Shellie. He can't do anything to you."

"You don't know him like I do."

"True. But he hasn't got a chance with all of us surrounding you. And Bob has security posted. He can't hurt you, Shellie. You have to believe that."

They heard footsteps on the stairs.

"Where is everybody," Bob called out.

"We're in the garden room, help yourself to some coffee. It's in the kitchen." Adrian reached over and squeezed Shellie's hand. "It'll be okay. You'll see."

She wasn't so sure.

"So, what's the plan for today?' Bob asked as he entered, full of energy and grinning from ear to ear.

"Well, first we'll have our coffee, and then when Janet and Rachel come down we'll have some croissants with cheese and onion omelets. Rachel's doing the cooking. Then we're on our own. Nothing else planned after that, until tonight." She lowered her eyes and peered into her coffee cup.

Bob and Adrian exchanged glances.

"Sounds good to me," Bob quickly responded. "That'll give me time to get some things done on the Simpatico this afternoon. I've some renters arriving on Sunday; they're staying for two weeks."

"You make pretty good money leasing the boats?" Adrian asked as he stood to go after more coffee.

"Oh, it's enough to pay my bills. My other investments are what make money. Janet's taken pretty good care of me in that department. She lets me know when to buy and sell. Real estate has been good to me."

"Janet said you have a house here in Montmartre." Shellie commented.

"Yes, I was living in it, but now I'm leasing it to a family from Spain."

Janet came through the door, sparkling and fresh, in a red kimono. "Good morning, everyone."

"Oh Janet, is it new?" Shellie touched the fabric of the silk kimono.

"Yes, I saw it yesterday, couldn't resist. You like it?"

"It's beautiful. I love the embroidered birds. We could frame it and hang it on the wall. It's a work of art."

"Good morning!" Rachel called out as she carried the coffee maker from the kitchen to the garden room. Adrian was following, carrying a canister of coffee grounds and filters.

"Our breakfast chef has arrived,' Shellie added gleefully. "Did you sleep well, Rachel? You were up pretty late."

"Oh yes, I slept soundly. By the time Paul went back to his hotel I was two blinks from a coma. I could hardly make it up the stairs. Thought about crashing in on one of the two of you since it's such a climb up to my floor," she gave Shellie and Janet a mischievous glance, "but when I looked in, it was too crowded in your beds."

"Well, we could have made room, hon," Janet added jovially.

Bob lifted an eyebrow at Janet, "What kind of operation is this?"

"That was my question," Adrian laughed.

"Well, I can assure you, I don't do *ménage a trois*." Janet crossed over to help Rachel set up the coffee on the wrought iron buffet. "And I'm a one-man woman. One at a time, that is." She winked at Rachel.

"Is Paul going back to Cornwall today, Rachel?"

"Yes, he is, Adrian. He's leaving this morning. He wanted to stay to hear Shellie sing tonight, but he felt he better get back to Belinda and those darling babies. You'd understand if you could see them. They are something else. My godchildren."

Adrian's quick glance towards Shellie was not lost on the rest of them. "I've always wanted to have children to carry on my father's name. Looks like that isn't going to happen."

"It isn't too late for you, Adrian. A man doesn't get too old to have children. Women are the culprits," Janet blurted without thinking. An awkward silence crept through the room.

"I wanted children at one time," Shellie offered. "But I couldn't bear the thought of bringing them into the world to be hurt like I had been. I just couldn't. And besides, I wouldn't know how to be a mother. Of course, now it's out of the question, I have a career to take up my time. Children would only get in the way."

Rachel frowned slightly as she turned back towards the coffee maker. Janet did the same. They looked at each other and shook their heads.

"Yes, you have a career now," Adrian added, sadly.

"Well, not yet, but I will."

Bob felt the tension building in the room. "So where are the croissants and omelets?"

Rachel quickly responded, "Coming right up. Shellie, come help me, will you? Janet, you entertain the boys."

CHAPTER 66

They arrived by cab. Janet stepped out of the back seat in front of Maxim's.

Jerold recognized her immediately. She was dressed in white and with her blond hair gleaming, she wasn't hard to miss. *The fuckin' cunt!* Seeing her reignited his anger and he held tightly to the railing on the bluff above the quay. Earlier he'd decided to stretch his legs and walk along the bluff after sitting in his car all day in the parking lot down below.

Another woman got out of the car who Jerold had never seen before. She followed Janet. Then he watched a hulk of a man step out on the opposite side of the taxi and reach back inside.

Out stepped Shellie. Jerold's heart started pounding; his ears were ringing from the rise in blood pressure. She was dressed in a short green sequin dress. He didn't like it at all when the man put his arm around his wife. He wanted to jump over the railing and down to the parking lot and grab her away from him and tell her he loved her and wanted her back. But, he knew he couldn't, he had to wait. Then he saw the man from the houseboat next to the Simpatico coming down the walk towards them. They all knew each other. Jerold stepped behind a tree and watched them go into Maxim's. He stared after them for a moment and then turned and ran back across the boulevard to his hotel. He was going to change his clothes and go to Maxim's for dinner.

Jerold managed to slip in behind a large group of people arriving for dinner on the floating restaurant. He walked to the back of the boat and asked a waiter there if he could sit in the far corner.

"Yes, of course. Usually no one wants to sit that far away from the music. The singer is exquisite. If you would like to move up closer, later, I'll see what I can do."

"No, thank you. I prefer sitting in the back."

"Would you like to order a drink before dinner?"

"I'll have a Bourbon and Coke." He sat and visually searched the crowded room for Shellie and her friends. He saw the big guy first. Even sitting in a chair the guy loomed over everyone else in the room. The chair beside him was vacant. Jerold figured that was Shellie's seat. He craned to see Janet and the other guy. They were cozy, the guy's arm was around Janet and she kissed him.

The combo was playing and he wondered about the singer the waiter had mentioned.

"Here is your drink, Monsieur, and here is the menu." The waiter bowed and stepped aside, waiting.

Jerold quickly found what looked like the word beef on the menu and ordered it. He hoped it was beef. He ordered a salad and a potato. Just like home, he thought to himself. But he was sure it wouldn't compare to a Kansas City steak. No way. No one could do it like a KC chef.

Suddenly applause began. All heads were turned towards left front. He couldn't quite see where the people were looking, but in a flash, Shellie appeared. A spot light followed her on stage. She was a vision of electricity, not because of the light that was beamed on her, but because of the light that emanated from within her. Her stage presence alone captivated the audience even before she opened her mouth and let go with the most melodious and clear sounds a human being could produce.

Jerold was spellbound. He couldn't believe what he was seeing and hearing. That was his Shellie? When she began the second number he slowly raised the glass to his lips and took the first sip of his cocktail. She'd changed. She seemed to be more deliberate, more sure of herself. It worried him. No, that was not his Shellie.

The waiter brought a plate of bread and the salad Jerold had ordered. It sat untouched through the next two songs. At one point, he reached for the bread and began munching. Then he picked up his fork and began eating his salad, all the while not taking his eyes off Shellie. The room was dark; the only light glowed from the candles on the tables. Jerold couldn't be seen by Shellie or her friends.

Just before her break, Shellie spoke to the audience. "I want to dedicate this next song to a very dear friend." She looked at her table of friends. "This is for you, Adrian. 'The More I See You.'"

Jerold felt a stabbing pain in his heart. The waiter arrived with his steak and set it before him. He couldn't respond when the waiter asked if he wanted anything else. He just sat there staring at the plate listening to Shellie sing to who appeared to be her new man. He was feeling anger, hurt and regret. Regret at how he'd treated her, hurt that she had found someone else, anger that that bitch Janet had made it all happen. He didn't know what he had to do, but he was going to do something. First, he had to calm down. He remembered Carole's words that repeated over and over in his mind. He began eating his steak. After he'd eaten and left cash on the table for the waiter, Jerold went to the men's room down the corridor off the room from where he was sitting. Bob and Adrian came in while he was there, but didn't see him in the enclosed stall. They stood at the urinals.

"Security's posted outside?"

"Yes, they've been watching him since the day he arrived. He sits in a rental car in the parking lot watching the boat. But of course, it doesn't do him any good because she doesn't live there anymore. And they're at the Marriott watching him, too."

Jerold froze.

It was after midnight and Jerold was sitting in the back seat shadows of a cab when the merry group came out of Maxim's. They were hugging and laughing. Janet walked with Bob to his boat and went inside. The rest of them stood waiting for a cab.

He had managed to slip out of Maxims with a crowd, same as he did going in, who then walked to the Eiffel Tower, lucky for him. The security people hadn't noticed him. Once at the Eiffel he grabbed a cab back to Maxim's and was waiting and watching from farther down the quay near the river cruise boats.

He knew the security people thought he was still in Maxim's, so he felt safe.

Security hadn't figured Jerold would be a problem in the restaurant, especially since Shellie was surrounded by people, so they hadn't alerted Bob that he'd gone inside. Bob knew who he was, anyway. He'd recognize Jerold, and they knew Bob was better at this than they were. He had been one of their trainers. Janet and Shellie knew Jerold, too. And with a huge guy like Shellie's friend at her side, they weren't the least bit concerned about her safety. They also had two men posted backstage.

The cab carrying Shellie, Rachel and Adrian pulled out of the parking lot. A few car lengths behind another cab followed. Security was still watching the entrance of Maxim's, Jerold noticed. Now he would find out where Shellie lived.

"Stay with that cab and it's worth a hundred Euros to you."

The driver seemed to understand and whipped in and out of traffic wildly, as only Parisian cab drivers do.

As the trio went through the front door of a four-story house on what looked like a popular square in Montmartre, Jerold remembered that he'd read about an artists' square in the magazine on the plane and thought this might be the one. It was well lit and there were still late night strollers and wine drinkers sitting about. He asked the cab driver to pull off onto one of the side streets and wait for him. He sat at a table where he could see the house and ordered a beer. Lights shone through the second and fourth floor windows. He could see Shellie's female friend through the wide diamond-paned window on the Fourth floor. She was sitting on what looked like a window seat, sipping a glass of champagne, talking on a cell phone. Then he saw Shellie walk to the window on the second floor, the guy was behind her. She closed the shuttered blinds.

As he sat staring at Shellie's window, he thought of all that had led up to that moment. He thought of his mean, domineering father and how much he still hated him. Thoughts of his wounded mother and brother consumed him. He had been tough enough to take the abuse, but his mother and brother hadn't been. His mother was dead, his brother was deaf from being battered and was emotionally crippled. He thought of when he and Shellie first got married, how much he had loved her. He would have done anything for her. But it had changed. He'd wanted to have children, at least a son, but she couldn't get pregnant. That had angered him. She had wanted to have a singing career and he knew that it would take her away from him, so that angered him. He felt as if she didn't want to get pregnant because she wanted to keep her figure so that she looked good on stage. He had wondered if she had been taking birth control. She'd denied it when he asked. He wondered if she'd been as devious about that as she had been about this new man in her life. He wondered if they had been having an affair right under his nose. Did they both come to Paris together? *This changes everything*, he thought as he stood, paid for the beer and walked back to the taxi.

CHAPTER 67

It was Sunday morning. Jerold had successfully moved, unseen, from the Marriott to a small Montmartre hotel the day before. He had sent his duffle bag ahead to prevent his watchdogs from knowing he was checking out. Then he boldly walked out the front door of the Marriott to the same coffee shop on the corner that he had frequented every morning. That morning, however, instead of having his coffee at a sidewalk table, he sat indoors. When the waiter brought his coffee and a pastry, Jerold took a couple sips then left the book he'd brought with him on the table, and acted as if he was going to the men's room. But instead he ducked into the kitchen and out the back door into an alley. From there he fled down a side street and jumped on the nearest Metro train which took him all the way to Montmartre.

Now he was again sitting on the square, watching Shellie's house. The open cafes and the artist displays in the center of the Place du Tertre were adequate enough to shield him from sight. He had seen Shellie's friend come out earlier and she was having coffee at a café near the house. He'd seen no sign of Janet or Shellie and her boyfriend. The day before they had stuck together like glue, and that night had all gone to Maxim's again, but he didn't bother to follow them.

His attention shot to the front door of the house. Someone

289

was opening it from the inside. Out stepped Janet, then Adrian who turned and hugged Shellie as she stood in the doorway. They walked over to Rachel, stopped a moment and spoke with her, then walked on out of sight. Shellie stepped back indoors and closed the door. In a few moments she appeared at the second floor window and opened the shutters.

Jerold left cash on the table and slipped by the artists towards the house, shielding himself from Rachel, although he didn't know her and felt she wouldn't know him.

A group of people were sitting at the table next to Rachel and had engaged her in conversation, so she wasn't looking at the house.

Jerold walked faster. He was about ten feet from the front door. He hesitated. He looked over at Rachel and saw that she was still in the middle of the group conversation. He took three long strides and pushed open the door of the house. He shut it quickly and leaned back on it as he gaped at the living area in front of him. He'd never seen such extravagance and artistic furnishings outside of an Architectural Digest or Home Magazine. The fresh floral arrangements, the gild-framed gigantic mirrors, the crystal and porcelain figurines, the statues and paintings, the silk brocade chairs and overstuffed chintz sofas . . . it was beyond anything he'd ever seen. His Shellie lived here?

He heard her singing, coming down the stairs. His first thought was to get the hell out of there, get to the airport and back to Kansas City where he belonged. But then she was standing on the stairs staring at him. She was so tiny and beautiful. Like a China doll. He'd called her his China doll before they were married. "Shellie?"

"What are you doing, Jerold? Get out of here!"

He took a step towards her. "Now wait, Shellie. I just want to talk to you." He slowly continued towards her.

Shellie began to back up the stairs. "Stay away from me, Jerold. I mean it. I'll call the police, my phone's programmed. All I have to do is push this button."

He stopped. "I just want to talk to you. Can we do that?

Can we just talk?'

"You don't know how to talk."

"Give me a chance. Please. Here, I'll sit over here." He pulled a chair out from the dining table and sat. "Please?"

Shellie suddenly saw him once again as that young boy she fell in love with at the beginning. She suddenly felt guilty that she'd abandoned him, knowing he had had a horrible life growing up and couldn't help himself when he hit her. She'd always felt it wasn't his fault, it was his father's fault. She took two steps down the stairs and hesitated. "If you get up from the chair, I'm warning you, I'll call the police."

"I won't move until you tell me to. I promise."

She walked across to the other side of the table, nearer the front door. "What do you want?"

"I want you to come home with me. I want us to start over. I'll go to counseling; I'll let you sing whenever you want. You were spectacular, by the way. I was at Maxim's on Friday night."

"You were there?"

"Yes. You sounded and looked like a star."

"I can't come home with you, Jerold. I have a life here now. Please understand that." Her face softened as she spoke to him.

He looked down at his hands that were clasped in his lap. "But, you belong to me, Shellie. You're my wife."

"I don't belong to anyone. I'm married to you, but I don't belong to you." Her voice maintained a soothing gentleness in its tone, almost as if she were singing quietly.

He hadn't heard this quality in her voice before, and he had never heard such finality. He stood and faced her with a beseeching expression, "I promise I'll never hurt you again. Come back to KC with me. I love you."

Shellie felt her heart break in half. She took a step towards him. "I'm so sorry, Jerold."

Suddenly the front door swung open and laughter filled the room. It stopped instantly. Adrian and Janet stood gasping in horror at Jerold reaching for Shellie. Adrian moved fast. He covered the space between the door and Jerold in a split second. He grabbed him and pushed him to the floor, bending his arms behind him up onto his back.

Janet was in the melee screaming at Shellie to move away from him.

Shellie cried, "No, no! Adrian! Stop!"

Jerold twisted out of Adrian's grip and got to his feet and knocked Adrian to the floor.

Shellie ran to Adrian, screaming.

Janet picked up a statue and was poised to swing it at Jerold. He ducked and grabbed her arm in midair.

"You're not going to hurt me again, you bitch. Never!" He slapped her across the face and she fell backwards onto the sofa.

Shellie screamed at Jerold as she caressed Adrian's head. "Stop it! You've killed him, you bastard! You've killed Adrian!" She laid her cheek on Adrian's forehead. "Adrian, please don't die. Please, my darling." Adrian hadn't moved, but was faintly breathing. Shellie quickly dialed emergency services and screamed into the receiver while she rushed to the kitchen for a wet cloth.

Jerold was taken aback at Shellie's demeanor. He glanced back and forth between Adrian and Janet. "Shellie, I—"

"Shut up, Jerold! Shut up!" She dropped to the floor beside Adrian and began mopping his brow. His eyes opened. "Say something, Adrian. Say you're all right."

"Did I have a seizure?"

"No, darling. Not a seizure."

Jerold raised a stunned Janet to a sitting position and propped her head against sofa pillows.

She touched her lip. "You asshole! You busted my lip."

"I owed you one," he said quietly. Then he straightened up and looked back at Shellie and Adrian. "I'm sorry, Shellie."

"So am I, Jerold. But my life is here, now. I can't come back to you. Surely you can see that."

"Yes, I can. I'm sorry. I'm so sorry." He turned and walked towards the door.

Shellie stood up quickly, "Wait!" She went to him and hugged him tightly.

He didn't want to let her go, but he knew in his heart she wasn't his anymore. She wasn't the Shellie she once was, and he wasn't who he once was. He wanted to go home. "Good luck, little China doll, I won't bother you again," he whispered as he reluctantly pulled away and disappeared through the doorway, closing the door behind him.

Janet watched Shellie facing the closed door wiping her eyes. "He means it, honey."

Shellie turned and smiled sadly at Janet. She felt tired and weary. She was glad she didn't have to sing that night.

Someone pounded on the door.

"Get over by Adrian, honey." Janet moved quickly and opened the door to the police and the paramedics. She could see Rachel behind them hurrying across the square.

"There is a problem, madam?"

"There was, but everything is all right now. No more problems. Come on in. Thank you for coming." She glanced at Shellie and Adrian and winked.

Adrian had moved to the loveseat and Shellie was by his side, holding his hand.

"What happened?" Rachel cried as she came into the house. "What's wrong?"

"Not a thing, honey," Janet answered, pressing a tissue against her bruised and bleeding lip. "I ran into a door knob and Adrian ran into a wall. Right kids?"

Adrian and Shellie replied in unison, "Right!"

CHAPTER 68

The weather in Paris had grown considerably colder with the holiday season approaching.

"Now, honey, don't stay away too long. This is your house, too, you know," Janet hugged Rachel as the cab driver loaded her luggage. Rachel had decided to fly back to Cornwall; she didn't want to spend a full day on the trains. "Are you coming back for Christmas?"

"No, I'll be spending Christmas with my godchildren and I'm hoping my son and his wife come for Christmas from Phoenix. They just moved from Denver to Phoenix."

"Well, at least come back for New Year's Eve. Will you? Bob decided last night that he isn't going to Vietnam this year since I've decided to stay longer. He's going to have a party on the boat. It'll be a bash on the river at the Eiffel Tower, so you can't miss that!"

"It sounds like fun, but I'm not sure how long my son is staying or what Belinda and Paul are planning, and of course I don't know what's happening with Pete, yet. But, we'll see."

"Okay, dear. You have a good trip. And I want to read that book as soon as it's out, you let me know."

"Oh, it'll be at least a year, takes that long. But I'll print out a copy of the finished manuscript when I get home and send it to you. Or email it to you."

"Email it. That way I can download it onto my desktop."

"You got it." Rachel stepped into the cab. "You take care of our girl in there, will you?"

"That's why I'm sticking around. Don't want to leave her alone just yet. She's been through a lot in the past few months. And she's looking a bit fragile these days."

"I noticed that, too. Well, must get going. Love you."

"Love you, too. Have a safe trip."

Janet shut the cab door and waved at Rachel as the driver moved from the square and headed down the hill.

Bob was rounding the corner carrying a bag of groceries and blew Rachel a goodbye kiss just in time.

"I'm going to miss her a hellava lot," Janet said.

"Did you tell her about my New Year's Eve party?"

"She doesn't know if she can make it, but I bet she will."

They opened the door and went into the house.

It was early evening a week later and Shellie was in the kitchen making a salad. Janet was sitting at the table with Bob talking about his New Year's Eve party. There was a knock on the door. Bob answered it.

Adrian stood with flowers in his hand and a bottle of champagne in the other. "I heard there is a special dinner here tonight."

"Come on in." Bob reached for the bottle, "I'll take that and put it on ice."

"Hello, lovely lady," Adrian said as he bent and kissed Janet on the cheek.

"My, my, it's Prince Charming in person."

"And where is my Cinderella? Ah, there she is, slaving away in the kitchen." He approached Shellie and embraced her with a lingering kiss. "That's what I've been waiting for. Here're some flowers for the table, darling."

Shellie took them and placed them in a crystal vase that was waiting on the dining table, already half filled with water. "These are beautiful, Adrian, just beautiful. Thank you so much."

She smelled one of the yellow roses and shifted a few of the white ones around to even out the colors. "Okay, back to the scullery. You stay in here with Bob and Janet."

"But I want to be with you." He had the look of a sad little boy on his face.

Shellie stared at him. "Are you kidding?"

They all burst out laughing.

"So what do you think about the party on New Year's? Are you going to be back from Switzerland by then?" Bob handed Adrian a glass of wine.

"It all depends on Shellie," he answered as he glanced through the opening into the kitchen.

She stopped what she was doing in the kitchen and looked across the counter at him. "Me? How's that?"

"Well, if you go home with me for Christmas week, then I can bring you back by New Year's Eve. You'll be performing at Maxim's, right? So, I was thinking if you could take off the weekend before, we could spend the week in Gimmelwald and return before New Year's Eve." He was sitting with his fingers crossed as he looked at Janet and Bob, his back to Shellie.

Shellie stood silent in the kitchen; her eyes squinted at the two faces that stared at her in anticipation. Janet nodded to her. Bob's eyebrows were raised, his head cocked and nodding. Adrian, more handsome then ever, turned to look at her.

"All right. You win. I'll go with you for Christmas."

Adrian jumped up and after three long strides, he picked her up and held her close as he spun around the kitchen, hysterically happy.

"Adrian! Put me down! Stop this, silly!" she cried through her laughter.

Before he set her on her feet, he kissed her full on the mouth and declared, "I love you, Shellie Singer. I love you."

"Well, you have to bring me back for New Year's, and I mean it."

"I will, I will." He went back into the living room, his eyes sparkling. He was taking Shellie home to Gimmelwald just as his father had taken his mother home to his family that first

Christmas. Adrian knew she'd love it once she got there. He wanted to call his mother right that minute, but thought better of it. He'd call her tomorrow. She'd be thrilled. She liked Shellie.

"So what will you do for Christmas, Janet, without all of us?"

"Don't worry about Janet, she's in my care," Bob answered.

Janet smiled at Bob's quick response and squeezed his hand. She had been putting off going back to the U.S. not only because of Shellie, but because of Bob. Now that the Jerold situation wasn't to be feared, for they'd heard he'd taken up with a woman in Kansas City; Janet could go home to California if she wanted. But she wasn't quite ready. She knew she'd have to sooner or later, but not yet. She'd been handling business long distance and in cyberspace and had even worked up another remodeling project in Paris with Bob's firm.

"What about Rachel?" Adrian lifted the glass to his lips.

"She's spending it with her God-children in Cornwall, and her son may be coming over from Arizona," Janet answered.

"Well, then, everybody's plans are settled for Christmas and New Year's Eve. Anyone want a glass of champagne? I'll open the bottle."

CHAPTER 69

Three days before Christmas was cold and stormy in Newlyn and Mousehole. The Atlantic sea along the Cornwall coastline was black and wild, lashing at the sea wall lining the port and crashing over the granite boulders along the beach and up across the road.

Rachel loved turbulent weather. It was like this when she and Ethan had spent Christmas there, the first time she'd been to Cornwall several years before. As she stood sipping ginger tea while gazing through the picture window, her mind suddenly flooded with memories of Ethan. Why had he been taken so soon? A man in his sixties with so much going for him, so much ahead of him. He had been her closest friend at one time. A soulmate. She still felt there was a possibility that they'd known each other in a past life and that someday they were destined to be together. She had the same feelings about Pete. Paul, too. And Belinda. They all had been an integral part of her life. So much had happened to each of them in the past two years.

Rachel felt as if she was teetering on the brink with Pete and she didn't know in which direction she would fall. She felt deep in her heart that he didn't love her enough to make a commitment. It made her sad. Everything was making her sad. She kept telling herself she should be happy. Her son was coming for Christmas, her stepmother Lee was coming from California, she had her newfound friends in Paris. But it seemed that everyone she knew was pairing off . . . Janet and Bob . . . Shellie and Adrian. That is, she was hoping Shellie and Adrian would pair. She was envious of their relationships. But then on the other hand, she was not sure that she could commit to a relationship anyway. How does anyone know if a marriage would work? She'd asked herself that question a thousand or more times and she still didn't have the answer.

Shellie telephoned her and told her about consenting to go to Switzerland with Adrian for Christmas. Rachel had literally jumped for joy. *Even Jerold has found a mate*, Rachel thought to herself. Shellie told her that he'd mailed divorce papers for her to sign. Janet called to tell Rachel how she was feeling about Bob. Paul and Belinda were madly in love, and so were Margaret and Philippe. "They're playing songs of love, but not for me," Rachel sang sadly and softly.

The phone rang.

"Hello?"

"It's me."

"Belinda. Where are you?"

"I'm at home. Are you all right? We've been worried about you because of the storm."

"I love this weather. Don't worry about me. Are we still on for tomorrow night - the eve before Christmas eve at the Ship Inn?"

"Absolutely! We wouldn't miss the boat light parade and the pasties for anything. I hope it stops raining. I've got a sitter for the kids, so we can all just go and enjoy ourselves. We haven't done that in ages."

"It sounds fabulous. So when does your mother get here?"

"Tomorrow afternoon, same as Paul's."

"His mother is coming?"

"Yes, he hasn't seen her since he was in California that time he rescued you. They arrive on the same train, as a matter of fact. We pick them up in Penzance. That should be an interesting ride for the two of them, all the way from London."

"I bet." Rachel laughed. "They're as different as night and day, from what Paul says."

"Oh yes. So when does your son arrive?"

"In the morning. I'll pick them up at the airport in Newquay. My step mother's coming, too. You remember me telling you about Lee. The artist?"

"Oh yes! So when did she decide to come?"

"A couple days ago. Devin convinced her. Bought her the plane ticket and told her she was coming with them. She's never flown. So they're going to have some stories to tell, I'm sure. It's been a long time since we've all been together. You'll have to come over tomorrow when they get here and meet them, and see my tree and decorations."

"I will. Call me when you get home. Have you heard from Pete?"

Rachel sighed. "Well, he called this morning. Said he's feeling good, has made some new discoveries, he loves it there, loves the warm weather and all. Yada-yada-yada."

"Oh. So he's not coming home for Christmas?"

"Doesn't sound like it."

"Well, we don't need him to have fun, do we?"

"Nope. Don't need him." Rachel's voice dropped to almost a whisper.

Belinda could sense her depression. "Rachel, why don't you come over tonight? We're having pizza and Little Jake would love to see you; he won't see you tomorrow night."

"I just might do that, since I'm all set for my company. Do you need me to bring anything?"

"No, just bring yourself. Six, okay?"

"Yes. See you at six."

CHAPTER 70

They flew from Paris to Zurich the day before Christmas. Adrian's mother and George picked them up and drove them back to Interlaken. The plan was to spend Christmas Eve with the Schmidts, then travel up the mountain to Gimmelwald the next morning to join the Van Allman family for Christmas Day. Adrian's sisters had been there a week and were already in Gimmelwald at the family farmhouse preparing for the feast on Christmas Day.

Shellie fell in love with Interlaken and the surrounding countryside the moment she arrived. She didn't have a chance to see much of Zurich, but Adrian told her she'd love it.

George drove by the Grand Hotel in Interlaken to show Shellie where they'd gotten married earlier that year, then drove to the middle of town and took a side street to his antique shop. He parked and they went inside. His was one of the most upscale galleries and shops in Interlaken. His merchandise ranged from jewelry to paintings to collectibles of all types – furniture, rugs, brick-a-brack, etc. Upstairs was a large apartment where they lived, and in back of the building was a cottage that had belonged to the previous owners. Most of the families in Switzerland built mother-in-law cottages behind their main houses. Shellie and Adrian were staying in the two-bedroom cottage that Gina had filled with freshly cut flowers and had stocked the refrigerator with drinks, cheeses and snacks that she knew Adrian loved.

301

Shellie was very impressed with it all.

After the two settled in, they joined Gina and George and his family at a nearby restaurant for dinner. There was a piano bar there, where Gina had met George on her weekly sojourn to Interlaken from the farm in Gimmelwald. It was their favorite night spot. They'd already told the proprietor about Shellie, about her singing, and after dinner he invited her to sing. At first she said no, but she was easily convinced. As expected, the patrons loved her. She sang a full set – seven songs. The band was thrilled to have her and told her she could sing with them any time she wanted.

Adrian applauded the loudest. He had been proudly beaming all evening. He would look around the room as Shellie sang and would give thumbs up to the people he knew.

Shellie had never seen him so happy. Actually, she noticed the change in his countenance and behavior as soon as they got off the plane in Zurich. There'd always been something missing in his personality, a bit of a reserve, sadness maybe, but now it was gone. She couldn't explain the difference, but there definitely was a marked difference.

Adrian held on to her and hugged her continually. He kissed her cheeks, her hands, the top of her head; he couldn't keep his hands off her all that day and even into the evening. At first it was too much for her, it embarrassed her, but she was getting used to it. She noticed that Gina was the same way with George.

As Shellie looked around the large, cozy restaurant, it was extraordinary how families behaved. They were laughing, singing, hugging and kissing each other. It seemed like a dream world. Surely this wasn't real. Shellie had never seen this type of behavior in her entire life.

At midnight they left the restaurant and walked back to the apartment above the store where they had a Brandy with Gina and George before going to the mother-in-law cottage. George's son and daughter and their families were staying in hotel rooms and would make the trip up to Gimmelwald with them in the morning.

In the middle of the night, Shellie woke up feeling nauseous. She made it to the toilet just in time to lose what food was left in her stomach. Adrian warmed a wash cloth in hot water and mopped her brow trying to soothe her as she continued to hang her head over the toilet bowl.

Finally she stood up with his help. "I must have eaten too much. The food was so rich. I'm sorry you saw me like this."

"You're beautiful even when you're sick, Shellie. I love you no matter what."

"You're too good, Adrian. Oh, no . . . it's starting up again. I want to lie down, maybe it'll go away." She hurried to the bed and curled up under the quilted coverlet and the down duvet.

Adrian came out of the bathroom a few minutes later and slipped under the covers next to her. He snuggled close and put his arm over her on the outside of the bedcovers. Without saying anything, not wanting to disturb her, he closed his eyes and fell asleep.

But Shellie couldn't sleep. She lay still, ruminating. This wasn't the first time she'd been sick lately. But this was the first time it happened this early in the morning. Usually it was later, around nine or ten, and lasted a couple hours before it dissipated. She found that soda crackers and oranges helped. *It's got to be the stress of Jerold and the changes. Maybe it'll go away.* She wasn't going to think about it until after Christmas, and as soon as she got back to Paris she would go to a doctor.

The trip from Interlaken up the mountain to Gimmelwald was beyond anything Shellie had ever seen or experienced. They took an earlier train than the Schmidt family to Lauterbrunnen. The lower mountainous landscape was still green with sparse snow. Then from Lauterbrunnen they rode a funicular to Grutschalp where they boarded a train to Murren. In Murren, they boarded a gondola and took the five-minute ride to Gimmelwald. The snowy inclines dotted with chalets and cabins were a Christmas card setting. As they approached Gimmelwald, Shellie's breath was taken away. The tiny village of less than 300 people sloped steeply to the edge of a cliff. It looked like a Department 56 village of ceramic houses and tiny trees nested in white cotton that one would display on a mantle or a ledge in one's home at Christmas time. Smoke curled from the chimneys of the multi-level houses made of timbers and stone, terraced on the mountain - some on stilts, some with rock retaining walls protecting them from steep hillsides that might slide. The narrow road that led through the village was traversed by golf-cart-like vehicles or on foot.

"This can't be real, Adrian," she said as she hugged his massive arm.

"It is real, oh yes, it's real. It isn't Paris, but it has an unsurpassed beauty of its own. There is no place on earth like this, and when you meet the people you will understand why I miss it so much."

"I already understand. And you lived here all your life?"

"Yes. Except when I attended university in Zurich, but I came home on weekends to help out on the farm. My father and grandparents were alive then, so I wasn't needed as much."

"It must be fabulous to be part of such a large family, Adrian - knowing everybody, living in such beautiful surroundings. I can't believe the size of these mountains. Just to be able to breathe this clear, clean air is a good reason to live here."

Adrian reached around her waist and pulled her even closer. "I'm so happy you decided to come home with me."

She cupped his face with her hands and gave him a sweet, loving kiss as the gondola came to a stop.

After Christmas lunch in the Van Allman farmhouse, the families and visitors scattered throughout the multi-level building, finding their own space to laugh and talk to each other. In the great room, which was an expansive area that was lavishly decorated with holiday ornaments, candles, mementos and dishes of sweets, breads, cheeses and nuts, Shellie sat in a hand-hewn rocking chair that had belonged to Adrian's great-great-great grandmother. She ran her hands along the smooth wooden arms and tried to imagine what it was like so long ago when it had been built, when the house had been built, and wondered how many generations of children had been born and raised within its walls. She felt a satisfaction she'd never felt before. She felt as if she were somehow a part of it, that she belonged there. She quickly shook her head, trying to clear the thought from her mind. *Don't be silly, I belong in Paris.*

"Shellie, I want you to meet my cousin, he just arrived. Had to have lunch with his in-laws first." Adrian reached for Shellie's hand, disturbing her reverie. "This is Hans. Hans van Allman. He's my father's uncle's son's son."

"A distant cousin." Hans laughed at Adrian's description of lineage. "But a van Allman, nevertheless."

"Hello, Hans."

"We grew up together in Gimmelwald. Roamed these mountains, chased rabbits and girls, and skied through puberty."

"And I miss that more than anything, Adrian. Spain doesn't do it for me."

"Oh, you live in Spain?" Shellie asked.

"Yes, left here when I went away to university and never came back, unfortunately. Except for holidays, deaths, and weddings. Last time I saw Adrian was at Mama Anna's funeral. A sad day."

Adrian's eyes lowered. It still hurt. He still felt guilty about her death. Felt he could have been gentler as he rescued her from the burning train. Felt that was the reason she didn't survive.

"So have you heard about Andria? She's moving back to Switzerland. To Interlaken."

"You're kidding? What happened?"

"He was having an affair with one of his students and she found out. Divorced him."

"Did she have any children?" Adrian asked quietly.

"No."

Shellie noticed a marked difference in Adrian during the conversation about Andria. "Who is Andria?"

"Adrian wanted to marry her, but she went away to

305

school and married one of her professors."

"Oh, so now she's coming back." Shellie's voice was barely audible as she attempted to relax a tightening in her dry throat. "That's nice."

Adrian picked up on the tone of her voice. "Well, serves her right for marrying a Frenchman." He grabbed Shellie's hand and led her towards the kitchen. "Maggie and Tara are upstairs, Hans. Go give them a hard time. They're here without their husbands."

They walked through the kitchen and out the back door onto the porch. Adrian placed Shellie against the outside wall and with his hands pressed against the planks on each side of her, he bent down so he could look directly into her eyes. "Now, I want to get something straight here, before it grows out of proportion. I love you, Shellie Singer. I have not given Andria a second thought since she left those many years ago. She made her choice and there's no going back on that. Yes, it hurt me and, yes, I was heartbroken for awhile. I was over her long before I met you. There is no one in this world for me, but you, Shellie, and there never will be. If I can't have you, I won't have anyone. I'll go to my grave as a crotchety old bachelor. So, is that what you want? Will you save me from being an old crotchety bachelor? Will you marry me and have my children? And don't say you're too old to have babies. My cousins and aunts all had them when they were in their forties. I love you. I want you to be my wife and I want your children, our children. So, what do you say? Can I go back inside and announce our engagement?"

Shellie was flabbergasted. She hadn't expected this. She knew how he felt, but she didn't expect this outburst. She looked into his earnest face and carefully thought about what she should say. She didn't want to hurt him.

"Will you marry me?" he asked softly while stroking her cheek.

She wanted to cry. He was so vulnerable and she didn't want to hurt him like he'd been hurt before. "I—Adrian, I don't know what to say, or how to say it."

"Just say, yes."

"Sweetheart, you know I adore you. You know that don't you?"

"So you're saying, no. Is that what you're saying?" He drew back, his face reddening.

"I'm saying this is not the right time for me. I came to Paris to be a singer. You know that. Like you went to Paris to be an artist."

"But I can be an artist anywhere. And I miss my homeland. I belong here and I want you to be here with me. You can still sing. They loved you in Interlaken. You can sing there on a regular basis, I'm sure they'd hire you for the weekends. We could spend the weekends in George's cottage and here on the farm during the week. We could raise our children here. Can't you see how right it is? We'd be a family, Shellie. You'd be a perfect mother, I just know you would."

It was almost too much for her to bear. "Adrian, please. Let's not talk about this now. Let's just enjoy the holiday, okay? You know I have that other gig now. You know that. I'll be singing at the Marriot two nights a week as well as at Maxim's. That's five nights a week. It's my dream come true. Something I've always wanted to do. So, please, let's not spoil Christmas with your family."

He took a deep breath and straightened up to his full 6-foot 6 inches. "I'm sorry. I lost it for a moment. But at least now you know exactly how I feel and where I stand. I won't be staying in Paris much longer, Shellie. It isn't what I thought it would be."

"I'm sorry you feel that way. I can't imagine being in Paris without you. But if it has to be, it has to be."

"Come along. Let's get back to the party. Will you forgive me?"

"For expressing yourself? Never." She laughed and hugged him tightly. "I think I love you, too." The words came out before she realized it.

"Yes, I know you do, darling." His eyes twinkled as he pressed his body against hers, backing her into the wall, again.

She playfully slapped the side of his thigh and exclaimed,

307

"Oh, you are such a tease."

They giggled and went back into the house.

CHAPTER 71

It was December 29. Shellie and Adrian had already returned to Paris from Switzerland.

Shellie answered when Rachel called to say she'd decided to return that evening. Shellie told her how wonderful it was in Switzerland and how Adrian had asked her to marry him.

Rachel in turn told Shellie about the spectacular Christmas in Cornwall. Not only had the pre-Christmas celebration in Mousehole been exciting, but Christmas Eve in Rachel's cottage for her own family had been very special, and Christmas Day dinner at the Newland's was the frosting on the holiday cake. Three events, each as memorable as the next. She told Shellie that her family had left to go back to the States, so she was coming back to Paris for New Year's Eve.

Shellie hung up and ran upstairs to get her purse. The doctor's appointment was scheduled for 11 a.m.; she had just enough time to get there without being late. That morning she'd vomited for an hour at least, crackers and oranges just weren't doing it for her anymore. She definitely needed something for the nausea, and needed to find out what was causing it.

Adrian had gone back to his own apartment when they had returned because Shellie had said she needed a breather. He wasn't happy about being away from her, but he respected her request.

When Rachel arrived that evening, she found Shellie sitting in the garden room drinking champagne straight out of a bottle. She was obviously inebriated.

"What are you doing? Save some for me." Rachel laughed and took the bottle from Shellie and poured herself a glass and was going to pour another for Shellie, but the bottle was empty. "My god, you almost drank an entire bottle! What are you celebrating? Where's Janet?"

"I don't know where she is." Shellie began crying.

"Sweetheart, what's wrong?" Rachel sat next to her and clutched her hand.

"My life is over! It's ruined!" She buried her face into Rachel's shoulder.

"My God! What has happened?"

Shellie lifted her head and looked up at Rachel, "I'm pregnant!"

Rachel was shocked by the news. Finally, "What do you mean your life is over?"

"Have you ever seen a pregnant singer?" she blurted through her sobs.

Rachel chuckled as she drew Shellie to her and stroked her hair. "Singers have children, sweetheart. They really do."

"Not this one."

"Why not this one?"

"I just can't."

"So, what are you going to do?"

"I can't have it."

"Have you told Adrian?"

"No, and I'm not going to."

Rachel frowned.

They heard Janet coming in the front door.

"Hello! Anybody home? Where are you?" Janet took off her coat and headed for the stairs.

"We're in here," Rachel called out.

"Well, tell me all about your Christmases and—" She

stopped mid-sentence when she saw the scene before her. "What's going on?"

"Shellie has something to tell you."

Janet quickly sat on the other side of Shellie. "What is it, hon? Are you all right?"

Shellie raised her head, "I'm going to have a baby."

Janet grabbed her, "A baby! We're going to have a baby, Rachel!" She hugged Shellie. "Wait'll I tell Bobby. When are you getting married, hon?"

Rachel frowned at Janet and shook her head.

Janet loosened her grip and tipped Shellie's face up towards her. "Why are you crying about this, hon? You should be happy."

"I can't have a baby."

"Why not?"

"I just can't. I have a career."

"But honey, if you have a chance to have a baby, and this might be your last chance, you'll just have to put your career on hold, won't you?"

Shellie was silent.

"Did you like Switzerland? Adrian's people? "

Shellie answered weakly, "Yes, it was a fairy tale."

"A fairy tale?" Janet smiled at Rachel.

"I mean, it didn't seem real. They're so sweet and nice, Adrian's mother, his sisters, his cousins, all of them. I've never been around a family like that before. They hug and kiss . . . no unkind words. They adore each other so much it shows. And the village is beautiful. I can understand why Adrian misses it. He's going back, he says. He's leaving Paris. Wants to go back to work the farm again. They don't even have cars in Gimmelwald. They have them in Interlaken, down the mountain, but not in Gimmelwald. You take trains and a gondola to get up to Gimmelwald. Can you imagine?" She wiped her tears and began smiling. "I've never seen anything like it. The farm house is over two-hundred years old. I felt like I belonged there." She looked down at her hands and stopped talking.

Rachel raised her eyebrows at Janet and quickly went

after another bottle of champagne. "Tell her what Adrian asked you, Shellie."

Shellie remained silent.

"What did he ask you?" Janet prodded.

She didn't answer.

Rachel returned with the bottle. "He asked her to marry him."

"Omigosh! Then it's all settled. You're getting married to the most handsome and kindest man on this planet, you're going to have his baby and you'll live happily ever after in a fairyland. What's so wrong with that?"

Shellie looked up at both their gleeful faces. Thoughts flashed through her mind about all the plans she had to become a famous singer, but then she wasn't so naive as to think that it would be simple and easy. She knew her career as such might be resigned to only singing in clubs in Paris. She knew that was a possibility. She hadn't realized how hard it was until she'd learned from all the other musicians how it worked or didn't work. She'd met other singers who came to Maxim's after their gigs. Sometimes they'd sit in and sing. She felt some of them were much better than she was and they hadn't made it. Some had been singing in Paris for twenty years and it showed on their faces. Most of them drank too much.

"Honey? What's so wrong with that?"

Shellie half-smiled again. "Nothing."

"I'd love to have a baby. Always wanted one, but didn't because I wanted a career. I was foolish," Janet smiled at Shellie. "Honey, you're going to have a baby. That's a little person inside you. He's alive already. It's a miracle."

Rachel added, "It sounds like a dream come true to me."

Shellie reached for the glass of champagne Rachel had just poured. "It does? Well, what about you and Pete? What if he asks you to marry him? Will you say yes? You said you didn't think you could combine marriage with your career."

Rachel raised an eyebrow at Shellie. "Oh. Well, that's different."

"Why is it different? And what about you, Janet? What if

312

Bob asks you to stay here? What if he asks you to marry him, would you? Would you give up your career in Los Angeles? All you've worked for?"

Janet winked at Rachel. "Honey, I can take my career with me anywhere I want to go. If Bobby asked me to stay, I think I would. In fact he already did and I said yes!"

"You did?" Shellie jumped up.

Rachel screamed, "You're going to stay? Really!" She gasped. "I don't believe it! You really are?"

"I'm going home next week and am closing up shop, putting my house up for sale. Bobby and I are going to be partners. We'll buy, renovate, and sell. Sounds like a terrific idea to me. And I kinda like him."

Rachel and Shellie hugged her, giggling and kissing her on the cheeks.

"Okay, okay. That's enough. Now what about you, Shellie?" Janet reached for her drink.

"Rachel's turn," Shellie said as she returned to the sofa. "Would you give up your career for Pete?"

"Well, first of all, Shellie, Janet isn't giving up her career, she's moving it. Right, Janet?"

"Right!"

"And she's taking a different direction so she can be with the man she loves. She does love him, whether she wants to admit it or not."

"Okay, okay. But don't tell him that, he's conceited enough as it is, the poor bastard."

"All right, so she didn't give up her career. She can have both. What about you, Rachel?"

"I can't answer that, sweetheart. I don't even know if Pete is interested in getting married or settling down. Sometimes he acts like it or says something that makes me think he is, but then he turns and goes off on a trip and it's like we're strangers all over again. He didn't even come back for Christmas. That really pisses me off."

"Do you love him?" Janet questioned.

"I wish I didn't, but I think I do. I don't know if I love

him enough to be married, though. And again, he hasn't asked, and probably never will. I'm listening to myself and am thinking I should get on with my life, to just forget about him and quit hanging onto something that might never be. I don't even know if I want it to be."

"But if he did ask you, would you feel you had to give up your career and follow him around the world? Or stay at home and be there when he returned?"

"It wouldn't be like that. I would never stop writing. Luckily I can write wherever I am. If he went to Africa and I wanted to go, too, I would. I could write there. If I didn't want to go, he could go on, and I'd still write wherever I am. Here, Cornwall, wherever my books are set. Marriage wouldn't interfere with my writing—" She abruptly stopped talking, hearing what she'd just said. "That's funny. I think I just argued against my own case."

They sipped their drinks in silence for a few minutes.

"Well, I don't know what I'm going to do," Shellie said. Will you promise me you won't say anything to Adrian or Bob about this? Please?"

"If you promise you won't make a decision about it until after New Year's and you won't do anything without telling us first," Rachel answered.

"And whatever you decide, hon, we'll support you," Janet added. "Just give it another week or so, okay?"

"All right. I will."

CHAPTER 72

Rachel came bounding down the stairs dressed in tight black satin pants and black spike heels and a tunic top of stretchy, see-through black lace, high neck with long sleeves. The black satin undergarment was low cut and revealed the upper curviness of her breasts that could be seen through the lace. She wore an emerald pendant encircled with alternating pearls and diamonds. The pearl and diamond earrings she was wearing were given to her by Ethan on another special New Year's Eve. She had been thinking about him all day, remembering their stay at the Ritz Hotel and then the excursion to Trafalgar Square just before midnight where she had kissed Paul, a stranger then, but not a stranger now. Midnight at Trafalgar had been an exciting one that year. Maybe Midnight at the Eiffel would be as festive and eventful, although it still hurt to think of Ethan.

"Ooo-La-La!" Janet exclaimed when she saw Rachel.

"Ooo-La-La to you, too. Now that is some party dress!"

"I must say we'll turn the rascals' heads tonight, won't we?"

"I hope so." Rachel laughed and peeked into the kitchen. "Where's Shellie?"

"She was in the bathroom when I came by her room."

"I'm so worried about her."

"Me too. She hasn't had much to say the past couple days."

There was a knock at the door. Rachel opened it.

"Good evening, Ladies!" Adrian stepped in with arms full of flowers. "These are for you." He handed a bouquet to Rachel. "These are for you." He gave another to Janet. "Where's Shellie?"

"She's not ready, yet. These are exquisite, Adrian," Rachel said as she headed to the kitchen for a vase. "You are so thoughtful."

"Hon, you are the most charming young man I've ever met. You know that?" Janet reached over and gave him a tight hug and kiss on the cheek. "And you're looking good enough to eat," she said as she stood back and gave him the once over standing there in his Navy tuxedo and pink silk shirt.

Rachel returned with a glass vase large enough to hold both bundles of flowers. "Here, I'll put those with mine and set them on the table."

Janet handed them to her.

Shellie appeared on the stairs. "I'm ready!"

They all three were mesmerized at the sight of her at the top of the staircase, showing off her tiny waist and curvaceous body in a stunning, strapless, clingy, pale pink floor-length gown. She wore a single pink camellia in her thick, shoulder-length, auburn curls, her complexion was glowing.

"You are more beautiful than ever. How can that be?" Adrian said as he stepped towards the stairs.

Rachel added, "I've never seen you more radiant, Shellie."

Janet whispered, "You're gorgeous, baby."

"Oh, thank you, thank you, you make me feel good." She carefully stepped down, holding onto the banister so she wouldn't trip on her dress. "Don't you all look spectacular? I can't believe this is happening, that we're all here like this in Paris. And I just want to say right now that you're so precious to me, all three of you." Her voice wavered. "Oh no. I don't want to cry and have to do my makeup all over again."

316

Adrian reached for her hand. "Here, Shellie. I looked all over town today to find these for you." Adrian laid the bouquet of pink baby roses in her arms.

"This is amazing, isn't it? Pink roses, your pink shirt, my pink dress? How did you know I would be wearing pink?"

"I didn't. Pink roses remind me of you every time I see them because you are as lovely and perfect as they are."

Janet and Rachel stood back watching the scene before them. Now both women had tears in their eyes and radiant smiles stretched across their faces.

"You're so sweet, Adrian." Shellie smelled the roses and walked past him to the table and added them to the flowers Rachel had just arranged. "We better get going. I need to be there in thirty minutes."

"Okay, let's do it. The car's waiting outside," Adrian winked at the girls, more jubilant than usual.

They grabbed their coats and went out the door to a waiting limousine.

"What is this?" Janet asked.

"We're riding in style tonight, girls, no taxi. This is a very special night, in more ways than one."

Before they could step in, tall, tanned Pete Bell stepped out of the limo wearing a black tuxedo and white open-collared shirt exposing a St. Christopher's medallion on a gold chain nestling in the spirals of gray hair covering his chest.

Rachel screamed.

Pete's laughing eyes were twinkling as brilliant as the mini-lights that were strung throughout the square. "Is that the only welcome I get? A scream? How about a hug?"

He grabbed Rachel and drew her to him and held her tightly. After a few moments they both leaned back to catch their breaths and to explore and gaze upon every inch of each other's face before they began to kiss more deeply than they ever had.

Janet and Shellie were clutching each of Adrian's arms, almost as excited as Pete and Rachel.

"How long have you known about this, Adrian?" Janet whispered.

317

"Since before Christmas. Paul called me to see if Pete could stay with me, because he wanted to surprise Rachel tonight. At first he was going to wait till midnight and appear on the bridge at the Eiffel, but neither one of us felt he should miss everything leading up to it."

"I am so happy he came, Adrian," Shellie said as she leaned her head against his arm and continued to watch them kiss.

Finally Pete came up for air, "God almighty, woman, I have waited much too long for this."

Rachel looked back at Janet and Shellie, seeming to say, *I love him. I have no doubts about it.*

Adrian ushered them into the limo, "Come along, we mustn't make my lady late for her gig. In you go."

They all decided to go from Maxim's to the bridge across from the Eiffel just before midnight. From there they could take in the entire view of the tower and the festivities. It would take five minutes to position themselves. Then they'd go back to Maxim's so Shellie could finish her gig. Afterwards they'd planned to join Bob's friends who would already be partying on the Simpatico. His party was to begin at ten, and he and Janet were to meet the rest of them outside Maxim's just before midnight so they could make a dash for the Eiffel.

So Bob joined them for dinner and afterwards had stolen Janet away to meet his friends on the Simpatico. Adrian told Rachel and Pete he wanted to make a few calls to his family, and would return in a while. So Rachel and Pete were snuggling at the table together as Shellie sang "It Was Just One of Those Things", when the waiter arrived with another bottle of champagne. He poured for them and left.

Pete lifted his glass towards Rachel. "I'd like to make a toast."

Rachel smiled and touched his glass with hers.

"But first . . ." He reached into his pocket with his free hand and brought out a huge solitaire diamond ring, holding it between his fingers, the candlelight making it flicker and flash.

318

He watched Rachel's reaction without saying a word.

Rachel didn't know what to say or think.

"It's a Brazilian diamond. I had to wait till it was made for you. That's why I couldn't come home at Christmas."

"It's so big." She didn't move.

"Will you be my wife?"

She couldn't believe the words she'd just heard. She was still holding her glass against his, still not moving, and barely breathing. As she stared at the ring he was holding out to her, she began to cry, gently. It wasn't a sad cry; it was a lovely, soft, quiet, happy shedding of tears.

"Please, say you'll have me, doll, will you?"

At the sound of his favorite nick name for her, she blurted out, "Oh yes. I'll have you, Pete Bell, if you'll have me. Yes, yes, yes!"

He set his glass on the table and reached for Rachel's left hand. He placed the ring on her finger and lifted it to his lips.

Rachel couldn't control her emotions no matter how hard she tried.

Pete brought out a handkerchief and dabbed her eyes. Then he leaned over and kissed her softly as if to seal the deal. "I love you, Rachel." He kissed her nose and then both her eyes and her forehead. "Now, I shall make a toast!" He lifted up his glass once more. "To us, to our future and a long life together."

Rachel's heart was beating so fast she was dizzy.

CHAPTER 73

Just before midnight Shellie left the stage and joined Adrian at the door as the band carried on. Everyone else was already waiting outside – Pete and Rachel, Janet and Bob. The night air was brisk and cold, making every human exhalation visible.

They hastened to the steps taking them up to the Pont d'Iena that crosses the river connecting the Eiffel Tower to the Palais de Chaillot and the Place du Trocadero on the Right Bank. From the bridge the view of the Seine and its left and right banks stretching in both directions was incredible on this eve of the new year. Maxim's and the Bateau Simpatico could easily be seen from the bridge as well as other celebratory boats. Straight ahead of them was the Eiffel looming with it's thousands of lights and thousands of people gathered beneath. There was music and spectacular fireworks.

Rachel and Pete embraced as they looked up at the tower and its blazing lights.

"We'll always remember this New Year's Eve, won't we, doll?"

"One I'll never forget," Rachel said as she turned and melted into Pete's sparkling eyes.

Her thoughts were of her father and what he would say standing on the bridge facing the Eiffel on New Year's Eve, celebrating his daughter's engagement. "I wish my father were here with us."

"He is, my sweetheart," Pete said as he held Rachel close.

Janet and Bob were in each other's arms swaying with the music closely and romantically, although the music was upbeat and blaring through the loud gigantic speakers.

"So, why don't we get married and have a double wedding with Rachel and Pete?"

"Ha! It ain't gonna be that easy, Bobby Baby. You got a lot more wooing to do."

Bob laughed and twirled her as they continued to dance.

Adrian held on to Shellie's hand as he pulled her from the bridge across the boulevard towards the Eiffel Tower.

"Where are we going, Adrian?"

"Not far, just hold on."

Rachel and Janet gave each other a wink and a smile as they watched the two lovers cross the street.

Adrian managed to maneuver through the crowds under the Eiffel through to the opposite side. At just the perfect spot, the Eiffel behind them and standing in the gardens of the Champ de Mars where trees with pink blossoms and rose colored crocus lined the pathways and an occasional velvety Magnolia bud perched on its tree branch, Adrian stopped and held Shellie tightly as if they were the only two people in the middle of the throngs around them.

The countdown to midnight began. *10 . . . 9 . . . 8 . . .*

Adrian lifted Shellie's tiny, delicate hand and slipped a diamond and amethyst engagement ring on her finger. It was the ring his father had given to his mother when he asked her to marry him.

"What is this?" She was astounded at the beauty of the brilliant stones and the gold filigree antique setting.

"You must marry me, Shellie. I love you so much that I'll do anything you say. You want to stay in Paris, we will. All I know is I can't live without you. Please say yes."

Shellie gazed into the handsome, insistent face above her and wondered if their child would have Adrian's dark, sexy eyes and long eyelashes. She wondered if she'd be happy in a family such as Adrian's who'd gather her to them as one of their own. It had never occurred to her that she would one day be part of a real family in the spectacular Switzerland Alps in a storybook village with a storybook husband and have storybook children all of her very own. She'd be crazy not to say yes.

"Yes, Adrian. Yes! I love you with all my heart. But, first, there is something I have to tell you."

Adrian bent down closer so he could hear Shellie's words.

"You're going to be a father," she said. Then she said it more loudly thinking he hadn't heard her. "I'm pregnant!"

He immediately lifted her up in his arms and held her tightly as he whispered in her ear. "I am so happy. You will never be sorry, I promise you."

With her arms around his neck and legs locked around his waist, Shellie kissed Adrian through the rest of the countdown and beyond.

Yes, another New Year's Eve, another year gone by, a bright future for some, but not for all.